# S P ROWELL

# ZETA

*Resin Pines*

# Contents

| | |
|---|---:|
| Chapter 1 | 1 |
| Chapter 2 | 8 |
| Chapter 3 | 15 |
| Chapter 4 | 26 |
| Chapter 5 | 37 |
| Chapter 6 | 48 |
| Chapter 7 | 58 |
| Chapter 8 | 67 |
| Chapter 9 | 74 |
| Chapter 10 | 81 |
| Chapter 11 | 88 |
| Chapter 12 | 102 |
| Chapter 13 | 119 |
| Chapter 14 | 128 |
| Chapter 15 | 143 |
| Chapter 16 | 154 |
| Chapter 17 | 163 |
| Chapter 18 | 169 |
| Chapter 19 | 178 |
| Chapter 20 | 187 |
| Chapter 21 | 197 |
| Chapter 22 | 212 |
| Chapter 23 | 223 |
| Chapter 24 | 233 |

Chapter 25                                          243
Chapter 26                                          249
Chapter 27                                          263
Chapter 28                                          276

# Chapter 1

Wedged within a shallow grave, pushing against an icy blanket of brittle leaves, Snipe wrestled the exposed roots of the downy birch. He clenched a shaking wrist, squinting, a blinding light loosened his grip as a shockwave tore the stranger from his view. His hands rigid and outstretched, a thudding, rhythmic beat echoed deep within. His eyes were the only part of him that were able to move. Stilted intakes of sulphur-tinged air stung Snipe's eyes as his muscles tensed, near to the point of snapping. The invisible force that had held him in place for no longer than a few seconds let go, as if it no longer had anything to prove. He staggered before falling back into the frosted cavity between the trees.

Why he was in a frozen pit, and who had shouted at him to *run*, to *get away*, he could not say. It was a blur. His body drifted from side to side, like a snowflake playing with the force of gravity. He felt no pain, no fear. Just falling.

Snipe's eyes flitted open at the sound of a drone hovering above the treeline. He reached for his gun. It wasn't there. Old-fashioned, mechanical gunfire peppered the air. Now curled in a tight, protective ball, he looked through spread fingers as the drone exploded in a cloud of gas.

A vehicle rumbled and clattered as it drove, unseen, into the distance. Alone in the dark woodland, Snipe strained to see anything or anyone around him. With laboured breath, he ran his fingers over his face. Pushing his tongue through parted, swollen lips, he tried to comprehend the events that should have ended his life, and what part he had played in them. Like a hand flicking through a pack of playing cards, his thoughts were scattered.

Sharp, snapping laser fire, followed by small arms fire, trailed off in the distance. Snipe ran through the thicket with adrenalin-fueled energy toward the flashes of light until he found a clearing. An old-style military truck, the sort only talked about by the town's elders, hurtled down a dirt track, leading away from the woodland. It was too dark and far away to make out who was firing at the sky. Snipe couldn't see anything above the truck as it swayed erratically, swerving and then braking as if avoiding incoming fire. A green laser combed the roof of the truck, scanning its interior. A single bass note hummed through the air as he watched it explode. There was nothing he could do to help the small band of rebels. They were dead.

The moon looked brighter, clearer somehow. Stars appeared sharper and more apparent than when he left. He walked in a full circle, all the time looking and thinking, trying to remember anything that might explain what had happened. His body was failing to obey his orders to keep moving as he followed the well-trodden track down the hill that would lead him home. His chest hurt like hell as he stopped to gain his composure. He looked back toward the woodland. The moonlit trees looked ablaze, but he knew it was only the truck beyond them, which bellowed out the kind of smoke that only comes from burning rubber mixed with the burnt flesh of freedom fighters.

*Freedom fighters? A rescue went wrong? Must be. But who was I rescuing? The camps are the other side of town.*

*Lexi! ... The tunnels ... Fuck! Why can't I remember?*

With every step forward, he recounted yesterday's events. He'd left around midnight after being tipped off about an assault on the underground camps. Lexi was down there, unaware that she, and anyone within the disused sewer, were in danger. The few remaining who were non-chipped were gassed while they slept; murdered by Zeta to further refine an ideology. An ideology which he and Lexi despised. An ideology that had taken decades to develop, and was now the world's norm. Not through choice or a democratic vote – such notions were as ancient as the guns used in the wood – the norm had been imposed over years of indoctrination by an unseen dictator that the people followed without question.

*I got to the camp in time. I remember. Lexi wasn't there, and then...*

The seasons had changed in the short time he'd been out. It had only been a few hours. Cold, moist air slowed his movement. The night didn't want to let him go; it seemed determined to turn his blood to ice and ground him where he stood. It wasn't like Snipe to be unprepared, without a backup plan. It was a humid night when he left Vic. He had been dressed in thin black army slacks, a black t-shirt, and a light jacket. He remembered slipping the hooded jacket on because it had several pockets. With stiffened fingers, he fumbled through each one. Empty. Survival kit, gone. His knife was missing, no firearm either. Medkit was also missing. But where had everything gone? If the strangers on the hill had stolen his things, then why was he still alive? They'd shot down the drone hovering above him, and the weapons they had used were obsolete; found only in museums and Harden Antiques.

Victor Harden was the proprietor of Harden Antiques, and he had been Snipe's guardian since before he could remember.

He'd never called him Dad or Mr Harden, always Vic. Vic had been chipped around the same time as it became law to implant women during pregnancy. For the past twenty years, kids had grown up thinking the biochip placed inside of them was a part of life itself. How else would they be able to access buildings, pay for things, or use transport? Public or private, there was no other way.

Dry-mouthed and weak, too tired to carry on but more fearful that if he stopped, he would seize up and never find the momentum to move forward again, he continued to tread down the yellow, frost-covered grass until gravity bore too heavily on his shoulders, and he fell to his knees.

Fatigued, he mumbled, "A few minutes. That's all I need." As if justifying his grounded stance, Snipe sat with his legs crossed and muttered, "It's over, and it's just me now. The fight's over."

He dug his fingers into his emotionless face. He should be dead. He was at a place he knew, but in a time that seemed impossible to fathom. Had years of fighting against the system stolen his soul and his memories? Was this the way it ended? Or had it ended already? Was he dead, or had he slipped into an alternate timeline? A different dimension, maybe, like the old movies he used to watch as a child? Right now, he took comfort in watching his body shake to some inaudible tune.

"Lexi."

Visions of her faded along with his state of consciousness. As soon as he had a fix on her, the picture in his mind took them both back to childhood. He was thirteen. It was one of those days; a day that reaffirms how beautiful life is. People seemed happier that day. The weather was perfect. Not too hot or cold, with just enough of a breeze to make breathing seem effortless.

After a scuffle with an older kid who was picking on a

young girl, he'd strolled into the shop, knowing he couldn't buy anything. Suddenly, a screech filled the room, and the doors locked themselves, leaving him trapped inside. The shopkeeper looked at him, and kept saying that he had no way of letting him out until the NWP released the door. NWP –the new world police. If they came, they'd take him away for sure. He protested, and told the man who stood shaking behind the glass counter that he hadn't stolen anything.

"You're not a registered citizen," the shopkeeper replied, edging back from the counter.

Snipe had thrown something heavy through the window; a stone statue or a garden pot, and clambered out. He'd made it back home just before the police arrived, and locked himself in his basement room. It was that night, sitting in the basement and crying, that Victor Harden had told him the truth. He told him that he was different. That he had been born outside of the system, and was handed to him by his father moments before an attack on their camp. That was the day Vic showed him his arsenal of weapons. Clunky, old-fashioned pieces of pure destruction.

Struck by a bolt of realisation, Snipe stood upright. "Vic… What if someone found out about his illegal stash?"

A thin layer of frost threatened to topple his tired body. He checked to see if his head and his ears were still there. They were, although they were as numb as his feet were in the lightweight trainers that he wore.

Through wispy clouds, he saw a flashing red light –a drone beacon. Another two miles and he'd be home.

"Stop right there," a raspy voice came from behind him. "Move and I'll—"

Snipe spun around. His arm hit the side of the man's neck.

The bulk of the man rocked before hitting the ground. Snipe dropped into the flab of his gut. He tried to move his fingers, but they refused, so he used the side of his hand to knock the gun from the man's thick, hairy fingers. The man's head shook from side to side; Snipe pushed his knee further into his chest.

"No— Please— Stop!"

Their eyes locked. You can tell a lot from looking into another man's eyes, and Snipe knew that he wasn't out to hurt him. He was alone. "You've got five seconds to tell me who you are before I break your neck." Transferring the weight of his knee from the man's chest, it came to rest on his throat instead.

"I'm sorry. We need food. I was hunting."

Snipe took the gun and stepped back from the cowering giant. Unclipping the charging unit, he threw it away.

"Don't tell them... they'll take me to the farm for conditioning."

The man stayed in the foetal position, and his pleading intensified, growing louder with every word. "I'm on my last warning. I have a family."

Snipe moved closer to the man's trembling bulk. He out-stretched his arm, then retracted it, knowing he wouldn't be able to lift him. "Stand up and shut up before you get us both killed."

"Thank you, sir; I'll be on my way."

"If you're not chipped, then why are you carrying a bio gun?"

A look of bewilderment stained the man's features. "Chipped?"

"You heard me. If you're not a free man, then why risk prison for hunting? You'll be caught for sure if the tracking drones fly past."

"I'm desperate," he said, lowering his head. "They took away the living allowances. I had a choice: either go to prison or find work, but there *is* no work, so I had to do it."

As the man lowered his head, Snipe saw a scar running just under his hairline, as if he'd been scalped, or he'd fallen out with his barber. Either way, he'd seen it before. Where, he couldn't remember. Right now, he couldn't think at all.

"What's your name?" Snipe asked.

"Fin," he replied, looking at the gun as Snipe examined it.

He threw him back his gun, minus the charging clip. "Fin, you never saw me, and I never saw you. Got that?"

"You're a legend, Snipe."

"You know who I am?" Snipe asked, half-wishing he hadn't passed over the gun.

The man hesitated, as if regretting his loose tongue.

"Snipe Siren, the outlaw. They said you got killed with the rest over a year ago. I always said you'd survived. You're a national hero. You saved thousands, rescued the enslaved, but never got caught. One thing I don't get..." Fin rubbed the stubble on his chin. "How've you been eating? And where've you been living? They searched every inch, and you can't leave the zone without them knowing, now that the scan pods are up."

"Scan pods?"

"Where have you–"

Snipe stepped back. Like a robot that had run out of charge, Fin stopped, frozen in mid-sentence. Buzzing from high above drew closer. Snipe shouted at Fin to run. For a moment, he thought he saw him look in the opposite direction, as if telling him to get away.

Fin was too large to carry. He couldn't be saved. And he knew too much for Snipe to let him live.

It was a decision he wouldn't need to make.

# Chapter 2

Like a spider casting its web, the silent mass hovering above Fin spat out an inky black substance. Shimmering liquid solidified mid-flight before fluctuating as if under control, encasing Fin within a tar-covered blanket. As silk would cling to a wet body, the sheet of doom sought, every crevice turning the man into a sculptured woodsman. The wet leathery sheet pulsated as it tore Fin skyward. Dragged by an invisible cord, it followed the drone at an impossible speed before disappearing into the night.

The flashing red light in the distance was his only guide. With renewed energy, he ran towards it, over broken branches and thick ferns, and headed down the hill. He should have been able to see the lights within his home zone by now, but there were none. Not even a sound.

Something was wrong. The town was in total darkness. There was no light from the street markers. The moon appeared from behind a cloud, lighting his way. Things had changed. Nothing significant, but everything was different, all the same. Every property had a white pole outside. The shop was yellow instead of green, and the skip bins had moved to the other side of the street.

Apart from the thin, white pole next to its entrance, Harden Antiques hadn't changed. Snipe walked around the back of the building. The trapdoor that led down to the cellar was missing.

A large pot, cushioned on topsoil, stood in its place, with grass growing around its base. He looked up at the tall building, just to make sure he was in the right place. Moving the pot, he used the side of his shoe to scrape the soil. It was how he'd left it; still booby-trapped.

He had to think. Hitting his forehead, he felt nothing.

*Why would Vic cover my only entrance? Was he warning me? Are they down there waiting with guns drawn, ready for me to drop? Maybe, maybe not. But if I don't get shelter soon, I'm a dead man.*

He pulled at the green wire and waited for the lock to release. The rope ladder had moved, unhooked from its place under the trap door. Lowering himself down, his grip gave way, and he fell on top of his bed... only, he didn't remember putting his bed underneath the hatch.

Shivering, he tried to stand, but fell back down again. The duvet, bound with string, sat at the foot of the bed. A pile of books balanced on top of the bedding slid over him, warming his lower half. His hands shook as he pulled out an old jumper that was sandwiched between the mattress and wall. He covered his head. His ears throbbed from the warmth of his makeshift pillow. His eyes fluttered, then closed.

A shadowy, arched figure entered the room. Snipe flinched and tried to turn over. The barrel of a shotgun pushed into the side of his neck forced him to face the wall.

Snipe laughed. "There's only one man I know with a gun like that, and he's older than God himself."

The gun clicked. Snipe pushed his head into the soft jumper and grabbed at the barrel, sending it flying across the darkened room.

"Fuck's sake, Vic, what's wrong?" He swung his legs off the bed, sending books flying toward his attacker.

The light turned on. Blinded by it, Snipe covered his eyes. "Vic, you old fool, what's gotten into you?"

"Snipe Siren… is it you? Prove it's you or ill–" Victor looked at his hands, and then where the gun had landed, as if he was only now registering that he was no longer holding it.

"Have you lost your mind?! You can see it's me!"

"All I see is someone who resembles my Snipe." Victor shuffled towards the gun.

"Vic, it's me, you crazy son-of-a-bitch. What have you done to my room? Where's my desk and my wardrobe, and what have you done with my locker?"

"Snipe?"

"Yes, I'm Snipe, and you're Vic… what's wrong with you?"

"Snipe, my boy, it *is* you." Victor closed his wrinkled hands around Snipe's face, his palms soft pads against his harsh stubble. "I thought it better to burn your things, so that when I die, they wouldn't be able to make a connection."

Victor drew closer to him, "Never mind that. Anyway, how have you stayed alive? There was nowhere to hide after the cleansing."

"Cleansing?" Snipe shook his head, as if trying to wake from a nightmare. "You know where I went. You tried to stop me, we argued. That was yesterday. Right?"

Victor, a frail old man in his eighties, seemed to have aged and become weaker overnight. Things had turned from being strange and challenging to outright weird. Nothing made sense. It was like he'd entered into another dimension. He'd read about such events. One minute you were going for a walk and the next, you woke up and things were just not how you remembered.

"Vic, either you've had a stroke and developed memory loss, or I'm dead and the Maker's sent me back to punish me."

Victor reached inside his brown overcoat; the only overcoat Snipe had ever seen him wear. He pulled out a candle, lit it, and switched off the light. The candle flickered, making the few items in the room come to life.

"Why've you switched off the light?"

Victor pulled up an antique plastic chair and lowered himself down into it.

"A lot has changed while you've been away, Snipe. I still can't believe you're here. Back home. How have you hidden for so long? How've you been eating? You're malnourished, my poor boy."

"Vic, what's changed?"

Although he was good at telling stories, Victor tended to get sidetracked and went off on tangents. He'd be halfway through an explanation and say a word that triggered a completely different one. Somehow, he'd always go full-circle and end up back where the story had left off. Most often, the sidetracked adventure would bolster the original story, and give it greater credence and plausibility. *Most* of the time.

Victor was acting like he hadn't seen him for years, and would love nothing more than to chit-chat. Snipe needed answers, but he would be careful not to rush the old man. One of his tangents could shed light on where he had been for over a year, and where Lexi was now.

Victor edged forward on his chair. "You look half-starved. I'll make something nice. A good, hot drink to stop you from shivering. I'd put the heating on, but you know how things are... well, if you don't, I'll explain. But not until you've had nourishment."

Snipe moved his head, and the room followed. Dehydrated, weak, and on the verge of collapse, every bone in his body ached to the core. Bright blotches of light danced before his eyes in the darkened room. The meaning of words took time to decipher. He closed his eyes.

When Victor re-emerged, he was leaning on the wall to steady himself. He walked down to the cellar one step at a time. Bowls clanked together, and steamy froth from cups of drinking chocolate spilt onto the tray.

"Phew, I made it. Didn't spill a drop," Victor said.

But it was too late; Snipe was down for the count. In all the years that Victor had watched him sleep, he never once heard him snore. He was always on edge and alert. Now, he was out cold.

Victor pulled the duvet over Snipe's body and tucked him in, just as he had on the first night he became his guardian. Must've been about six then, give or take a year.

At the side of the bed, he bent down until his back warned him that it was far enough. Looking at him all scrunched up reminded Victor of when Snipe was a boy, and less tainted by the growing divide between the citizens and those who chose not to conform. Snipe never had a choice, and Victor kept his word in maintaining his anonymity. It was easier back then, before the media turned normal folk into vigilantes. They'd encouraged and rewarded those who turned in anyone who hadn't volunteered to become a citizen. And by "citizen", they meant *chipped*. The deadline had long since passed. The law had no room for those who chose not to fit in.

There were many criminal outcasts who didn't slot into one of the three camps: those who followed the rules without question; the weak-minded fools who feared the world would return to the chaotic state it once was; and those who were awake enough to understand, but felt powerless against the disillusioned masses.

Until the cleansing, they'd shown sympathy to the few who evaded control and tyranny: the unchipped. The uncontrollable few who didn't fit into any camp. Those who fought for true freedom.

Although chipped himself, Victor valued the freedoms of the past. Not that he didn't embrace useful technological advancements; far from it. In fact, when he was Snipe's age, he was an inventor. But what he *didn't* embrace was the control element embedded in the new-fangled gadgets of today; gadgets that promised freedom, but only if you stayed ignorant of the fact that the freedom they offered came at a cost. That cost was control. He'd watched it spiral from way back at the turn of the century. Everyone knew everyone's whereabouts anytime they switched on a mobile phone. They were filled with applications designed to distract users from being human and doing human things. Victor craved anonymity. But it was too late for that now. Most argued that the new world which came after the event was a positive one, and Victor would be the first to admit that crime was at an all-time low. Prisons had shut down, and were turned into robotics factories. Money was a thing of the past. Shops had given way to cold warehouses run by functional robots, overseen by AI humanoids. Robots that decided on a course of action, emulating human behaviour. Programmed and operated by Zeta, a man never seen in person, whose success had cloaked the world in a bubble of hope and progressiveness. That's where Victor drew the line.

Snipe's father escaped the oppressive movement, settling instead for a simple life in a gipsy camp. He'd showed an interest in antiques, and spent many a day discussing things from the past. Rush Unix had always been a guarded man; a man of secrets. Victor had warmed to him all the same. When Rush asked him to protect his son's human rights, he'd agreed to do so, and from that day forward, every day had become more of a challenge.

Victor looked down at humanity's last hope: The half-starved, beaten man he first knew as a green-eyed gipsy boy, full of life and wonder. He placed the tray on the floor next to the bed, left the candle alight, and shuffled his way over to the door. He watched Snipe toss and turn in a restless, haunted dream. Sleep is what he needed. Questions could wait until the morning. He smiled. His Snipe was back from the dead.

He climbed the wooden steps, stopping as one creaked. A thought washed over him. *Everyone thinks he's dead. A dead man who lives is truly a free man...*

The thought drifted off as he muffled a yawn.

# Chapter 3

Snipe hadn't planned to save Lexi. He knew nothing about the impending attack. Every police drone and citizen patrol vehicle would be out looking for him. An informant said that the old barn was in use as a slave camp. He went to check it, and there were four men keeping two non-citizens hostage for their pleasure, and the pleasure of anyone who credited them enough units. The tip-off came from a reliable informant, a non-citizen called Rex. Rex was a lowlife, but he was talkative. That night, he talked.

The unchipped women were doomed if they remained locked up, and doomed if the police got involved.

A new mission for Snipe Siren.

His plan was merely to assess the situation. Screams and pleading cries changed all that.

Without hesitation, Snipe entered the barn, ducked, and a hole appeared where his head should have been. The largest of the four men had opened fire. Snipe dropped to his knees, blasting off four shots, each one as accurate and as deadly as the first. Screams, muffled by gags. Splattered bits of flesh hung from just about every surface.

The women looked at Snipe with fear in their eyes, expecting the worst. He was untying the second woman when two men approached the barn. The youngest of the three women, just out of her teens, puked from the mess he'd made, covering the older one who was the spitting image of her. A mother and her daughters, he reckoned, looking similar in every way. Brown, rough-cut hair, slim bodies, and matching large noses.

The male voices outside rose in pitch, giving way to ecstatic chatter. Snipe hid behind the door and waited for them to enter. He looked at the bedraggled females and placed his finger on his lips. The women held each other close and fell silent.

The door creaked open. Two men entered, one a stodgy bald guy and the other a larger-than-life hillbilly type bearing a scar across his forehead. They stood with open mouths, staring at the end of Snipe's Smith & Wesson.

"We– We– There's a party. I–" they both stuttered, overlapping each other.

Snipe cocked the gun and drew closer to the hillbilly. "The party's over."

A shriek from behind pierced his ears.

"Leave and live a good life, or I'll find you."

He watched until they'd vanished out of sight, regretting that he hadn't ended their lives.

The women were shaking and mumbling. The older one gave him a combative look, while the other two cowered behind her.

"Which camp are you from?" Snipe asked.

"You may as well kill us," said the mother in a deflated, matter-of-fact way.

"You're free to go back to the tunnels," he told them. "Come on. Hurry."

An insane, tortured smile filled her dirt-smudged face. "They're going to cleanse the tunnels and gas any remaining non-citizens," she said.

"Who told you this?"

A drone flew overhead. "It's happening," she said.

He held the door ajar, turned, and said, "Go back. You're out of options."

The drone buzzed past, leaving only the sound of crickets from the nearby blackberry bush.

Ramblings from the abused. Four citizens down and police on the way left him with no choice but to lay low for at least the next few days.

He couldn't shake the words that echoed in his head: *They're coming to cleanse the tunnels.*

*Lexi!*

Snipe's eyes rolled open. The shadow of an empty chair danced on the wall. The candle sputtered. Half-awake, he tried to raise his head from the sweat-soaked pillow. The flickering movement of the burnt-down candle matched the fluttering of his eyelids.

*Lexi!*

"Where's Lexi?" he shouted to every passing person. Those that didn't acknowledge his cries, he grabbed in desperation.

"What's happening? Why is everyone leaving the sewers?"

At last, someone he recognised. A young boy. He knew him as Spud. He was about six years old, of mixed race with long locks that made him look more like a girl. Lexi had taken him in after finding him wandering around a squalid camp run by undesirables. She'd told Snipe that he didn't look like a street kid, and offered him a home with her in the tunnels.

Snipe grabbed his shoulders. "Spud, where's Lexi?"

"They took Lexi and everyone last night," the boy cried. "I was out hunting... and now this."

"Now what?" Lowering his voice, he knelt, and his eyes met the boy's. "Why is everyone leaving?"

"Someone said they would gas us."

Spud ran off as the air turned hazy grey. The swirling gas had a life of its own, as if it was somehow conscious.

*Lexi! Lexi!*

"Snipe, I'm here!"

It was a man's voice.

Snipe threw his covers off and took a swing at the voice, not registering that it was Victor Harden.

"You were dreaming, my boy." Victor looked down at his wrist. "You've slept the morning away. I made breakfast, but it's long gone, so how about we catch up over brunch? I've got your favourite sautéed potatoes. They've not moved out of the deep freeze for over a year. I thought about cooking them when they stopped the allowances, but a part of me... I just couldn't bring myself to eat your favourite comfort food."

Snipe chuckled at the thought of the old man eyeing his sautéed potatoes but feeling as if somehow, it would be immoral to eat them. Victor raised his eyes. His bushy grey eyebrows danced. And there it was. That half-slanted smile that came from chewing on the end of a pen all his life.

"Vic, I'm glad I made it back. And that you're still you."

Victor pulled his face back. His baggy skin followed. "Still me?"

"Still you, Vic. If I'm in another realm, at least you're in it, too."

As the water hit his skin, Snipe breathed a lungful of warm steam. In his mind, he'd only been missing one night. Vic said it had been over a year. He'd been presumed dead by everyone, and nothing made any sense. Things had changed. The white poles outside, for one. The hunter guy in the woods called them scan pods. The skips had moved, as they did every winter. It was summer when he set out two nights ago.

18

After de-clogging the shower's dirt shoot for the fifth time, his body was finally clear of the mini-ecosystem that had used it as a playground for God knew how long. His mind, however, was full of unanswered questions; questions that he wondered whether he'd ever get the answers to.

Wrapping a towel around his waist, Snipe felt his ribcage. He'd always been lean and muscular, but now he resembled a starved refugee from the old world.

The kitchen, situated over the main storefront, was alive with the smells of food. Snipe breathed in the smell of fried brunch as it wafted down the hallway, past Victor's bedroom, hitting him just as he closed the bathroom door. Victor kept a stash of lard and a freezer full of proper food. It had all been illegal for as long as he could remember. Victor, ever the law-abiding gentlemen on the outside, was a rebel at heart.

Victor called from the kitchen, "Snipe, my boy, your breakfast's getting cold." Something he'd always said. This meant he was just about to dish it out.

"Yeah, coming!" Snipe shouted.

"Your gown is hanging up in the hall."

*Gown?* Snipe often wondered just what would happen to his street-cred if the bad guys could eavesdrop on some of the things said in this place.

As he fed his arm into the sleeve of the dressing jacket, he saw the name: *Lexi.* He'd scratched it into his arm with a pin twelve years ago, when they were both fourteen. It was so faint that it would go unnoticed unless the hairs on his arm were parted, and even, then he had to squint to see the scar.

Victor had laid the small wooden table as if expecting royalty. The red tablecloth matched the blinds, and the plates rested on bright white napkins, which appeared unused. They still had the fluted creases that only ever appeared on new fabric. A small beaker with a single flower sat in the centre of the surrounding dishes, which were loaded with an array of breakfast items and salad.

"Bloody hell, Vic. It's like we're on a date."

Snipe sat down facing him. A sliver of sunlight lined the windowsill from beneath the blackout blinds.

"Vic, I need answers, and I need to find Lexi," he said, picking up a handful of the little square potato bits, dropping them back down as they burnt his fingers. "Thought you said it was getting cold?"

Victor frowned. "I say a lot of things, Snipe, but you need to listen to me now."

Back-and-forth questions lead to countless dead ends. Where had Snipe been for over a year? Guesses, including the bizarre and ridiculous, were considered. One of the saner explanations was that amnesia had struck him and he was taken in by a non-citizen, as any normal person – even a sympathiser – wouldn't risk their lives for an outcast. Victor had skirted around the idea that Lexi was dead. Snipe knew different; she had to be somewhere. He couldn't comprehend the world without her.

Like reaching the top of a helter-skelter and finding out that there was only one way down, just when they thought they'd figured things out, logic made them slide back down to the beginning again.

Trying not talk while he chewed out of respect for the old man, Snipe covered his mouth. "So, what else were you trying to tell me?"

"Well, we're not getting very far in finding out where you've been." Victor filled his beaker. "Orange juice?"

"Yes. Thanks. You said I'd better listen to what you had to say."

Snipe lowered his head. A solemn veil covered Victors face. "You're out of options, Snipe. I never thought I'd say it, but—"

"I know. The scan pods, right?" Snipe asked.

Victor sighed. "You're trapped here. Every area's separated by scanners," he gulped. "Our zone starts at the high bank, which includes the woods, and stops at the end of our road."

Snipe grinned. Nodding, he said, "And if I cross over, they'll be all over me... Shoot me down like they tried to in the woods."

"Snipe, I fear I will not be around for long, and when I go, there's no one left who would dare buy you food or—"

"So, I go out fighting... nothing else I can do." Knocking the juice back in two gulps, he continued, "Or I'll head down south, dodging the bastards all the way."

Victor smiled, showing a full set of yellowing teeth.

Snipe returned his smile. "See? You *do* see the funny side."

"I needed to hear the words, Snipe. Now, I have something for you."

Still seated, Victor reached under the sink and brought out a small wooden box. "This is from your father; he told me that if you ever ran out of options, I should give it to you."

Mixed emotions ran through him as Victor slid the box across the table. He was more disappointed than angry that Victor had kept it hidden. He'd never even spoken of his father before, let alone mentioned that he had something of his. Snipe had been out of options from the day he'd arrived, and only now did Vic feel it was necessary to hand it over... whatever *it* was.

Snipe looked down, hesitant to flip the gold hook from its eye. *What if it's a gun? What should I make of that —no options and a gun? There's no way I'd take my own life. What if it's an heirloom, or pictures and information about my past? Right now, I'm not sure whether I can handle that, either,* he thought.

"Well, come on. Open it," Victor said.

"Tell me what's inside first, Vic."

"I don't know. Well, I was shown, but that was twenty years ago." Victor opened and closed his fingers, but didn't reach for the box. "He told me that the freedom fighters planned to build a hideout in the southernmost part of the island, and that they've built a network of support there. He wouldn't say where. The map doesn't give much away, and the contraption doesn't work, so it might come to nothing. I thought it might give you hope."

Snipe's eyes widened. Could things get any weirder?

"Hope?" Snipe frowned. Victor moved back in shock. "I could have done with hope before today, Vic. You had no right keeping this from me, and if my father was that concerned about my safety, he wouldn't have left me with you for the past twenty years."

Victor shook his head, then bowed it, unaware that a sea of guilt had already washed any anger and resentment away.

Victor spoke into his chest. "I'm sorry I–"

"You've got nothing to be sorry for; it's not you that I blame," Snipe said.

He opened the box. Inside, there was a map bound with green string and compass. He looked for a note, a message, or instructions. There was none.

He'd seen a paper map before. It had sold for a small fortune. Everything was paperless, and had been for most of his life. The shop still had books, paper scrolls and picture sleeves which used to contain plastic discs that somehow played music.

As Victor cleared the table, Snipe unfolded the map, but it was really more of a diagram or an architectural drawing. There was no North or South pointer, and the only hint of location was the sea and a hill. Or the hill could have been the base; there was no way of telling. One thing he was sure about was that it was a human-made structure, showing different levels, platforms, and areas. All had measurements with abbreviations written alongside them. Labelled as Resin Pines was a drawing of trees and a pond, which after twenty years, could be a building or another factory by now.

"Vic, what do you make of this?" Snipe said, looking at the drawing. He shook the antique compass. The needle had a point on one end. As he moved it, the needle moved with him, wobbling on its axis as if it was broken.

Nose touching the paper, Victor said, "It looks like the outline of a base." Spreading his gnarled fingers to flatten it, he added, "Look at the measurements."

Snipe raised an eyebrow. "Might be useful if I needed to build a secret base, I suppose."

"Look closer." Victor tapped his finger on the first number, then stood back. "Look at all the measurements and tell me what you see."

He did, and saw what he had before. Just measurements. "Vic, I'm not in the mood for games. These things are useless." He held up the compass. "I still see measurements."

Victor pulled a quill pen from his jacket pocket, then tore off a corner of the diagram. Snipe gritted his teeth, then swallowed the hateful words his mind was telling him to say.

Chewing the end of the pen, Victor wrote down the first number of each measurement. "Think like your father."

Snipe shook his head. "How the… how would I know what he thought? I don't remember the creep. Besides, what good would it do to find him, and some hideout he dreamt up twenty years ago?"

"Do it for the people you've saved." Victor chewed faster. "You sent them down country because it was the safest place for your sort, and besides, your father would be older than me if he was alive. The chances are remote."

Snipe slid his elbows across the table, cracked his knuckles, and raised his head. "My sort?"

Victor gave a wavering smile and gazed over the top of Snipe's head.

Snipe stood up. Lightheaded, and his gut in knots, he walked out of the room without speaking.

"Snipe, come back. Sit back down."

"I'm going out for a while."

"Not through the shop. The scan pods will bring an army to the door."

Snipe entered the cellar. The room, *his* room, looked empty; void of memories, just like his head. Regret swept over him. *The old boy means well, but I need answers, and I need Lexi. And I'm fucked off with hiding!* The voice in his head ran rampant. Inner chatter telling him to go outside, to walk through the scan pods one by one. Wait for them to turn up and go out, guns blazing.

Fresh clothes at the foot of his bed were a welcome sight. He couldn't recall Victor putting any there, but he was glad to see them. A pair of black slacks, a navy blue open-neck shirt, and a week's worth of smalls.

After hanging the rope ladder back in its rightful place, Snipe walked over to the hatch situated under an old empty trunk. The combination hadn't changed. It led to a crawl space under his room. Three feet deep, packed with old weapons and ammo boxes, it ran the full length of the building. He pulled a string cord, and the area lit up. Green tins from some old war formed a tunnel that fanned out into an area under the shop. There was wooden shelving stacked to the brim with ammunition, and a steel set of drawers held sticks of dynamite and grenades, all with the pin wedged in tight, waiting for someone to bring them out of hibernation.

Today might be that day.

# Chapter 4

Snipe froze upon seeing something scurry across the floor. The hairs on his arms rose and his legs tightened. He rubbed his clammy hands together. His eyes stayed fixed on the spider that sat between him and his goal. The light source cast his shadow on the wall, and then another shadow joined it, its legs long and gangly. He backed away, aware of the hold that this harmless eight-legged devil had over him. He knew that this deep-seeded, irrational loathing was only a figment of his imagination, but irrational or not; he wasn't staying in here with it. He backed up through the tight space, snatching an old .303 rifle, a box of ammo, and a small firearm. As he shuffled back, the spider moved toward him like a guard seeing off a trespasser.

Snipe nudged the hatch open with his head, stood up, and pushed himself out.

"Find what you're looking for?"

"For fuck's sake… Vic, you scared the shit out of me," Snipe said, wiping his brow.

Victor laughed. "You'll be needing more than that, my boy."

"I was just going for a walk."

"Good. Test the pods, find a way out, and make a plan." Victor waved his finger. "That's the Snipe I remember. Level-headed and on the ball. I'll come with you."

It was unlike Snipe to lose control, but on the rare occasion that emotion pushed logic out of the room, Victor knew just the right words to bring him around and make him see beyond the moment.

With a trace of weariness, Snipe walked from the rear of the building to meet Victor, who was leaning on the white pole to the left of the door. Victor was dressed to impress in a grey suit, black socks, and shiny black shoes; his tartan bow tie clung to the collar of his pastel blue shirt.

A blanket of fog settled over the town. Shards of sunlight penetrated the yellow-tinged clouds, making for a cool but pleasant morning. A frosty breeze hit Snipe's face and brought with it a musty smell of uncollected rubbish. Vapour clouds formed from his hot breath hitting the coolness of the day.

Snipe cleaned the lenses of his vintage sunglasses, playing along with Victor's suggestion that they'd disguise him from the locals. He'd concocted a story for why a stranger was in town; a story Snipe couldn't remember. He looked around the road. It was deserted; void of all life. Not even a bird or a stray animal passed them as they walked across the street.

"Something you're not telling me?" Snipe asked.

"We'll walk to the last scan pod. The road's bigger now, by twenty plus houses."

"Bigger... how's that work?"

"More demand for cheap housing, I guess. They're printing them from the foundation to the roof in less than three days." Victor jerked his head sideways for emphasis. "Quite remarkable, considering in my day, it took months, if not years, to build a single house by hand."

"They're printing buildings now... did I vanish for one year or ten?"

"Ah, it's quite a sight. The print drone has a pattern that it

27

follows, like a spider spinning a web."

"I see," Snipe said. "So why is the place so empty?"

"They opened the new power plant eight months ago. Remember the proposed site?"

"Yeah, they wanted to demolish the school," Snipe said.

"Well, they did. No need for schools and traditional education anymore. Not now that everyone works for Zeta's power plant." Pretending to take in the sights, he said, "Governments worldwide –well, what little crawled out of the nuke bunkers – gave in and sided with the terrorists, and why not? They had a solution. They were the ones housing people, giving hope that society could continue. They restored control. People following the logic of machines… who'd thought it? But someone pushes the buttons, and this someone isn't the public-facing type."

"That someone is most likely the government you're talking about. Who else could it be? How would a terrorist group form so fast when everyone around is struggling to comprehend the event?" Snipe slowed his pace to a shuffle alongside Victor. "They'd have to have had that technology stashed years before mother-nature threw a wobbly."

"I'm not so sure. Question everything, Snipe. Remember that, and you'll live as long as me." Coughing, he spoke with a wheeze. "They can take your things, even end your life, but they can never take your soul."

"What about the kids?"

"Kids?"

"From the school," Snipe said.

"Working," Victor replied. "The only reason they still let me have the shop is that I'm over the hill, but when I'm gone, the state will claim the building, demolish it, or turn it into accommodation."

The only convenience store looked different. Not in size; the main structure was the same, but now it was yellow, and the windows were no longer windows. They had been replaced by giant screens, the kind you might find in the city, not a small town. There were no shopkeepers, just one big vending plant that supplied food and necessities. The shopkeeper who locked the doors on Snipe when he was fourteen had died of a sudden brain tumour. The day after, the shop had become the biggest vending machine in town, spewing out everything from food to a new Physi Print Box, which built anything from replacement parts for a home to a living pet, albeit one with little consciousness.

A boy of about ten years old, wearing the latest flight jacket, walked out the store, a nutrition tube in hand. He spun his shaven head toward them and pressed something resembling a wrist sweatband. A hologram appeared. Two monsters were tearing shreds out of each other as he munched on the brown sticky tube.

Snipe called the boy, "Is that a think pad?"

"Think pad? That's so last year. This is my new Hollie-Band. Where've *you* been?"

"What do you mean, where have I been?" Snipe asked.

The boy looked confused. "*Everyone* knows what a Hollie-Band is."

The boy walked over to them, eager to explain the new gadget. "Look. You can play in sight mode. Just flick your eyes, and it does whatever you want."

Snipe watched a grey alien dance in mid-air. "Do me a favour, kid." Snipe looked at Victor and then back at the boy. "Think: *scan pod perimeter.*"

"*You* think it. I've not got it in locked mode. You can think it

29

yourself."

Victor shuffled forward, and for a moment, Snipe thought he'd do it. He held out his hand to stop him. He couldn't risk Victor's thoughts being traced through that machine.

"I want to see what you can do on it," Snipe said.

The boy looked at his wrist, and a hologram appeared with a simple explanation of scan pods.

"Think *location* or *scan pod map*," Snipe suggested.

"I am, but that's all it gives me. Check this out." A waterfall and a rainbow appeared before their eyes. "You can think the weather too. Have a go."

"It's okay, kid. I'll skip it," Snipe said.

Snipe found it difficult walking at a snail's pace. Taking ever shorter steps, he stopped and gazed up at the tall buildings, allowing Victor to catch up and rest.

A box moved from across the street; another in the doorway next to it. Victor watched as Snipe slid his hand inside his jacket, ready to draw his holstered weapon.

"Hello Curt, everything alright?" Victor asked the shadowy figure as it emerged from the doorway of a printed building.

"Victor, my friend Victor, can you spare a few units? I've not eaten in days," said the bearded, bedraggled looking man. Snipe couldn't gauge how old he was. His skin was pale. The only thing of colour on him was a red ring, slipped around his bony finger. His eyes were glazed pearly white; the soiled rags he wore hung loosely, hiding his frame. Snipe saw others approaching from across the street. Two men, not as ragged, but still downtrodden. Another, much older man appeared from behind them and Curt.

"A year, you say?" Snipe asked under his breath.

Victor didn't reply. Snipe reached into his jacket and unclipped the gun from its holster. His knuckles whitened around the trigger as he drew the pistol from its hiding place, spun around, and pointed the barrel end toward Curt, then the man behind him, then the ones that had joined them from across the road, and then back to Curt.

"Move one more—"

"No need for that." Victor lowered Snipe's extended arm, then turned toward the ever-growing crowd, which now included a family of five, a couple, twin boys no older than five, and a teenage girl.

Victor turned to face Curt. "You know better than to ask me for units. My allowance stopped when yours did."

"Yeah, but you've got a shop and a roof over your head," Curt said. "And who's he, anyway? He doesn't look short of units."

Victor coughed, laughed, and broke wind at the same time. "He's come to look after me. Make sure you eat once a day. Kitchen's open as usual tonight, but the rations going to be less. None of you've brought anything from the hunt. How do you expect me to feed you without food? My stocks are running low."

Curt raised his voice. "At least you *have* stock. We've got nothing."

With one swift motion, Snipe had his gun between Curt's glazed eyes. "Don't *ever* raise your voice towards this man." He cocked the pistol. The front of Curt's trousers changed colour as he stood in a puddle of his own urine.

"Okay, okay."

Victor rose his arm toward the gun. Snipe lowered it again.

"Now let us pass." Snipe holstered the gun. "And let that be a warning to anyone who–"

A drone snapped into sight. Snipe twisted on his heels and ducked his head. The delayed reaction from the bystanders surprised him as much as the drone did.

Stone-faced, lips a mere sliver, Victor said, "No, Snipe. Don't do it." It was as if he was expecting his next move.

Wispy sun-soaked clouds cloaked the nearly-invisible disc, making it hard to see as it waved from side to side above the road.

An old-style electric sports car came into view. The drone lowered itself to head-height. Snipe slid his hand inside the breast of his jacket. Victor embraced him, pushing his frail chest up against his. The hum of the car trailed off, as if its charge was failing. Snipe looked through Victor's mop of grey-peppered hair as the car came to a stop. The driver, a smartly-dressed man in his thirties who was too tall for the car, pushed up his door. The hiss of the door's hydraulics matched the wheeze from the driver's chest as he stood, posed in a running motion. His feet fixed to the road, eyes wide, mouth agape. Frozen mid-flow by the metallic drone, not so much a mussel twitched.

With the drone's attention fixed upon the stiff on the road, Snipe and Victor edged away from the pavement. Snipe's eyes flicked between the shimmering drone and the suited figure.

Curt retched. Vomit joined his already soiled trousers. A man broke away from his family and ran to the stiff's aid. Stopped mid-flow, he joined the suited mannequin.

Gritting his teeth, Snipe knew he had to protect Victor. Thoughts of the man in the woods, cocooned and pulled up into the sky, flashed through his mind.

Needing no encouragement, Victor ambled down the two-foot passage between the residential buildings. Like a door, Curt covered the entrance. Still retching, he waved them on, providing a human shield between them and the unfolding scene. Certain that he'd be next, Snipe hurried Victor past the backs of the buildings until they came to rest at the rear of the food store.

"I need to stop," Victor said between gasps. "You go."

"We're alive. I don't know how, and I don't know why, but we're alive," Snipe said.

A distorted voice rippled through the air. *"You're charged with evading an official named T4970 at junction 9 at 7:23, on the morning of March 10th, 2067. Stay in your position."*

Leaving Victor half-bent, hands on his knees, Snipe moved to the front of the store.

Above the stranger's head, the drone spoke. The other man snapped out of his frozen stance and continued forward. Cries from his waiting family provided enough motivation for him to turn back.

A sound flooded the air: *"Citizens, you are free to go about your business."*

Victor came to join him at the front of the store. With laboured breath, he leaned on the wall between the two display screens. The screens were showing how anyone could travel the world as an armchair tourist, or while sleeping in the comfort of their own bed, injecting the notion that it was needed, and that it would somehow bolster their otherwise mundane limp lives.

"We haven't much time." Victor took in a deep breath. His voice quivered. "Go to the basement."

With a wavering smile, Snipe said, "I'm not leaving you here. Take your time, and we'll go together."

Linking his arm with Victor's, he shuffled across the road. Snipe glanced toward the drone. It flashed and pulsated as it orbited the head of the suited statue. Victor pointed his gnarled finger skyward in the opposite direction. Squinting, Snipe followed his finger. A sound that he'd heard before woke his senses. He had visions of the hunter in the woods and the wrap-around cast, smothering his body like preserving black tar. The speed at which it rose into the night sky.

Victor said, "Drones are always in scan mode, you'll be... just go." His face contorted and his pale blue eyes narrowed, emphasising the word: *Go.*

As quickly as the sun had pierced his vision only moments ago, now a shimmer of blackness tore through the air. A shockwave raced through Snipe and Victor as the drone zipped over their heads. If it was scanning the area, it would be too late for Snipe to get away with Victor in tow.

Victor's face had turned ashen, as if the thing that had flown past had snatched the colour from his otherwise rosy cheeks. He'd never seen Victor in such a frail state. He knew that his guardian was on borrowed time. Snipe had always looked death in one eye and laughed while spitting in the other. But this was different. This he couldn't control. He'd protect Victor with his own life; without thought, but the ageing process was a fight which no human could win, and if there was a cure for it, they damn sure wouldn't make it public knowledge.

Victor shrugged off Snipe's attempts to help him cross the road as naturally as Snipe shrugged off Victor's pleas for him to hurry off without him. Like an old car pulling off in third gear, they headed in the direction of the oldest looking building in town; the building Snipe called home.

Victor covered his mouth with his left hand. "Keep looking forward. Pay them no attention," he said into his palm.

Snipe saw the suited man being smothered by inky blackness. The drone pulsated as if gathering the strength to lift the covered statue. Both vanished skyward at an impossible speed, leaving the man's two-seater car standing idle.

Victor unlocked the shop's door, and Snipe ran to the trap door. He knelt to enter the combination. A shiver ran down his legs. The sensation of something hovering tightened his chest. Like a throbbing wound, the frequency made his body spasm. Facing the trap door, he leaned on his left hand and crawled his fingers over his jacket. Like the spider under his floorboards that had crept up on him, he knew that any sudden movement might spur it into action. He'd seen enough of these things to know that he was a dead man kneeling, but he wasn't going out without a fight.

Transferring his weight onto his left arm, he felt his hand reach the snapping point. He rolled to his left, drew the gun from its holster, and fired. Missing, he fired again, flat on his back he continued shooting at the near-invisible flying object as it darted from side to side, mocking his attempts.

He'd blown the bigger drones out of the sky, but this wasn't one. This was a scan drone that seemed hell-bent on taunting his every move. After firing his last shot, he scrambled to his feet. With his back arched forward, the weight of his head threated to send him toppling from where he stood, fixed to the gritty topsoil. If the thing was talking, he didn't hear it. The only sound was a throbbing beat, hidden somewhere within the confines of his skull. Unable to move his neck, he flicked his eyes in a circular motion to get a fix on the drone. If he could have gasped, he would have, as his eyes rested on a much larger, solid shape that had joined the smaller, almost transparent flying object.

A wide thin pane of light brightened the ground below his feet. It moved up his legs, gut, chest, and neck. A pain hit the inner workings of his head as it moved towards his eyes. He saw Lexi reaching out to him, pulling him towards her. The smile on her face comforting him as he felt his body pulled.

"I can't move–"

*"Scan complete. Protected AB negative. Retina scan complete. Authorization code confirmed. Access denied."*

Lying face-down with his arms stretched to both sides like a toppled crucifix, Snipe heard the swish of parting air followed by a duller, more menacing vibration taking flight.

Victor pushed open the heavy fire-door. It hit the wall with a thud. A sparrow landed on a bush inches from Snipe, its song giving life a new meaning. The bird flapped off, increasing the distance between him and it as it flew. Standing, he brushed himself down and looked at Victor.

"Snipe, my boy, what's—"

"I'm alive." Snipe laughed the words. "I'm alive."

"Well, I can see that. Come on, I've made you a cup of tea."

Victor, unaware that anything had happened in the small garden, frowned, then raised one eyebrow as he had when he'd caught Snipe in a lie when he was a child. Snipe had no confessions to make, but he did have one hell of a story to tell over tea.

# Chapter 5

Deep underground, level seven was known as *the zoo* by adults, *the school* by anyone under twelve, and *a waste of time* by Lexi. It was busier than ever today; a lack of teachers being the problem. All adults had to submit their ideas for a lesson: science, history, cookery, and anything else Mr Ranger thought appropriate.

Over forty years ago, he handled a thousand senior schoolchildren. After *the event*, as it was known within the base, he now taught children with no understanding of normal life. He checked submissions from adults for accuracy –not that he could verify the validity of every subject, but he passed what he thought to be correct, and allowed the teaching of opinions to broaden the minds of the young. Everyone had taken their turn, from dinner ladies and handymen to soldiers and scientists. All but Lexi and a handful of others, who, for several reasons, Mr Ranger felt had nothing of value to offer the young impressionable students.

Spud, like most children alive today, was of mixed race. Unlike the other boys who'd become hardened and weathered, he had long brown curly locks and a feminine-looking face.

Spud didn't know his age, but he must have been about seven when Lexi rescued him. He'd latched onto her from that moment. It had taken over a year for him to sleep in his own bed. Today was his first day at school, and the first time he'd been on level seven.

Lexi frowned as a tear rolled passed Spud's button nose. Going to school would benefit both of them, but that didn't stop her from feeling like shit. He'd enjoy mixing with the other children, and a break for her wouldn't go amiss, since her only alone time was when he slept. When he was asleep, she'd sneak out and walk. Nowhere in particular. Anywhere, just to be alone. Lexi entertained herself and often climbed through air vents that lead to different areas. She stayed ahead of the game that way. She knew in advance who would be in a bad mood the next day because of an argument she'd eavesdropped on the night before.

Lexi knelt, licked her finger, and combed it across Spuds eyebrows.

"What you doing that, Lexi?" Spud asked.

"It's *why. Why* you doin' that," Lexi replied.

"I don't wanna go. Don't make me. Please Lexi, please."

"We've gone over this a thousand times, Spud; the teachers know things that might be useful for you. Anyway, that kid you keep looking at will be there. You might make friends."

Lexi straightened his slacks, rolled up his shirtsleeves, and lead the way to the elevator, which Spud was looking forward to riding. He stayed on level two with Lexi, only venturing down to level three for dinner and entertainment for over a year now. Restricted outside exercise had lead Spud to develop a fear of the outdoors. It was driving Lexi mad being cooped up and seeing the same faces day in and day out. Today, she was looking forward to seeing the outdoors. Not that there was a view. A few tents, an exercise park, green dotted around, and not much else. She knew the ocean was on the other side of the base, but access was strictly prohibited, as was the access to all open spaces, for fear of being spotted by flying scanners. She felt imprisoned.

Mr Ranger stood by the elevator to welcome Spud on his first day. He watched as it stopped on level six, only to rise to level two. This went on for a good five minutes before the doors opened on level seven.

"Sorry, Teach. You know boys, right?"

"Er... right. Well, hello..."

"His name's Spud," Lexi said.

"Well hello, Spud. Your lesson's about to start. Follow me."

Lexi followed behind them. Spud looked over his shoulder to make sure she was still following.

Mr Ranger shoed her away with a wave of his hand. "You need to leave now," he said, giving a final flick of his fingers.

Spud turned to face Lexi. Lexi winked and said, "I'll be right here waiting for you, Spud." Then she blew him a kiss.

She'd eyed an air vent that she thought might lead to the classroom they'd entered. It was worth the risk of getting caught– not that she intended to; Snipe had given her the nickname Squirrel for a reason. She was petite, with size three shoes and the flexibility of a gymnast. If anyone could fit through small spaces undetected, it was Lexi Teal.

Spud sat in the second row from the back in a class of ten students. The room had twelve small touchscreen desks. Mr Ranger held a thin cane that had a leather loop wrapped around his index finger.

"Good morning, children."

The children sang their reply: "Good... morning... Mr Ranger."

Sinking lower into his seat, Spud avoided eye contact with the others.

A thin plastic strip that had gone unnoticed by Spud ran the length of the wall behind Mr Ranger. He tapped it twice with the cane. The wall seemed to come alive, like the view from a window. Spud's eyes grew wider at the sight of a patchwork of green and yellow fields. There were also hills, lakes, and oceans with waves that washed down the wall.

He watched as Mr Ranger tapped on a speck of land. It grew before his eyes, becoming clearer and more real as trees appeared alongside buildings and mountains joined lakes. It made sense to him. This was a magical fantasy land, like the ones that Lexi made up at bedtime.

"Above this line," Mr Ranger moved the cane, separating a small piece of jagged land. The line overlapped into the sea. "Was Scotland. Let's inspect." He tapped again. Buildings appeared, people walking dogs stopped to talk to one another, and some of them were stepping onto what looked like a moving building.

"Is that building moving, sir?"

"That's what we called a *bus*; a thing that took people where they were going," Ranger said. "Today, we'll be looking at schools from the old world." He looked at Spud's lowered head. "But for the benefit of anyone new, we'll cover the change from the old to the new world as well, including why the land we live on looks different, and the accepted theory for how this change happened."

"God did it," said the boy behind Spud.

Spud shuddered. Laughter bounced from desk to desk.

The boy behind Spud laughed out the words: "Could've been! Better than what *you* say happened. My Gran said God made it, and then he got rid of most of it because we kissed girls."

"Silence. Speak when I ask you to, and not until then. Understood?" Mr Ranger said.

Heads dropped, including the head of the boy sitting behind Spud who'd made the remark.

Mr Ranger continued. "Please tap the pink dot in the left-hand corner of your desk."

Spud followed the actions of the girl sitting in front of him. He'd forgotten what *left* was, and was hearing the word *pink* for the first time. The long shot of the land he'd seen on the wall now appeared on his desk, including raised hills, flowing water, and a patchwork of greens and yellows. There was a strange shape, narrower at the top and broadening out at the bottom with jagged edges. It almost joined the other land, but not quite, and a slim sliver of water separated the two.

"This will be an overview of–"

"What's an overview, sir?" asked the same boy who'd spoken before. Spud risked a glance at him.

"A short explanation of how the new world came about. A whole lesson in just a few minutes." Mr Ranger gave the children a look which reinforced the silence he'd suggested earlier. "This land, the United Kingdom, was a small, but very influential country. We had our government and a monarchy."

Ranger condensed the history of Britain into a half-hour lecture. He had little hope of anything sinking into the young minds that sat before him. Most yawned, one had fallen asleep, and glazed eyes were plentiful around the room. The only thing spurring verbal momentum was the new boy, Spud. He was lapping up every word as a pet would lap up water.

"The elements." Ranger cleared his throat. "The weather, had been changing quicker and quicker before the event. Things were in place to stop anything from hitting the planet. There were backup satellites and power generators too, should a solar flare knock out our communications. We'd prepared for just about anything that could threaten the human race. We could spot a small meteor heading towards us three years before it could ever pose a threat. Who could have imagined that an entire planet, five times the size of Earth, would enter our solar system?"

"Did it smash into us?" asked the girl in front of Spud.

"No, and we've been over this before. How about you tell us what you remember from the lesson, Mazzy? Think back now. What happened?"

Meanwhile, Lexi got into an air duct that should lead her to the classroom and Spud. The square metal tunnel – one of many internal ducts – had a cool breeze blowing through it. Voices echoed toward her. She was close. She planned to listen to what the teacher had to say so that she could answer any questions Spud might bring back with him. She'd never been to school and wanted to learn along with him, maybe even teach him something other than how to fight and steal. He wasn't a natural fighter and clammed up at the thought of stealing anything. Too old to sit in on lessons, she would steal knowledge instead. Taking what she needed was a trait she had mastered. With arms stretched forward and her toes pointing down, she edged forward toward the voices.

"Dunno," Mazzy said.

Mr Ranger shook his head. He wondered whether anything he said was getting through to the children. "Just as well I'm going over it again, then," Mr Ranger said. "Now, press the pink dot on the top left."

Spud was the first to do so. The map collapsed in on itself, zooming out until it vanished, leaving a blue ball with patches on it, floating above the desk.

"Now, I will give you hope, and explain just how lucky you all are."

Mr Ranger made a conscious effort not to use any big or

confusing words. Otherwise he'd have to explain each word, and he would never get onto the subject of old world schools.

"That's planet Earth, where we live. Now, I haven't got anything showing the event, so I need you to use your imagination here, and if you don't understand something, make a note of it and ask me after the lesson. The rogue planet went around our sun, and the magnetic pull caused a pole shift." Ranger tapped the wall, and the Earth appeared, rotating on its slanted axis. "Imagine a ball moving this way."

The cane sliced through the globe and hit the wall. The projected planet moved. The children watched as the football-sized globes moved above their desks. Someone yawned, but not Spud; he loved it.

"Now, the effects of this were catastrophic. Our satellites were the first to go; over eleven hundred in total. Planes, cars, and even submarines had no direction. The loss of communication only added to the chaos that followed. The sea bulged over the Pacific, and the Earth moved under a blanket of air and water, causing tidal waves which reached one hundred miles inland; records show they were over two hundred feet high. The weather was a mess. Tornadoes wiped over hills and destroyed the valleys beneath them. The ash from erupting volcanos buried nearby communities, and heavy metals within the ash poisoned the drinking water of millions. The whole world suffered from magnitude nine earthquakes. Towns, cities and built-up areas vanished. Torrential rain backed up rivers. It took weeks for them to drain. Liquefaction, a sort of quicksand, prevented reoccupation. So yeah, we're all lucky to be here after that. I'm glad you guys weren't around to witness any of it. And your parents, some of whom might still be alive to tell the tale, would have been at least one hundred miles inland; hundreds of miles away from any volcanic activity and on high ground. Otherwise, they would never have been able to make you."

"My Gran says I'm made of clay," said the boy sitting to the left of Spud.

Laughter filled the room. Spud wanted them to stop. He needed to know more.

Mr Ranger continued. "We were more advanced back then than we are today. We had satellite communication, GPS systems, and the internet was unregulated and open to all users."

Mr Ranger swallowed hard, blinked, then rolled his eyes up to stem any escaping tears. His throat threatened to strangle any words of hope he might have for these children. There was no place for non-citizens in this world. The rebellious became the outsiders. The demand was to conform, and those who didn't became isolated, condemned, and left to starve. The kids within this room did not differ from their teacher; they were all hunted. Culled like cattle while the good citizens of the world turned a blind eye, justifying their ignorance by repeating: *We had a choice. We had notice. The gate on the pen was open for us cattle to stroll in.* But these kids had no choice. With the pen gates bolted, their only option was to survive long enough to see change.

Mr Ranger loosened his necktie. "Okay, now I want to show you schools from the old world."

Spud raised his arm. His question outweighed his apprehension. "Sir, are we bad people because we're not allowed to… well, you know… go where others can? Lexi says we need bigger guns."

Mr Ranger wiped his brow, tapped the wall twice, and the map disappeared, along with the floating globes above each desk. Spud gulped, thinking he'd asked the wrong question.

"Come on, guys, let's all sit in a big circle." He pushed the desks aside. "Come now, let's all sit together and build a pretend fire in the middle."

Mr Ranger gathered books and ripped up the homework he would have handed out after the lesson. Legs crossed, the children followed, forming a circle around the pretend fire.

"I want to tell you a story about a man called Mohandas Gandhi," Mr Ranger said.

Lexi's elbows burned as she edged forward, and the balls of her feet were swelling from her continuous forward motion along the square duct. The one-minute shuffle along the air duct to reach the classroom had taken her somewhere else. Where, she didn't know. She'd followed a man's voice for what seemed like ages, thinking it was Mr Ranger's, but knowing that it couldn't be. What had started out as a laugh, something to ease the boredom and impress Spud with her understanding of what he'd learned that day, had turned into pure frustration.

She stopped to gain strength for the backward wiggle when a door closed. The same male voice she'd heard at a distance spoke.

"Any word from Mathews?"

Lexi pressed her ear flat against the cool metal to listen – and to rest. A line of pain had developed on the back of her neck. She felt foolish, no doubt about it, but knew she needed a minute's rest. After all, she'd followed this voice, so she may as well earwig on the conversation.

"Presumed dead."

"And what about Siren?"

Lexi flinched upon hearing his name, and her head hit the top of the air-duct. She held her breath as she lowered it. Their voices kept changing in pitch, and sounded muffled. Convinced that she'd heard Snipe's name, she listened with more intent, catching a few words between mumbles, desperate to find out whether fate had brought her here to find out about her Snipe.

"They must have followed Mathews. Thought they'd kill two birds. We lost our first team. The second made it. They found him wedged between two trees. He's a lucky man."

"They could track him. Is he conscious? Said anything?"

"He lost sight of Mathews in the wood. The last time he saw him, he was reaching out to him, then all hell broke loose. He's being taken to quarantine outpost two."

As if Lexi had gained weight while laying with her ear pressed against the duct, the metal under her popped, and she gasped. The voices below fell into a silent whisper.

"Mike – did you hear that?"

Tyrone eyed the room. Didn't take long; the large open desk was clear atop and under. The walls were clinical white; a pull-down screen fastened to the far wall remained steady on its clasp. Tyrone shrugged. "We'll bring it up at the meeting. Might as well go in now; it's not like Rush is in a rush."

"I wouldn't joke about Rush Unix. He could appear right in this room if he wanted to," Mike said.

"He can't. Can he? Appear where he wants?"

Mike twitched his eyebrows and smiled.

Lexi heard footsteps and a door closing before she let out a breath that she was unaware she'd been holding. Like a snake retreating from a predator, she wiggled backwards, then found a sliding motion. With her toes lifted, she pushed back on her palms.

Laughter came from behind as she eased her way out of the air vent. A group of teenagers, five in total, challenged her on what she was doing.

"Maintenance," she said, before heading toward the classroom.

Peering through the window, she saw Spud, sitting on the floor with his friends, smiling. She smiled, too. She'd done the right thing sending him, and now she'd do the right thing in finding Snipe Siren.

She stood, arms folded in the narrow passageway that led to the operations room; a room which only a few people could enter. Lexi faced the wall as Kat Brenna, a high-ranking operations manager, ran past. Kat had been perspiring and blinking fast.

Had Snipe arrived?

# Chapter 6

Lexi slid her back down the smooth cold wall, then brought her knees up to her chin. She was already breaking the rules by being this far down the passage that led to Rush Unix, the man who created this vast underground complex. He was rumoured to be a recluse, hidden away from the people he protected, and it was said that he lived beyond the operations room.

Lexi didn't believe the rumours. She'd done the maths, and he'd be over a hundred years old if he were still alive. No, she was sure he was a creation; a godlike figure that didn't exist; a puppet giving wisdom to the few gathered in the room. A scapegoat if it all went to hell, and a prophet if it all worked out how they'd planned.

Lexi had gathered testimonies and a large list of names from those who Snipe Siren had either rescued or helped find their way to safety. She'd approached Kat Brenner with countless reasons to find Snipe, but she'd said that the risk was too high, and the gain was too little.

It was only after Rush Unix gave the go-ahead that they sent a rescue team out to the drop-off point; a wooded area not far from the prison. An insider at the farm named Mathews worked in the prison morgue. He was supposed to break him out and take him there. What could have gone wrong? Something had to have happened for Kat to be running and the team not to be back. She had to know, and sitting around wasn't answering her questions.

Kat took a deep breath before letting it flow out between her pert lips. Had she seen Lexi back there? She wasn't sure. All that mattered was reporting to Rush Unix, and how he'd react to her newfound knowledge.

Mike and Tyrone sat in a low-lit room. Mike tapped the seat next to him as Kat Brenna entered. The room resembled a home theatre. Nine fixed seats faced a raised platform. A curved screen arched the stage, and a circle of lights shone green from the centre of the floor.

Kat took her seat on the front row next to Mike. All were silent; they knew he'd appear at any moment. As rumour had it, behind the screen, within a separate room, his body was being kept alive while they downloaded his consciousness into the base's mainframe. Being unable to speak or too hideous to look at were just two of the tales whispered among the few who knew about his existence.

They watched as green lights spun around the plate-sized circle until they joined, making a complete ring. A hologram of a man in his late thirties appeared as suddenly as a light turning on in a dark room. The hologram was a handsome man of average build with bright green eyes and shoulder-length hair. He was outfitted in clothes which looked more fitting to a hippie camp or circus: a bright red and purple patchwork jacket over a plain, white top, striped trousers, and army-style boots.

Kat often wondered what age she'd want to be and what she'd dress in for eternity, if she could create a holo-clone of herself.

Rush Unix smiled before saying, "Thank you for coming. Any progress with finding Snipe Siren?"

Tyrone went to speak, but Mike jumped in and said, "Sir."

"Rush," the hologram said back with a wink.

The action unnerved Kat. Not so much the wink, but more the persona of a man in the form of a hologram trying to be nice.

Mike cleared his throat and said, "He's arrived, safe and sound. Quarantine two, sir... er... Rush."

"Ah, good. Well done. Give the team who rescued him my thanks and tell them I'll reward them."

"I'll tell them, Rush. Mike and I have instructed a full scan report and medical. You'll have it when it's complete," Tyrone said.

"Miss Brenner, you were saying?"

"I know I'm not privy to why he's so important, or why we sacrificed five men getting him here–"

"Sacrificed?"

Tyrone interrupted, "I was about to tell you. We lost our first team, and Mathews is missing. Presumed dead."

"I hope he's worth it, that's all," Kat said, shuffling in her seat.

"I was unaware, and I'm sorry for the loss. Please inform me of any family members of the brave soldiers. I'll pay my condolences and make sure they understand that their loved ones haven't lost their lives in vain. And Kat, I feel your frustration, but saying it was worth it sounds like a throwaway comment. I didn't know that rescuing my son would cause the death of others."

"Your son?!" Kat shouted.

"And the saviour of almost half the people here. Yes, Kat. My son. His guardian, the man who raised him in the shadows, also helped him free other non-citizens. He's helped many, and needed my help only when he had no other options."

Tyrone and Mike sat on the edge of the moulded plastic seats with their hands covering their faces; they looked wide-eyed through spread fingers. Kat couldn't believe what she'd just heard. If five people hadn't died trying to rescue Snipe Siren, it could have been almost amusing to think of a hologram having a son, and how his son would look. Only five people *had* died, and Kat thought less of Rush Unix now than when she'd entered the room.

Kat was losing patience with these meetings, this camp, and the people in it. She used to hold a high military position within British Intelligence, and albeit doing mostly administration and PA work, she'd seen things; documents of high importance and influential people. Her title, Communications Intelligence Officer, had little meaning. Having next to no communications coming through, she organised who was doing what around the base. The most important things that were discussed in meetings were hygiene and exercise. She wanted an end to the mystery of who Zeta was as much as the next person, and a hologram with a fixation on family preservation would not answer the damn question.

"Your son? You've put everything and everyone at risk for one person–"

"Kat," Mike said.

Holding up a palm to Mike, she said, "No. He... if he *is* a he, then he needs to know what shit he caused." She stood up. "I'm sorry, but I can't listen to this anymore. I'm out. Finished. I quit."

As she reached the door, she heard it lock. She waved her hand at the sensor to no avail. "Open the damn door. I swear I'll... Mike, get it to open."

"Katrina Brenna, please take your seat. You can leave after you've given your report. We're a team, and you are a big part of that team."

The hologram took on a pleading look; a thing normally reserved for human behaviour. Rush Unix spread his palms, his eyes narrowed. "Kat, please take your seat," he said, waving an arm made only of lights towards her empty seat.

"Okay, but only to tell you what I know."

Mike and Tyrone shifted their legs to the side as she walked by to retake her position in the seat next to Mike. She sat, crossed her arms, huffed, and said, "Lost ears on all posts. It's as if there are no underground cables. Like they've been cut."

Mike shook his head. "What post? What underground cables?"

Kat paid no attention to Mike's comment, nor to Tyrone, who was leaning over Mike, getting closer to her.

"It looks like the underground exchange at Kelvedon Batch and Porton Down is disconnected. I've got intelligence on Corsham," she said.

"Hold on a minute. Am I the only one who hasn't got a clue about anything she's talking about?" Mike asked.

"Where are these places?" Tyrone asked, leaning further toward her.

Kat blew out the side of her mouth. "Look, numbnuts, I'm not here to give you a history lesson. The hint's in the name. Corsham's in Wilshire. You know, not far from here."

"I meant, what are these places?" Tyron said.

"Please let Kat explain, without interruption," the hologram said.

"Our people; I heard them die. Wiltshire's under attack. I heard them shouting and crying, saying they couldn't see it. Well, whatever it was, it silenced them one by one. They kept saying it was invisible. The last call I received was terrible."

Mike and Tyron looked on, wide-eyed.

"They said a staff member exploded from the inside-out, and

when his blood hit the others around him, they were eaten from the outside. Whatever it was passed from person to person without detection. At first, I thought it was biological warfare; a super-virus. But it passed right by the imprisoned citizens. I think they're still alive. I could hear their calls for help long after our guys were dead. That was before the line got disconnected. It wasn't local; it's as if the exchange no longer exists. I can't even detect a location signal."

"And what about the enemy bases?" Rush asked.

"The opposite happened. All imprisoned non-citizens are dead. The citizens were still alive. Whatever this thing is, it's attacking non-citizens only. It's intelligent, and we didn't create it."

"How do you know?"

Kat's head jolted backwards. It was the way he said, *How do you know?*

"They tried fighting it, but claimed there was nothing to fight. It was invisible. I almost broke call silence just to ask what the hell was going on, but that would have blown our cover, so I listened and cried. The sounds were horrific."

On the edge of his seat, Mike fidgeted and said, "So we have – I mean, *had*, guys in a base. There are other bases I didn't know about, all occupied by the enemy, and neither us, nor they, know who Zeta is. They follow his lead based on video links alone, and now we have a new enemy. Am I getting warmer?"

"Citizens aren't the enemy," Rush said. "They're human like you are. They're just working for a greater good called Zeta."

"Are you telling us Zeta isn't human?" Kat asked.

"I'll explain when Snipe Siren arrives," Rush said.

"Greater good?" Kat said.

"Bring Snipe Siren after the checks are complete."

The hologram of Rush Unix vanished as quickly as it had appeared. Kat climbed onto the platform and moved her hands over the curved screen, looking for an entrance door. Mike hissed the words, "Kat, leave it. Let's go."

Mike left, and Tyrone followed. Wanting to prove the rumours, Kat knocked at the walls on either side of the platform, hoping to discover a hidden door. Whatever was powering Rush Unix had the answer.

Lexi stood and paced toward the heavy grey door with her right hand raised. The door opened, and Lexi hopped back. Mike and Tyron walked by quickly.

"Lexi, I told you not to come down this far," Kat said, closing the door.

"Have you found Snipe?"

Kat lowered her head, bridged her forehead with spread fingers, and looked at Lexi. "We lost a team doing so."

"His he alive?"

Kat's eyes narrowed, and her top lip raised, revealing her gums. Lexi stood aside as she marched past.

Turning, Kat said, "You know what? We've lost a five-man team and could have lost five more trying to find your boyfriend." Taking in a deep, quivering breath, she added, "To be honest, I never want to see the guy."

"I'm sorry. I knew nothing about the second mission. I thought they were delayed. Thank you for approving another team."

"I didn't."

"But I thought you said—"

With a twisted smirk, Kat said, "Who am I to question the all-powerful hologram?"

"Hologram?"

"Never mind," she gulped. "He's just arrived at quarantine area two. Three days and you'll be seeing him. No doubt he'll receive the hero's welcome you all want to give him."

With a military turn, Kat marched down the long passageway. The noise of her boots striking the ground echoed long after she was out of sight.

Lexi knew the passageways well, even the No Access ones. They all carried sound, and she'd used that to her advantage when trying to find out what mood someone was in before approaching them with a question. She'd grown up on the streets; being switched on to every sound meant she'd live to see tomorrow.

Lexi turned toward the closed steel door. Her longing to see the operations room had turned into a need to discover what Rush Unix was. She flicked her matted dirty blonde hair and tucked it behind her ears, then raised both hands and placed her fingertips on either side of her head, letting them rotate in a clockwise motion on both temples. Information overload had set her head throbbing like a cake rising and falling each time that the oven doors opened. The ingredients were a mixture of excitement and relief that her soulmate was alive, and sorrow for the five who'd lost their lives finding him.

She knew that she'd soon come into contact with the bereaved or those who knew them. By the last count, the facility held two thousand. It was easy to distance yourself for a day or two, but paths always crossed eventually.

Lexi joined the dinner queue. The menu flashed on the far wall; a red cross indicated another meal wasn't available, then another. By the time she'd reached the counter, the choice was hydrated chicken curry or Molsh. She'd never been keen on curry and didn't trust the chicken, even though it wasn't meat, but Molsh contained the week's leftovers; bits of genetically engineered stuff that had fallen from the packet or become damaged.

About to ask for the curry, a bearded woman with a wart the size of a grape flopped a dollop of Molsh into a bowl and handed it to her without speaking.

"I'd like chicken curry, please."

"And I'd like my husband back, but I guess we're both shit out of luck." Her expressionless face made the mole on her cheek seem more prominent today. Lexi lowered her head. She hadn't noticed Kat standing behind her. Without asking, a piping hot chicken curry was given to Kat.

Lexi eyed a two-person pod in the far corner and made her way over to it. If heads turned, she didn't notice. Navigating her way through a sea of denim-clad legs, she stopped at the only empty eating space.

"Lexi."

Lexi turned. Kat's top lip quivered as she forced a smile. Lexi gulped and gave a nod before sitting at the square dining pod.

"Here, have mine. Never liked the curry," Kat said.

"Me neither. I'm alright with whatever…" she looked down at the undefinable slop, "…*This* might be."

"Suit yourself, but just know it's not your fault. I apologise if I made it sound otherwise. I've told everyone where the order came from and if they take issue with it, they can try their chances."

Lexi looked up at the women behind the counter and received a submissive half-hearted wave in return.

"Your man should be out in a few days. We've had to quarantine him and run checks, but I've not heard anything back from the scan checks, so he's chip-free. He's the first to escape the farm. On a positive note, everyone thinks he's dead, so he'll be a valuable asset."

"Asset?"

"And a valuable boyfriend, too," Kat said, patting Lexi on the shoulder. "Why don't you rest today? You look beat. I need you fit for tomorrow. Your boyfriend's caused quite a stir."

Lexi focused on a dried stain on the table, just above her dinner tray.

*The New World Police will know he's alive after he wipes them out, and when he does, he won't take shit from you or anyone, that's for sure.*

"Lexi, have you heard a word I've said?"

Lexi pushed the tray across the table. It fell over the other side and onto the floor. "Yeah, I get it, but let me tell you something. When he arrives, we're off. I might put up with your rules, but Snipe doesn't follow the rules, he *makes* 'em."

"Then you'll both be detained until you know which side you support." Turning, Kat flicked her hair back in a way that said more than words ever could.

She was unsure herself where the line was between both sides, ever walking the tightrope. The day of reckoning would soon be upon her. Like a discarded jigsaw, all she could do was place one piece at a time, in the hopes that none of them were missing.

# Chapter 7

With a smirk and a pooched bottom lip, Snipe handed Victor the four-inch kitchen knife and a handful of washed nettles. He unclipped the Ka-Bar Marine Hunter from above his right ankle and brought it down hard on the wooden chopping board, cutting through the thick root.

"It needs slicing, not chopping. I'm expecting a good crowd tonight."

Snipe wafted away steam from the large pan of broth as it bubbled away next to the array of foraged food from the same woodland he'd escaped. Every time the knife sliced the root, he had a flashback of the man called Fin.

"I'm leaving tonight."

"And just how are you going to do that?" Victor asked, throwing nettles into the pan.

"I've been shot at and damn near killed more times than you've thought about eating my sautéed potatoes."

"More the reason to plan this thing out."

"I should be dead, Vic, but I'm not. I should be looking for Lexi, but instead, I'm feeding skip rats."

"You've changed in the year you've been away. What's happened to the compassionate Snipe?"

Snipe lowered the heat on the pan for no other reason than to dampen the sound.

"Vic, they could have killed me in the woods, and right outside before you opened the back door. They were right over me; completed a scan and then fucked off as if I'm chipped and innocent of any crime."

"You're not well. A few more days rest won't hurt. Plus, we need to plan how to get you through the pods."

Snipe knew he was right; he almost always was. What choice did he have? He had to find Lexi; he also needed to know what had happened to him and where he'd been for the past year.

Their eyes met. Victor said, "Your mind's made up, that much I can see. After you've helped me feed the needy, I'll show you a way out."

"So now you know a way out?"

"Does the wind blow?"

Snipe waited, but there was no follow-up comment from Victor; no punchline. Victor was too involved with the task at hand, and turned his attention back to the pan of thickening green goo that would pass as food for whoever was turning up tonight. After what had happened today, Snipe wondered why Victor was unwavering in his ambitions to feed *the needy*, as he called them, but he knew that was what made Vic the man he was. After all, he'd given the best years of his life to raising a gipsy kid under impossible circumstances while keeping his word to his real father; a man Snipe would never meet.

Unclipping the thin leather holster, Snipe removed his firearm. "I'll keep guard and watch over things."

"You'll do nothing of the sort. I don't need crowd control, but I do need you to give out ration packs while I serve something a little more substantial."

Feeding over fifty people – people even Victor didn't recognise as being local – had taken its toll. Snipe knew that he wouldn't be leaving tonight. It was close to midnight by the time the last had finished their fill. The soup, and the other, more natural culinary concoctions had been spent within minutes, leaving only the ration packs; unlabelled silver packets from a war long forgotten, some containing dried porridge oats, others filled with a sweet-tasting slime.

Victor licked his finger and held it skyward. Women, children, strangers, and the elderly were leaving the makeshift garden kitchen. Six men – one of whom Snipe recognised as Curt – stood in the shadows of the weeping willow tree and Victor's outbuilding, which, until today, Snipe hadn't given much thought to.

Curt shouted across at Victor, "Are you sure you want to do this tonight?"

"It's on a trailer. Just bring it around the side of the shop and hook it up to the truck."

"Planning something?" Snipe asked.

"Planned, my boy. Planned."

Victor explained Snipe's escape, which involved a hot air balloon, a flying suit, and a parachute.

"Have you lost your mind, Vic? You want me to make a break for it in a slow, bulbous, colourful, non-controllable airship? This better be a joke."

"I've given it a lot of thought. Well enough to know it might just work."

Victor factored in the direction of the wind and the area that the scan pods covered. That's where the idea for using the balloon had arisen. He didn't own or have access to a helicopter, so it seemed like the perfect answer. Snipe was supposed to glide down to a selected spot, and the parachute would slow his descent.

"I'll be shot out the sky."

"The best plans are the most elaborate plans… only a fool would try to get away in a hot air balloon," Victor said. "And only birds have wings."

It took the strength of seven men, Snipe included, to pull the trailer over to the vintage 4x4 truck parked at the side of the shop, hidden behind a flimsy fence. A large metal object covered by stretched canvas sat upright on the truck bed. Snipe wondered if it might be a crane of sorts. The trailer holding the balloon slipped into place on the toe bar. Victor fired up the red, dirt-covered truck. A thick plume of smoke clouded the driveway. Sandwiched between the wall and the house next to it, they all held their breath until it cleared. Victor pulled away, and Snipe and the other six men walked behind it as it rocked down the road. Its destination was Walker's Field, one of the last remaining private fields, now used to grow crops and guarded by the Walker brothers. Both in their late sixties, they were as protective of their land as a dog was of its master.

The frosty air bit into Snipe's neck as he joked about walking behind his coffin to the others. None laughed or returned his banter. They had all been paid by Victor with extra food, and their stone faces served as a reminder to Snipe of what he could expect the other side of the scan pods.

Two men positioned the wicker basket on its side, the open end facing what seemed like miles of thin material. Victor pointed out demands to the others, and they followed his instructions by padding down a patchwork of red, yellow, and green. A man wearing a hat wheeled a large petrol-driven fan up to the sheet's open end. Curt had the job of pulling the cord. Air flowed into what would be his ride out of town. The thin, tent-like material flapped and fluttered before creating a rolling wave as it reached the top of the balloon. The balloon inflated.

Snipe put on the flight suit and parachute, having no intention to use either. He planned to get out when it landed. He listened to Victor's advice, which came thick and fast. The old boy was chewing on the end of a pencil faster than Snipe had ever seen him chew. He told him how to use the suit and how to land, along with how to release the chute when he needed to. He was on the part about bending your knees when flames appeared. With fuel fetching a higher price than precious metals, Snipe hoped that there would be enough to get him across the invisible line that held him prisoner.

"Vic, I've never known you to skydive."

"I haven't. I did a one-day training course when I was younger, but never jumped."

The basket rose from its side as the balloon lifted. Victor instructed the men. Now in the basket, Snipe shuddered upon seeing the light of the moon shining through the top of the balloon. Steadying himself, he tried to get Victor's attention as the old boy headed toward the truck.

"Vic!" Snipe cried through roaring flames. "Vic!"

Victor stood facing the truck, thinking of the last time he'd cried. The thought drifted skyward, along with the balloon behind him.

Victor's eyes welled as he turned and looked up at the basket. "Godspeed, Snipe. Godspeed, son."

Snipe wiped his brow. The material of the black flight suit did nothing to absorb the freckles of sweat that pooled together above the bridge of his nose. His short crewcut hair stood at attention as the wind gathered speed the higher he went.

Moments later, Victor and his motley band of degenerates became just a speck on a patchwork blanket.

The balloon was lifting, but not moving in the direction he needed it to go. Then, as if the god of the wind himself had heard his pleas, it drifted in the direction that Victor said it would. He passed the scan pods, and it climbed higher with every blast of fire.

For the first time in his life, Snipe was free, and at one with a higher, unexplainable, almost godlike presence. Trembling, the unseen hairs on his body spiked to attention, not because of the biting wind, or that he'd discovered a fear of heights. No, this was elation; a newfound hope. He *would* find Lexi. She *was* alive. The chills that he felt were her calling to him; willing him to whisk her into the air, to touch the stars and be free at last.

He'd always wondered whether the soul or free will existed, or if an unalterable plan was already in place. In part, he blamed Victor for his inquisitive mind. He'd encouraged him to question everything and always keep an open mind. *Keep an open mind, but not so open that your brain falls out*, he'd say.

"Lexi," he called into the flame, as it roared her name into the blackness.

Below, he could make out flecks of uniformed lighting stretching out and veering off into pockets of clustered speckles that shone like a ring on the figure of a sleeping giant. Above him, the stars; a random set of brilliance; an illusion of time already faded.

A roar of wind seemed to change in frequency, becoming higher-pitched and more menacing. Snipe fell to his knees, bringing his body below the rim of the basket as if it would somehow cloak him from the electrical charge that was drawing ever closer. The wicker basket, which only moments ago had been as open as the sky itself, was now more like a cage. Night became day as a drone scanned the basket and the hunched body below its rim. It was too late to jump, and there was nowhere to hide.

The drone steadied itself, as if hanging on invisible threads. It had no propellers or any visual means of sustaining flight. Its smooth, metallic surface reflected the moonlight, the basket, and the curvature of the balloon.

Snipe stood, gun poised between both hands. A howling wind threw him to the side of the basket. His hand hit the rim, sending the gun flying towards the drone. Without hesitation, he climbed out of the basket and clung to its side. The drone zipped around to face him as he brought his knees up to his chest. The weight of his body turned his knuckles white. With his feet now flat, pressed against the wicker, he thought of letting go and pushing out to clear the balloon's ties.

The thought, along with his body, flew away from the drone in an uncontrolled tumbling fall, carried by the same airstream that had disarmed him.

Snipe's internal organs moved up against his spine as he freefell, the flesh of his cheeks flapping. The pressure on his eyes took away any hope of seeing the drone that matched his speed three feet above. He went to reach for the cord to deploy the chute, but the shoot was still in flight within the wicker basket. He moved his arm across to his back. His body twisted and changed direction. He pushed his other arm out and twisted again, this time in the other direction. The force of the upward squall pushed both his arms and legs out. He flew upward past the drone, missing it, but sensing its mass. He was now looking down at it. The sight of his reflection was hard to comprehend.

The drone scanned him and fed the results through its database, filing it under unnamed flying mammal. An unlikely threat, with a high probability of it being a warm-blooded vertebrate showing attributes of a large bird. It processed the information as an unknown biological species requiring further verification. The drone informed the nearest air base of its find and retreated.

Snipe thought his bowels had emptied as he struggled to gain control of the thermal he'd entered. He was defying gravity, floating upward, as he had in the basket. Unaware of how far he'd fallen, and with the ground not yet visible, he glided, regaining composure. Aware that he was now alone, any relief that he should have felt disappeared. Death now the only thing he could think of.

He checked his back again for the chute while fighting against the wind. Trying not to spin out of control, he saw pockets of light beneath him. They were growing in size. He flapped like a bird, but this only made him plummet downward. With his journey – along with his life – nearing its end, he relaxed, spreading his arms wide, his legs closer together, his upright stance changing as he leaned back. The rush of air sent him into a backward roll. Over and over, spinning backwards. The lights on the ground flashed, strobe-like, with each spin. The tumbling motion stopped when he hit something; something where nothing should be.

Pressed against the basket, he let out a euphoric scream before being taken away by a gust that blew him sideways, away from the gently drifting wicker box. With small bodily movements and eyes focused toward it, he willed himself to reach it, and he did, this time hitting the balloon's deflating bulk. He slid, grabbed, and wrestled his way back into its enclosure.

The fire roared through its opening, slowing the balloon's descent. He saw the buildings below growing at a rapid rate. He was heading towards a tower. The tower's red light flashed, as if warning him to move or change direction.

Sliding his arms through the parachute's harness and clipping it into place, he bailed, pulling the cord as he fell. The chute opened, and within seconds, he felt the roof of a family transporter fold around him.

He woke to the sound of echoing voices and the sight of men in uniforms. His eyes focused on the three white letters plastered across their chest line.

*NWP.*

# Chapter 8

She'd been watching the warden dose off for over three hours. Every time she went to make her move, he'd snort, then look around as if the sound of snuffling back snot had come from somewhere other than his nose.

Her only plan was to get past the overweight warden who sat guard next to the exit of the tunnel. What laid beyond, and how many security measures were in place, she didn't know. All she knew was that the tunnel was long. She remembered walking along it with the few who survived the gassing of the sewer camp. The tunnel led to Snipe… she hoped. There were several leading out of the compound. Certain that this was the right one, she waited, in the hopes that the warden would leave his post.

Voices. Two, both male, echoed through the corridor behind Lexi. With only the open space of the cafeteria, and the dozing giant – his bulk spread over the chair, covering it until it seemed as if he was levitating – and the other two men approaching from behind, she had little choice but to give up, and claim that she couldn't sleep, so she was taking a walk.

She heard the name Snipe.

Lexi dashed across the corridor and hid behind the bin. Its interior had been cleaned only hours before, but the back of it made her gag. Putrid drips of curry, tainted with the smell of industrial bleach. Using her sleeve as a makeshift filter, she gasped in a breath and squatted in silence, anticipating what they might say.

"We can't feed ourselves properly, so how'd they expect to feed another stray? I thought they closed the gates. No one comes in, I was told."

The electric buggy they drove stopped beside the bin. The one who'd just spoke threw something through its opening. For a moment, Lexi thought they'd spotted her, so she scrunched her shoulders in to try and make herself smaller.

"Don't tell me you haven't heard of Snipe fucking Siren. I'd watch what you say, mate. He's the one who took out an army of Zeta's lot, an army of gun drones, and still managed to save a bunch who were being kept captive. He's young, but he's a hard fucker. A real Billy the kid," the other bloke said.

Slurping the last dregs of his drink, Lexi heard it bounce off the innards of her hiding place.

"Billy who?"

"Billy the fucking kid! You don't know your history, do ya?"

Lexi looked past the bin and saw a cart bolted to the buggy's rear, displaying the words *Quarantine Supplies* written across its corrugated side.

"Oi, lard ass!"

Lexi cowered closer to the bin, her face nearly touching the slime as she watched the rear wheels bounce.

"Creep up to him and shout in his face."

"You call from inside the tunnel, and I'll stand in front."

The wheels bobbed again as the other left the vehicle. Like a pair of giggling schoolgirls, they tiptoed over to the sleeping guard.

Sliding out from behind the bin, Lexi rolled up the side of the cart. As the two men lingered around the guard, plotting their next move, Lexi pulled out a tightly-packed something-or-other and rolled it down the corridor before squeezing herself into the space it had filled. A rush of adrenaline that she hadn't felt since she was last with Snipe flew through her body. She thought about getting back out and rolling the bedding further, as they might spot it on their return.

A series of shouts and a slap, followed by laughter, rang in the air. Lexi found herself saying, "Come on, hurry up already."

The cart rocked with the weight of the driver and his passenger. It jolted into motion. The guard snorted as they drove into the tunnel. A clang nearly made her gasp as something was thrown at the cart.

The ride had been smooth so far. The loud but distorted voices of the two men up front made the conversation hard to follow, although she did get the gist of it. They'd been talking about her Snipe – a real softie as far as she was concerned, but regarded as a fearsome warrior by those who exaggerated his abilities. Or had they? Was she the one who was wrong about him? After all, he had saved half the people at the compound; a compound that Snipe didn't know existed. He'd always say, *Head south*, as it was a well-known fact that people in the southernmost part of the island were sympathetic with the nonconformists. Back then, southern safety was a rumour, but today it was a fact. The compound offered a sanctuary to the damned.

The two voices were joined by others as the supply trolley slowed and finally stopped with a jolt. Lexi, ever the opportunist, hadn't thought this far ahead. It hit her harder than the slap on the snorting guard's face. Now what?

Snipe would never be confined to the city below ground, and after Kat's threats of detaining them both, she had to warn him. Better to live free and in danger than to be a comfortable prisoner.

The side flap opened without warning.

"I hope there are snacks in there."

"Just bedding," the driver said.

A raspy voice spoke, "Just bedding?"

Lexi recoiled as a hand hit her gut. She let out a winded cry.

"Okay, drop it on the side and take the other one back to base… and please bring the entertainment next time, or a few snacks at least. We're going out of our minds stuck out here."

"What's the load?"

"Rubbish and empties, mate," said the one who'd thought he'd punched a pillow.

Lexi was thrust forward as the trolley was detached.

What little air there was within the small space she occupied had turned arctic.

*Okay. Think, girl. The two idiots are driving back now, which gives you five minutes tops before they find the bedding in the hallway. You're outside getting frostbite all by yourself. You heard three other voices and a heavy door close. So, you have two choices: Knock on the door, be their entertainment, and hope Snipe's able to save your ass, or stay in here for the night and hope you wake up alive. And if you do, what then…? Stupid, that's right fucking insane. After all, he'll be out soon, and then we can go on our way. It's not a prison camp, it just has tight rules. Leave, and stay gone. Don't believe them, though; no one's ever left, so how do you know? Take your chances, she said. Can't trust that bitch. Can't trust anyone.*

The underground quarantine building had a gradual slope that provided the only way in or out. It was small; only thirty feet by twenty. Its original purpose was an entrance where freedom fighters and casualties would be funnelled through into the tunnel that led to the base. This tunnel joined another, which went to the heart of the base, safe from any outside threat. It was only when one of the rescued non-citizens brought a virus that disabled half of the people inside that they decided to use it as a checkpoint. There was a clean room, where individuals were recorded, washed, scanned, and vaccinated before they were allowed to enter. The room was lined with tent material, which served no real purpose or protection. It was merely a showpiece, meant to blend in with the other empty tents which surrounded it. To anything flying overhead, the structures looked like an abandoned settlement, of sorts.

Lexi opened the trolley's side, one louvre at a time. Click by click, the frosty air hit her exposed skin. She had her hand pressed to her chin. There wasn't a building or a heavy door. Instead, she stepped out into a military tent. There was a reflection of moonlight on the flapping material, and no sounds to be heard or people to be seen. The place was empty, as if the three voices, the slamming door, and the unintentional poke in her stomach hadn't happened. The thought of needing bedding in such a large, open area gave her little comfort. Lexi walked over to the door that was tied with rope and then back to the trolley.

The ground fell from beneath her feet. Lexi's open-mouthed, wide-eyed expression was wasted in the dark, painfully cold tent. She tumbled further before coming to a sudden, numbing stop. Then numbness turned to pain, and Lexi released every swear word invented, and others belonging only to her. The smooth surface of the steel door clung to her padded jacket. The day's moist air had turned it into a Velcro ice sheet, just waiting for bare flesh, or an equally moist jacket, to be pressed up against it.

The door flew open. Lexi's eyes slammed shut, blinded

by a rush of artificial light. She had no time to process her surroundings, or the people standing over her.

"Lexi."

A stifled bang.

"Lexi – leave her alone, she's with us. Lexi!"

Snipe's shoulder-length hair flew back and forth with every pound of his clenched fists. Dressed in an orange prison uniform, the numbers 08080 danced across his chest with every movement.

"So, you've followed him here? Who's with you? How many others are in your party?"

"Snipe!" Lexi shouted. Using one of the men to pull herself up, she stood and pushed him away before looking through a transparent wall. "Snipe! Snipe!"

"Just hold on a minute." Two of the three men held her back from the composite plastic-partitioned wall. Snipe's punches went unheard; his head tilted to one side as he smiled at Lexi before drawing his attention to the men restricting her movement. He pounded again, covering the screen with spittle.

The man she'd pushed stood between her and the five-inch-thick screen. "Calm yourself, little lady."

As she raised her leg to kick out at him, one of the others rose his hand in a backward motion, and another pulled her backwards.

"Stop! We're not going to hurt you. Calm yourself."

Lexi lowered her head submissively, waiting for the men to hover over her, before quickly raising the palm of her hand and knocking one of them back into the see-through wall. Snipe flew, hitting the solid surface. Overpowered, Lexi was wrestled into a glass enclosure. The door hissed shut as one of the men pressed a button on the adjacent wall. Twisting, she sped over to Snipe, hitting a clear dividing sheet of polymer instead.

# Chapter 9

The force of water jolted Snipe's head backwards. He opened his eyes and mouth between the high-pressure spurts that came from a hose held by one of the NWP. Having no recollection how he'd become tied to a steel water pipe, he pushed against it, and rocked from side to front in the hopes of freeing himself. This only triggered more water, carrying with it the laughter of a room full of uniformed soldiers.

Processing his surroundings, exit points, loose items that could be used as weapons, and too many men to count, he lowered his head and closed his eyes. The room fell silent. Aware that someone of importance had entered, Snipe peered through his eyelashes.

"So, this is the bird in question."

Snipe clenched his fists; they were of no use tied to the pipe. The man wore the same uniform as the others who stood in silence with their arms pressed to their sides, but looked different; crisper, more refined.

"Your name."

Snipe didn't answer.

He moved around the pipe. "You are a non-citizen. Not much meat on your bones." Eyeing Snipe up and down, he said, "This building's older than Jesus himself. Wood Stove... you'll burn for an hour or two."

Snipe raised his head, and following him with his eyes; he said, "Why not just throw yourself in? Then you'll have it working until Jesus returns."

A slam to his temple. A fist maybe, he didn't know. A solid object?

Pressure under his chin forced him to raise his head. He looked at the baton. His body twisted, his fingers tightened, and his spine went in on itself as a bolt of electricity flew through his body.

Words entered Snipe's mind like a slow, dull tone. "Take him to the shed. And keep him conscious."

Snipe fell to the floor. He needed to fight back, but his body wasn't allowing movement of any sort. They dragged him across the floor before lifting him to his feet. The temperature of the air changed as they manhandled him. His limp body was sat upright in a chair. Whatever the baton expelled had rendered him powerless as his arms and legs were strapped to its frame. The men retreated, a door clicked shut.

Snipe was alone. The space was airtight black. Vapour from his breath fell back into his face. He sensed that the so-called shed he was in was little bigger than the chair. The compact, pitch-black space allowed him to hear his captors speaking outside.

The conversation that they were having was as clear as it was nonsensical. They were talking about him being somewhere else. He listened as they argued between themselves, wondering how he could be in two places at once. One of them suggested that he was a twin, and another said he was a clone. Another chipped in with the idea that his robot-self was at the base ready to strike, aiming to wipe out the remaining non-citizens.

Japing with each other over who'd ask the questions, one said he'd be sick if he stayed, blaming tonight's meal for repeating on him.

"Guys, I've finished," Snipe said.

Laughter followed, then a kick to his cell. It was wood; thin wood. Snipe struggled with the plastic ties that bound his ankles and hands to the chair. Every movement only tightened them further, the straps cutting into his skin.

"What? You finished? We've not even started yet."

"How's a man going to clean himself up? Wait, this isn't the toilet?"

Hilarity had got him out of more scrapes than he could remember. He needed to buy time; enough to figure out how to break free from the restraints. He couldn't plan past that.

As if a conductor had waved his baton to silence an orchestral choir mid-song, the chatter and bravado outside stopped. Snipe listened as a strong, husky voice addressed the crowd. It was the man who carried a *different* sort of baton.

"You two replace sentry four."

Snipe bent his thumb and index finger inward to overlap his little finger, making his hand as slender as possible. It was no use; the more he pulled and twisted, the tighter the strap around his wrist became. He moved the heavy chair a fraction of an inch. It wasn't anchored, but even if he could stand, there was no way of escaping with it in tow.

"You two ladies take the watchtower, and you two relieve sentry one."

Snipe listened to a chorus of *yes sirs* before hearing the door open and shut.

"The rest of you bed down for the evening. I'll see to Mr Siren."

Snipe rocked the chair back and forth, testing it for any weak points. He stopped upon hearing two people whispering outside.

"Are you sure you don't want me to stay, sir?"

After saying that the order came from Zeta, the door slammed again. Snipe was alone with the baton man.

"I think we got off to the wrong start, Mr Siren." The voice had moved behind him. "I will ask you questions, and you will answer them. If you answer them, I will make sure that your death is quick and painless. On the other hand–"

"Couldn't you have found a place with thicker walls?"

Snipe tasted salt as sweat ran off his top lip. The straps cut his skin and his palms pooled with blood.

"What did you say?"

"It's just… your fucking breath stinks, so if you're going to ask questions I'd like thicker walls."

"I'll leave you to think on your own while I get a drink," the man said matter-of-factly.

There was a tapping and scraping from the back of the shed. Twigs broke as the man rounded Snipe before leaving. The outside door that the others had used slammed.

Snipe was alone.

Something scurried along the rim of his ear. A sharp pain, followed by numbness, struck him. He shook his head and gritted his teeth. A pinch below his knee. Another lower down, toward his ankle. Like a wire brush combing the back of his neck, soldier ants ran around it and through his hair, stopping only to let their scissor jaws strike the softness of his skin. With every slice, they released a dissolvable acid that burnt his punctured flesh. Slaves, given an order to hunt for food, the scout ants wouldn't stop until they'd disabled their prey. Only then could they spread the scent of success.

Throwing his head back, Snipe trapped several within the crease of his neck. Front and back, side to side in a circular motion, trying to break free from the straps that held him in place.

Tiny legs tickled his cheeks. One entered his mouth. He bit its little body, spat, then curled his bottom lip up over his top, forming a seal. Batting his eyelids open, shut, open. A tickle, a pinch, and then a blinding pain travelled up through his head. Tears pushed their way through his closed eyes, wetting his cheeks.

He screamed.

The scream turned to breathlessness before he passed out.

Unable to see, only able to distinguish between light and dark, the ants scurried across the flight suit and Snipe's now motionless skin. By passing out, Snipe had halted their voracity.

The hose, this time not as powerful, struck him again. He woke with a gasp. Artificial light ran in a straight line from the door, leading into the room with the pipe. After the first shock of icy water hit his body, Snipe felt relief as the ants flew off, hitting the wood that surrounded him and the chair.

The water slowed to a dribble.

"Sorry. I forgot to make you a drink," said the man.

Snipe ran through his response in his mind, but this time, he chose not to speak.

"Question one..." The man studied the screen held in the palm of his right hand as if the questions were not his own. He said, "Who provided the airship and where did you leave from?"

"That's two questions, you fucking idiot."

"So, my little friends didn't do their job. Maybe a few buckets full will convince you, or maybe should I pull your toenails out."

The man's sadistic scorn told Snipe all he needed to know. It was only a matter of time before the pain would overcome his will to live. As a consolation, he'd die without answering any questions.

"Answer me."

A soldier ran over to him.

"Sir, we have a breach. A red vintage truck. It's passed the outer signs. Might be nothing. Sir, permission to intercept?"

"Just one vehicle?"

"Yes, Sir. One old truck with one elderly driver."

"Send a patrol car."

"Yes, Sir!"

Snipe's eyes widened as a dry, painful gulp moved down his throat.

*Vic, you old fool! Bloody hell, Vic! Why? Why?*

The man drew closer. "Now, where were we?"

Throwing his head and upper body forward, the chair toppled out of the open door. He landed face-first on the wet ground, twisting his face as both airways sunk into the sludge.

His head twisted back as the man's boot smashed into it.

"Where do you think you're going?"

Snipe's plan was as simple as it was desperate. Head lowered, body in the sitting position, he rocked the chair onto its side. The man's boot came down again, this time dislodging the chair's back leg. A rain of kicks and punches came at him. Each time, Snipe rocked the chair. The man saw red. His tensed body shook as he lifted the chair to position Snipe's head for the final strike.

Snipe spat blood, then said, "You need to work on your upper body strength. Hell, I've seen kids stronger than you."

His childish comment paid off as the man lifted the chair from behind, intending to drop Snipe on his head or use it like a kickball. The chair's frame creaked. The man held out a baton; the same baton that had delivered the knockout shock inside the hall. Using the weight of his body to swing against the upward pull of the man, the chair's frame collapsed. Snipe fell and rolled to his right with the two chair legs tied to his feet like a pair of skis. He pulled the blood-stained spindles from between the plastic ties and the flesh of his wrists, shaking them off as he stood. The man charged, swinging the baton toward him. Snipe ducked and grabbed his testicles, throwing his head forward. The man's nose crunched from the impact.

Barbed wire ran atop the mesh perimeter fence, and the gate to the side was padlocked. Two shots rang out from the tower. Snipe dived and rolled toward the building, stopping short of the open door. Shouts and elated calls drew closer from inside the building. Flattening his back to the wall beside the door, he was out of sight of the tower. Thudding boots echoed through the building and out into the open yard. Snipe waited until one turned toward him. Using the frame of the door to swing himself inside, he slammed it shut behind him and twisted the lock. Two soldiers stood between him and the front entrance door. Their fight-or-flight faces did a double-take.

Snipe held out the baton they'd seen in action earlier. They went for the bio-guns that hung from their waists; the only modern things in the room, but then chose instead to raise their hands.

Snipe ran for the door, pushing them both aside. Two shots zipped past him. One took out a chunk of the door frame. Shots from above sprayed the dirt that stood between him and the little red truck, parked beyond the wire fencing.

Snipe hid behind a parked armoured vehicle. "Bloody hell, Vic."

Through the dust cloud, Snipe saw two men firing from the tower, a car approaching Vic with soldiers inside, and more gathering at the side of the building.

He was trapped.

# Chapter 10

Smeared lip marks on the transparent screen stood between Lexi and Snipe. Although it was soundproof from the outside, the dividing sheet inside, although as strong as steel, allowed them to hear each other.

"You look younger. What's with the long hair?" she asked.

Snipe smiled back. "Well, I tried to see the barber, but you know… thought it better to escape. Plus, the queue was huge." Placing his palms onto the screen, covering Lexi's, he said, "You've not changed. Still as fiery as your mother."

"You never knew my mother."

"Well, they say the spawn of the devil's horny for a reason."

"And you are Snipe Siren."

Snipe looked different; younger even. He hated long hair, and the regular prison meals had made him gain a few pounds. Lexi didn't need convincing; he was her Snipe. Same sense of humour, same penetrating stare, still strong and handsome.

"Babes, what's in there?" Snipe asked. "They call this a holding pen. They're making sure I am who I say I am, and not AI or chipped. I believed the fuckers, too. So, what's going on, Lexi? What have they done to you?"

Lexi had to shout back her response, which didn't come across how she wanted. She used body language to soften the words as she said them.

"They're the real deal." Raising two thumbs, she continued. "I needed to find you. I was going crazy in there." She spiralled her index figures in a circular motion around her temples. "Once you're in, there's no getting out. I mean, you *can* leave, but they're not gonna risk exposing the base. I don't trust 'em. They say the leader, Rush Unix, is a hologram and–"

"Lexi. Lexi." Snipe followed her tear-filled eyes with his own. "I'm here now. Nothing will hurt you. I need to get into the base. If I sense trouble, we'll leave together. *Together*, Lexi. You have my word."

Calls were made. Lexi was missing from her room. They were instructed to detain her and fast-track the quarantine process.

After Snipe's arrival, a scan drone was spotted in the outer rim; Rush Unix had ordered a lockdown. Entrance and exit points were sealed.

Struggling to hear one another, Lexi and Snipe reminisced. It was difficult to have a proper conversation, although reliving their adventures together became easy. They met at the tender age of fourteen. Lexi loved to recount the way he appeared from behind a tree and told the older boys to leave her alone. She remained adamant that she could have taken them. Snipe smirked and went along with it.

She recalled the way that he had swaggered over to the obvious leader of the six boys who had her surrounded. To this day, she wasn't sure what they'd have done if he hadn't arrived. Chewing on a straw, he'd said, *"You must be deaf and dumb. I said leave her alone."*

The boy must've been seventeen. He looked as mean as hell, and stood a good foot taller than Snipe. She remembered him saying something like, *"Nothing wrong with my ears, mate, so fuck off before–"* It was then that Snipe jumped into the air and slapped his hands on either side of the boy's head before headbutting him.

*"There is now,"* he'd said.

The others had helped the leader of their pack up and didn't even bother fighting back. Lexi always said he took out all six, and not one of them left without knowing his name. She liked it when Snipe rolled his eyes and told her it was nothing. That was the day he went missing after being locked in a shop. Lexi had looked for him everywhere, not knowing he was across the road in the basement of an antique store.

Two men entered. One approached and opened a panel on the screen that contained them. Snipe and Lexi turned toward him. "You two calmed down yet?"

The other man handed him two silver packets. Steam rose as he tore the seal apart. "Ration packs tonight, folks. Due to your stunt, little lady, we're out here until your test results come back."

"Why? Are you not allowed back in? We don't need a babysitter," Lexi said.

"The base is locked down. A drone followed you," the man said.

"We'd be dead if it had," Snipe said.

"Might still be. There's no telling what's on its way. I hope you were worth the hassle. Anyway, eat this and rest."

Slipping the packet in, he said, "Shouldn't be long before you're allowed inside, but know one thing." His eyes fell on Lexi. "We are the good guys, right? Here to help, and if I seem a little pissed, it's because we've risked everything to get your boyfriend to the base, and you're acting like we're the enemy. That, and the fact that it's freezing out here and half the bedding went missing off the trolley."

Lexi lowered her head. She'd bitten the hand that fed her, but she wasn't about to apologise.

"Sorry, guys. Lexi's sorry too, and thanks for the grub. When are we getting out?" Snipe asked.

"As soon as the doors open. The test results for you are complete; your ID checks out. We're waiting for the ones on Miss Teal."

"But I came straight from the base. You know I'm not chipped or infected," Lexi said, aware that she'd put them all at risk.

"Standard protocol. You might've been switched, and the real Miss Teal could be gagged and bound someplace else. I don't know."

"Bullshit," Lexi snapped.

"It's this bullshit that keeps us alive."

Snipe looked at Lexi. Lexi looked back at the man. "Okay, you're right, and I'm wrong. Okay."

"Just consider yourselves lucky that it's temperature-controlled in here, and if it gives you any pleasure, the people who saved your boyfriend will cuddle up together in the next room like swingers who got the wrong keys."

They both left. Guilt swept over Lexi. Snipe smirked as only Snipe could.

The silver packets contained sweet slime which this Snipe had never before tasted, but had been served to the needy by the other only a few hours ago.

The armoured vehicle allowed Snipe only one viewpoint: toward the little red truck. Vic's truck. He suppressed the urge to warn him; to shout at him to leave. He knew full well that if he did, Vic would be killed on the spot, or worse; captured and tortured until he gave himself up, and then they'd both be killed. His only hope was that Vic could talk his way out of this one.

"Vic, no. Drive off. Drive off, god damn it."

Under fire from the tower, Snipe watched Victor open the door to the truck and use it to pull himself out. The greeting party stopped, blocking the road. Two soldiers, dressed in black and bearing the NWP logo, got out and walked toward Victor with their guns raised.

Snipe tried the door to the armoured vehicle. Locked. All he could do was watch as Victor raised his arms in a half-bent, frail stance. Two shots rang out from beyond the perimeter fence. Snipe's heart skipped a beat. He watched as the two armed men fell to the ground. Curt and one of the Walker brothers ran over and helped Victor back into the truck. Mr Walker ran back to the ditch where he'd been hiding.

Curt's body jolted several times before it fell onto the road. The NWP fired from the tower at the corpse, making it look like he was still alive and trying to get away. They turned their attention to the truck and returned fire that came from the draining ditch which ran alongside the road.

There was a whooshing sound, and something flew over Snipe's head. The tower exploded. Snipe crawled under the car, nearly missing a storm of bricks. There was a crunching sound, followed by a whistle made by the parting air as the remaining tower fell onto the armoured vehicle. Dust filled the space between the ground and the underbelly of the vehicle, choking and blinding him as he sidewinded out on spread elbows.

The zipping sound of modern handheld weapons fired from his rear. In return, the peppering sound of machine gun fire silenced them from far in front. Snipe ran through the broken, twisted wire fence and over to the truck, stepping over Curt's dead body. There was a glint of light from a large red glass ring that Snipe remembered Curt twisting around his index finger during their last encounter. He covered his face; dust clouded his vision as two motorbikes skidded toward him. It was the Walker brothers, handguns outstretched, firing past him. Snipe glanced up as he opened the passenger door and saw a weapon mounted in the truck bed; part machine gun, part anti-tank missile launcher.

"Vic. Vic." No other words came to him.

"Snipe, get out. Stick to the plan: Find the base, find Lexi."

"Let me drive, reverse… back up, Vic."

One of the Walker brothers flew off his bike. Fuel gushed from twisted metal. It was missing a wheel, and the buckled handlebars looked unrecognisable. Vic held out a joystick control device, black plastic with a red switch on the handle grip and a small, raised button on top. Snipe felt the truck rock as Vic's homemade gun turned.

Victor smiled as he pressed the small plastic button. The truck vibrated with each rapid burst of gunfire. Snipe didn't see the body lifted on the back of his brother's bike; it wheel spun past the truck and away into the distance.

"Come on, Vic. Retreat."

Victor placed a shaking hand over Snipe's, covering his bloodied knuckles. "Snipe Siren, I have always thought of you as a son."

"Vic, what–"

"Let me die like a man." He pressed the button again. As he did, a small hole appeared on the truck's thick windshield. Tiny bricks of glass rained down onto Snipe.

"I'm not leaving without you, Vic."

"Then you'll die with me."

Vic pressed down on the accelerator. The truck rolled forward toward the incoming fire. Performing an emergency stop, they both jerked forward. Victor raised a handgun at Snipe. "Out."

Snipe opened the door.

"Get out, boy. Take this." Victor handed him the gun. Hesitantly, Snipe got out.

He didn't get the chance to say he loved the old fool. A spray of gravel skipped behind smoke-filled tires as Victor streaked toward the base with the passenger door open. Snipe dived for the drainage ditch and ran away from the base with his knees bent and his head bowed, stopping when he could no longer hear the truck's engine. Turning, Snipe saw the truck smash through the perimeter fence, stopping when it hit the building. Snipe turned and started back.

Victor's finger hovered in readiness to flick the switch. Ten, maybe fifteen soldiers fired at him. Like a plague of locusts, they closed in on the little red truck.

Victor glanced through the overhead mirror. "Godspeed, my boy. Godspeed."

Snipe flinched as the truck blew skyward. The explosion took out everything around it, including the base. Everyone in the perimeter of that hellhole was dead. Fragments fell from the developing mushroom cloud above what was once Victor Harden.

# Chapter 11

Snipe kept walking. He put one painful foot in front of the other, repeating the process, just as he had done since leaving Victor. Through stinging, narrowed eyes, he saw a building standing alone next to a shimmering mass of water. That was his next landmark; a self-imposed goal to keep moving.

He hadn't noticed the temperature drop below zero. The flight suit clung to him like a second skin. The night had passed without noise; the first thing he recalled hearing was a family of birds singing, as if in an attempt to lighten his blackened mood. Hours had passed, giving him enough time to reflect on what had happened last night, enough time to plan his next move, and enough time to think about Lexi, Victor, and the shop. However, he hadn't thought at all; his only focus was getting to the next landmark. Ambling and dazed, he pushed forward in singular, focused movements.

He'd paid no attention to the sun rising, and gave no thought to its brightness fading as fine, icy raindrops glistened as they blew in from the east. If there were people before now, he hadn't noticed them either. He moved his head for the first time to survey the area; there wasn't a soul in sight. He was in the middle of an unattended field that had once been used for growing crops, and was now only a wasteland. Weeds sprouted out of the uneven ground. The occasional foreign object, such as a child's broken toy or a toothbrush, littered his path as he walked. The building was getting closer.

As he approached what looked like an abandoned barn, it occurred to him that by now, he must have passed a scan pod, or should at least be close to one. This thought joined the ever-increasing bottomless pit.

A river ran in front of the barn. The frame of what was once a wooden slope entered it from the rear of the building.

The building was mounted on stilts and stood a good six feet from base to waterlogged ground. Rain flew, soaking his side. Two thick pieces of wood jutted out from beneath the door on stilts. Two sturdy bolts hung from where the steps used to be.

Compelled to enter the building, Snipe's subconscious mind sent irrefutable survival messages to him. He looked for a way up. Entering the water and using the frame that was once used to launch boats into the river, he grappled upward onto the wooden, slatted base of what he now knew to be a derelict boathouse.

He rattled the bolted door, its frame long since rotted. One shove and he was inside. Chains hung down from the roof. Heavy tools placed within drawn outlines and a canoe stood upright, balanced in the corner as if it had just been placed there yesterday.

Three stacked wooden pallets blocked the double door facing the river. Sitting down, Snipe covered his face with open hands, pinching his eyes shut. Like a living entity, dust flew through his spread fingers. The rain fell harder now, sounding like distant machine gun fire. Gunfire; the thought alone made his eyes well up. A single, salty tear rolled over his top lip, reminding him of his thirst.

Thoughts which had been absent throughout the night flashed through his mind in rapid, vivid bursts. Vic had been his mentor in life, and his hero in death. He tried to recall happy times; to pick a day when they both had smiled.

*We smiled the night I left to warn Lexi. Glad to be alive after foiling a non-citizen rape club. I was in high spirits. Vic warned me not to go. Damn near pleaded. I laughed; told him I'd be home soon and to get a hot chocolate ready. He wiggled his silver caterpillar eyebrows and smiled back. I remember that.*

Snipe peered through his fingers at the head of a raised nail sticking out from the beam opposite him. As time passed, the room became narrower, until it was only a haze of nothingness.

*The young boy. Lexi wasn't there. Where is she? The light from above. I was blind. Frozen. Black tar covered me. Strangled, unable to move. The ground disappeared.*

Snipe had entered a trance-like state. His eyes flickered and his body felt weightless as he recalled the wind blowing against his body. He wasn't wearing the flight suit; he wore a light summer jacket, pockets packed with survival aids, just in case.

*An armed guard greeted me. "We've got ourselves an RH? Welcome to the farm," he'd said. It wasn't a farm; it was a prison. Sounds, screams, and pain. I heard the pain. Restrained, but not beaten like the others, they took me to a room. It wasn't like the other cells I passed. It was an operating room with computers everywhere. I tried to move, but couldn't. I was strapped to the bed. Everything in the room was white and clean, not like the other cells.*

*"Mr Siren, I'm Mathews. I work for Rush Unix. Can you hear me, see me, and do you know where you are?"*

*He asked loads of questions. Left me alone for a while, then when he returned, he told me that what he was about to say I needed to listen to, no matter how crazy it sounded. He said he'd only have forty seconds to explain everything, and then told me to trust every word he was about to say.*

*The white room plunged into darkness. Computers faded and winked as they, too, vanished under the room's black cloak.*

*Mr Mathews covered my face with his own; his hot breath met mine as he spoke in a concise, almost robotic way. "You will be put to sleep. When you wake, time will have passed, but you'll not be aware. They're planning to clone you. A rescue date is set. Freedom fighters will be rescuing who they think is you. The clone is to take your place and infiltrate their base. My job is to dispose of your body. I'll make the switch, smuggle you out at the same time, and kill the clone before your friends arrive. Snipe, it's imperative that when you wake, you do not struggle or fight. I will get you out. Trust me. I'm legit."*

*A swirling light above my head flashed red as the room filled with other voices. The lights and the computers turned on.*

*Ice cold.*

*Ditch.*

*An arm is reaching for me.*

It was a single droplet of water that made his body spasm where he sat. Another fell from the timbers above his head. He was back in the room, awake and more alert.

A crazy high-pitched giggle left him. "There was two of me."

The muscles in his face retracted. A wave of anger washed over him at the thought of an imposter hitching a ride back to the base.

As if someone had flicked the off switch, the rain ceased, leaving only the tapping of single droplets that fell onto the pallets after their journey along the rafters.

There was no telling how long he'd been sitting there. The sun hadn't fully risen, giving the clouds below it a yellow tinge, reminding him of something that Vic used to call *custard*. He moved the pallets and swung the double doors open. Squinting, Snipe bridged his eyes with his right hand to shield the brightness of the sun. A settlement stood past the neck of the river. The buildings were brick or clay, not a printed house in sight. His gut growled in a wheezy call of hunger. His sandpaper-dry throat needed water. To find nourishment, he needed to cross the river.

"A canoe with no ores."

He spun the canoe on its tip toward the open double doors. Daylight seeped through a crack that ran its full length, shining a line on the damp wooden wall behind him. The line shortened as a rowing boat drew closer. It might not stop.

Snipe stood the canoe in the corner, wedging it under a shelf so as not to alert anyone to his presence. Keeping his back to the shaded wall, he moved over to the double doors. There were two men: one was rowing, and the other had a gun. One of his, perhaps, as it was an old-style Smith & Wesson sawn-off shotgun. Snipe stuck his handgun through the larger of the two knot-holes and peered through the other. It was heading right for the building.

He watched as the boat got dragged partway up the bank; the wooden, skeletal remains of what was once the slope stopping it from drifting down the river.

Two men, both in their forties, stood by its side. They looked up. Snipe recoiled, then looked back through the natural peephole. They were non-citizens, unchipped and trapped between scan pod communities. They had to be; he could tell even from a distance. The two men, both dressed in black slacks and wearing coats with thick, human-made fibre padding around the hood, moved closer. The one holding the gun looked older, as he had a full beard and was taller and heavier set than the other, who, like most non-citizens, looked half-starved. He had a gaunt face with bulging eyes which stared up at the wooden building on stilts.

"Duffy, I fink he was seein' fings."

The man holding the gun jabbed at the man with the gaunt face's ribs. "He saw things, stupid. What you think? That you would find a bat the size of two men?" The gun was pointing up at the open doors. "Hey, bat thing! Come out before I shoot your wooden cave into splinters."

The man with the gaunt face laughed, then snorted until the bearded man pocked him with the butt-end of the shotgun.

"Nowt in there, Duffy. Go on. Blast it to bits."

With his figure poised on the trigger, Snipe aimed at the shooter's hand. A part of him hoped this wasn't going to go down. He had no beef with these simple people, but he knew that the thin wood would not protect him from a sawn-off shotgun blast.

"You go in," Duffy said.

The scrawny man didn't question Duffy, and it was obvious to Snipe that he'd been inside here before today. Like a ferret, he climbed the sloping frame, stopping short of the opening. Snipe backed off into the shaded corner and straight into a cobweb. He felt a sudden rising paralysis flow upward past his forehead and into the tips of his short hair. The irrational fear of what could be inside the spiralling cobweb outweighed the gun pointing up at him. The scrawny ferret hadn't taken the gun from Duffy, not that it mattered; from where he stood, the blast radius would find him, regardless.

A bony face poked through the door. "All clear, Duff."

"Go inside proper!" Duffy shouted back.

Walking through the building at record speed, the man stopped at the far end, next to the upturned canoe. He walked back to the open doors, this time dragging his feet and swinging his head from left to right. Snipe held his gun to his chest, both hands on it, almost as if he was praying; praying that he wouldn't have to break the ferret's neck and shoot Duffy, and praying that whatever was tickling his ear hadn't come from the funnel of the cobweb.

Duffy called up, "Well?"

"All clear."

As the words left his mouth, his eyes widened, and his jaw dropped upon seeing Snipe. Snipe curled the arm that held his gun around the ferret's neck and slammed the palm of his left hand above the bridge of his nose. The ferret's limp body fell to the ground.

"Bobby, stop fucking around and get back out here."

At least now Snipe knew both names. One down, one to go.

"Bobby, I swear I will beat you if you don't come out right now."

Snipe swiped at the cobweb in the corner with the barrel of his sidearm. Nothing came out. He backed up into its place, hoping that Duffy would enter before Bobby came to his senses.

"That's it. I'm coming. You've pushed me too far this time."

As soon as the glint of metal came through the open doors, Snipe grabbed the barrel. Twisting it out of Duffy's hands, he pushed his gun into his temple.

Duffy's voice quivered. "Whatever you are, we mean you no harm."

"Turn around."

The man turned toward him. "You're a bat."

Snipe tried to disarm the gun and found the chamber empty.

"Empty your pockets and place the ammo on the floor."

"Ammo? There are no bullets. Not been any since ever," Duffy said, before repeating himself: "You're a bat."

"Ah, the suit. It's a flying suit. Never mind. I need food and water."

With a toothless, uneasy grin, Duffy handed him his water bottle. "You don't look like a baddie."

"A bad... baddie? What?" Snipe's teeth filtered grit as he gulped down the full bottle of water.

"You don't look like no citizen. You look like a bat. You gonna eat us?"

"No. There's not enough meat on your bones."

"Er..."

"It's okay. No, I will not eat you. Why would you think I would eat you?"

"Dunno. Just with you havin' wings an' all."

It took ten minutes for Bobby to wake up, and another ten minutes to cross the river. After the first shock of seeing what they thought was an oversized human bat, they told him what to expect back at the camp, and that Trig was the head of the two-family camp. Apparently, he was grumpy, and not to be challenged.

There were at least twelve abandoned buildings, all without windows and doors, stripped of any flammable material.

"What happened?" Snipe asked, looking around at the ruins.

Waving his arm in a circular motion, Duffy said, "Come and meet Mam. She knows everything."

Based on his meeting with these two, Snipe pinned little hope on learning anything useful, and was still on his guard. After all, he had just knocked out the ferret.

Snipe followed them both, weaving between slabs of building debris, car tires, and rotten swill bins. They arrived at a building which, from the outside, looked no different from the others, only this one displayed material for windows and had strings

95

of beads hanging from the top of the door frame, tied midway down with a belt. These guys were basic, all right; no sewer system and no organised areas of any kind. Whether food was available or not, Snipe wondered how much longer his gut would stay within his body. The smell of shit was triggering his gag reflex.

"Guys, thanks, but I'm just passing through."

"Who's there?" came a voice from beyond the beads.

A small woman with a hunched back waddled through the opening, stopping only inches away from Snipe. Her pearly white eyes looked straight through him. Holding up her hands, she spread out her grimy fingers. Snipe flinched as she ran them over his body.

"A demon. You brought a demon home." She stepped back, shaking as she did. "Begone, demon. I command you, be gone."

"It's a flight suit. There's a man inside it. He could have killed us, but he didn't."

"Who sent you?"

Snipe surveyed the area as he answered, "I'm just passing through."

"You're one of them. You're a citizen," said the old woman.

"No, I'm like…" He stopped himself from saying, *I'm like you.* "I'm a non-citizen."

"Liar. If you were, you wouldn't be passing through. They know when we move too far from home."

Smoke rose from behind one of the buildings. The shimmering heat distorted the air.

Duffy and Bobby eased the women back through the beaded doorway, whispering something as they did.

A portly man walked over. "I told them I saw something over the river. Didn't think that some*thing* was some*one*. I'm Trig, by the way."

"Snipe Siren," he replied.

"So, you met the goon family, then. They're not a bad bunch. I feed them and keep them alive. You never know when times might get lean."

Snipe didn't know what to make of his comment; he smirked as if agreeing with him, then said, "I'm going now. Nice meeting you."

"Have a bowl of food for your journey. We have plenty." Trig pointed over to the fire, where the largest pot that Snipe had ever seen was hung. "Here. Meet my family and sit for a while."

The smell of shit wasn't half as bad here as it was over where the goons lived. And he *was* hungry.

Six upturned barrels ran down either side of a makeshift table. Snipe thought it strange that they would eat outside when it must be close to zero. Trig rolled over another barrel; its contents sloshed when he turned it on its head, leaving a curved bottom that would act as his seat.

Five others joined them; four males and a female. All of them looked like Trig.

"These are my kids. Their mother died last year when everything froze. She saved us." Trig nodded his head, agreeing with himself.

The kids looked as old as Trig. They were ragged inbreeds, similar in almost every way to their father – or their abuser; Snipe wasn't sure which. All of them looked as if they would kill first, ask questions later, and as if they would do whatever Trig asked them to. An uneasy, instinctual pulse throbbed between his eyes. The last time he had felt it was when he spoke to Spud, the child outside the camp, just before the drone arrived.

Leaning back, Snipe gave a casual 360 glance. He saw the

goons hiding and watching him. "So, what happened to the rest of you?" He pointed to the abandoned buildings that littered the area. "And how do you manage to find food between scan pods?"

"They all vanished. Might've tried to leave the area and got caught. NWP is everywhere. It's better for us, you know. It's our cover. They think it's abandoned."

"And the food?"

"Plentiful. The area's big, and things just wander into camp."

A girl wearing a tattered dress looked into the steaming cauldron. She fished out a ladle and filled metal tin containers with the watery substance. The others made primitive, animalistic sounds as they received their fill. Snipe thought they would serve Trig first, but their system – if they had one – started with the youngest. Tins were placed in front of them in order of where they sat. Snipe got his last. Trig went before he did, flicking something out the tin before it reached the table. Snipe looked in and saw a mixture of meat and roots. All looked fresh enough.

"Let's toast to our new find," Trig said, before the girl had even finished pouring what looked like river water.

The four men grunted as they ate. They hadn't spoken a word, and they probably couldn't. Snipe asked them whether they liked it here, and was met with twisted faces without words. Trig spoke for them. "It's all right. No bother. We have our patch, and they have theirs." He pointed over to a forested mound in the distance. "Over there's Mount Pass. Upper-class folk live there."

"Citizens," Snipe said.

"Sympathizers."

"Didn't think any remained with the risk being so high."

"Religious people put God before danger," Trig said. "They wouldn't dare mess with us. Killed a few who strayed over here."

The girl – more woman than girl; she looked in her forties but could well have been thirty – ate with her left hand. She was holding a large carving knife in her right, although she had already carved the meat. Two of the four men had their left arms hung low, eating with their right hand. They twitched their left under the table, as if holding something. Snipe looked once more at the large knife before returning his eyes to Trig.

Beakers were raised. Snipe looked down and saw a glass ring, wrapped in skin. He looked closer and watched as fluid ran from it, revealing its redness. There was a glint of blades under the table.

Snipe closed his eyes. Visions of pointing his gun at the man who was begging Vic to give him units whooshed though his head as bile rose from the depths of his gut. The same man who aided Vic in his rescue from the NWP camp. The man shot dead by his captors. His bullet-riddled body jerking before going limp beyond the perimeter of the compound.

As if in slow motion, he turned to Trig, then to the others, as they devoured the flesh of Curt.

The makeshift table moved as Trig jolted upright. A glint of failing sunlight sparked from the blade of the stained machete he held. Three men stood alongside him. One held a hunter's knife the other two slapped their palms with short iron poles. Trig glanced at his daughter, who revealed the carving knife used to butcher Curt's body.

"Cannibals."

"We is free, and you ain't leaving," Trig said. "We eat strays, and you're–"

Trig's eyes darted to Snipe's side. Snipe, already aware of the two approaching, quivered as rage surged through his veins. His chest tightened when he went to speak, to reason with them, to spare their lives. No words surfaced, only the sound of his teeth grinding as he pulled the gun from a concealed pocket.

Kicking the table over, he turned and fired. Bobby and Duffy crumbled before Snipe silenced the screeching women standing behind them with an instinctual squeeze of the trigger.

Trig's daughter squealed as her brothers and father slashed the air around the upturned table, trying to get at Snipe. A pole, swung by one of the men, accidentally made contact with Trig's knife, sending it flying. The man freaked as his father went for the knife. Snipe glimpsed the knife through a gaping hole in Trig's neck made by his fourth bullet. Ducking as a metal pole swung past his head, Snipe knelt and fired twice. Both men lay sagging across the table's edge like animals waiting to be skinned.

Snipe convulsed as he turned to the girl. Her face twisted as she snarled through rotted teeth. She edged forward, then backwards upon seeing the gun. Blinded, not by anger or fear, but by sorrow for the women who had relied solely on others for protection and food, Snipe realised he couldn't leave her to die alone; to be at the mercy of the NWP with the only food being that of her family.

He waited for her to advance before grabbing her arm and twisting it. He sent the carving knife to the ground before expelling the remaining bullets into her chest.

Snipe had killed out of self-defence. He'd killed to save the innocent from pain. Today, he killed everyone in the camp: the women, Trig, Duffy, Bobby, everyone.

His fingers, still on the trigger, turned pale. His bullets were spent. His head tingled, and an emptiness ran from his head to his throat. Like the family that had offered to feed him, he was powerless, drained, and guilty.

Snipe knelt, picked up the red glass ring, and squeezed it into his palm. With a heavy heart, he raised his head. Washed away by tears, the scream never came. He shuddered at the thought of what he'd done.

Without looking at the bodies that hung limply across the table and beyond, he walked toward the pin head that was Mount Pass. It was a good day's walk across unknown territory, and he needed supplies.

The thought vanished the second a waft of rotting flesh hit him.

# Chapter 12

The Church stood at the centre of a spiral of printed new builds which housed the good citizens of Mount Pass. With a population of over five hundred, it was a real community, and the last place you'd expect to find non-citizens, but they lived amongst the citizens, blending into the community and its surroundings with ease. Their only restraint had arrived as zoned areas, which included everything that laid between the wastelands, Trig's camp, and the NWP base that had gone up in flames.

They prayed for the souls that had died in the fire. Both citizens and non-citizens gathered within the grounds of the Church and prayed side-by-side.

The un-chipped lived a normal enough life. Their children attended the local school, they attended Church, and even the eating house had a different method of payment for them. It was a dream life for the condemned.

The gap where the Church bell had once sat contained a speaker. An artificial, yet realistic, bell sounded three times.

Reverend Stephen Phillips released his finger from the hand-held device after the third chime. Villagers followed their calling and made their way over to the Church. The shopkeeper finished serving and left, along with his customers. Zip Walker, the chef who worked within the only communal eating house, flicked the off switch on the oven and cursed under his breath before saying, "This better be urgent."

The school gathered the thirty-seven students that attended, guided them along the corridor, and into the dining hall before leaving via the fire escape. They formed a single-file line and made their way over to the now-crowded Church. People left their homes, adding to the thickening layer of bodies that stood outside the Church's packed interior.

Reverend Phillips cleared his throat; the sound echoed around the settlement. "Thank you, brothers and sisters, for coming here today. We're gathered here today to welcome a newcomer amongst us."

Zip mumbled, "Shit, that's all we need."

"You have all found God. Some of you later than others." Reverend Phillips pointed into the crowd. "The town grew smaller the day the devil tried to cleanse our town of what they call *non-citizens*." The room fell silent. "The town grew smaller the day they restricted our movement."

Agreeing whispers spread. A nod here, a smile and sideways glance there. Poppy, the school teacher, shouted, "Praise the Lord!"

Others followed her lead, until Reverend Phillips raised his hands to silence them once more. "And what did we do? Did we falter? Did we fall? Did we buckle under the pressure of their threats? No. We rose. We became stronger. We became one in the eyes of our Lord."

As if under hypnosis, everyone both inside and outside the Church nodded in unison – except Zip, who thought his bread must've sunk in on itself by now.

"I'd like to introduce you to Fin."

Fin joined Reverend Phillips at the podium. There were gasps as Fin's towering bulk stood next to him. A scar, visible under his hairline, looked as out of place as his ragged, torn clothes.

Fin lowered his head, but kept his eyes raised as he scanned the congregation and gave a quivering smile. The stench of homelessness wafted through the crowd. People standing by the gravesides on the Church ground shuffled closer to the open double doors to steal a glimpse of the newcomer.

"God has brought our new friend to us today to test our compassion once again. He, like a lot of you, arrived here needing help from our community. I'm asking you to search your heart and to offer this man exile and protection. The house of God will provide shelter until suitable accommodations are found."

Multiple whispers bounced off the Church walls like an out-of-tune choir rehearsal.

"Fin will share his story with us after morning prayer this coming Sunday. Meanwhile, I ask for you to show him discretion and kindness. He needs our love and protection… and a shower."

Laughter rang out. Fin gave a nod and smiled.

Snipe had pushed his body and his mind to their limits. The suit was the one thing that he felt he needed to shed before anything else. He'd walked for two hours, and now he understood why it was called a flying suit.

The morning had come and gone. What he did to the cannibals would stay with him for the rest of his life. The voice in his head was filling him with regret. If he'd only taken out Trig, he could have overpowered the others. He might not even have had to, with their leader gone. What had they done wrong, anyway? Eating people was the way they survived. Maybe he hadn't been on the menu. Maybe they would have let him walk away without a fight.

He stopped, shook his head in an attempt to stop the persistent internal dialogue, checked the compass, and continued. Mount Pass was his next landmark; his only saving grace. There, he'd eat, drink, find clothes, and change out of the suit. It helped his mental state that Mount Pass wasn't taking him off-course. The thought of not being able to get the things he needed when he arrived hadn't entered his mind. There was no longer any choice, and no one was going to stand in his way.

The ground crunched. Frozen clumps of earth underfoot felt as solid as rocks, making the trek more tiring than it should be. The closer he got to the mound, the more it grew. Mist covered the ground, so thick that it left foot trails. Once a mere pinprick on a barren landscape, the hill now resembled a mountain.

Speckles of icy rain dotted the black fabric of his flight suit, creating circular patches that spread as the heat from his body melted the nuggets of hale. They bounced off the ground and his head. He'd long since lost the helmet, and the tail and arm wings that had helped soften his fall onto the bonnet of a car. He wished that he still had them, as the helmet would be a middle finger up at the persistent icy bastards that pinged off his exposed head. A scarf and face shield could have been made from the tails, which would have been a bonus, but he had neither.

It was coming down thick and fast now, pelting pellets firing straight toward him. He stopped, turned, and lowered his head. The thudding sound on his back, along with the rocking, sideways wind threatened to unearth suppressed memories of the last moments he'd had with Vic. He drank from his cupped hands and cursed the finer cubes that bounced off his heated palms.

A buzzing, popping sound interrupted the constant peppering

of ice on his back. He looked up at a wash of dirty, yellow-grey sky. The trees on the hill would provide the perfect shelter. The popping, cracking noise drew closer; he searched the sky, then turned to face the direction he thought it was coming from, convinced that he'd stepped over the invisible line drawn between scan pods. Was a drone looking at him, waiting to strike? The noise didn't sound like a drone or anything else in Zeta's arsenal. More like Vic on one of his dinosaur-fuelled machines. Whatever it was, it was heading right for him. With nowhere to hide and no strength to outrun it, he sat to lessen his body mass and thought once again how useful the unzipped wings and helmet would've been.

He finally recognised the sound as a small, petrol-driven bike; not the ones that the new world police rode, and too high of a throttle to be anything more menacing than a couple of kids using the open land for frills and wheelies.

He wet his throat, but still felt lightheaded from dehydration and hunger. Needing to push on, he rose and turned toward the hill. It was no longer visible through the spray of what was now fast-falling snow. Looking down he saw the broken ground he'd trodden.

"Just need to keep going forward."

The thought of a warm bed and a good meal were as remote as the invisible bike. Snipe strode forward. The rest had given him a more focused pace toward the hill and the fading, popping sound of the motorbike.

There were pockets of applause, intense conversation, and a random "Wahoo!" from Poppy as the Church cleared. Suspicion, worry, and elation were all held under the umbrella of the oneness that the Church provided.

Zip returned to the bakery as soon as Reverend Phillips had

finished explaining the reason for the urgent gathering. He understood more than most; after all, he too stood next to Reverend Phillips with a lowered head, full of shame, two and a half years ago. Back then, he'd rebelled against the doctrines of the Church. He'd used them for what he could get and was making plans to leave. Then he realised what the future held for those who'd missed the deadline to become a citizen, and that, no matter what he thought about the dogmas apparent within the small community of Mount Pass, the people here were genuine and caring. If they needed a Church to make them that way, then so be it. For the first time, Zip felt loved and useful; it was now his duty to welcome this stranger, in the same way he'd been welcomed two and a half years ago.

"Joshua, come now. We all need to get inside," Poppy said. "You too." She pointed to Rond, who was a non-citizen like Joshua – not that she would dream of calling anyone unchipped, a non-citizen, or any of the many derogatory nicknames used by people outside of her community. "Girls, come on. Gather 'round, single-file."

Jetta and Mibby were cheeky little things, but somewhat charming. Their father had joined the Church after a non-citizen killed their mother at the time of the cleansing. They had been held hostage within their old-world manner house, two settlements to the east. It still stood as the oldest building around, and one of the grandest. The girls didn't speak for six months after they arrived at Mount Pass.

Blake, the father of the two, had hatred in his heart and loathing for non-citizens. Hiding it for the sake of his daughters, he would nod and smile while the fire inside intensified with every encounter.

Minutes marched into hours, the morning to the afternoon,

and prime daylight to a falling, chilling dullness. The sun, hidden for most of the trek, had shown up only to tell Snipe he'd better move his ass if he wanted to make it to Mount Pass before sunset.

Smoke whirled from the trees on the mound. Mid-day moistness had solidified everything that was exposed. Snipe tried to silence the crunch of fresh snow underfoot, something he had only experienced one other time in his life. A distant memory from a time when he still viewed the world as a magical place. A hint of that innocence, still buried in the wiring of his brain, ignited upon seeing shadows dance and the flickers of flame. Was someone up there? If there was, he had the advantage; not that of higher ground, but that of near-invisibility, his black suit blending into the shadows of the trees. His path was up and over. He had no idea how long it would take to walk around the raised mound, or whether his body would even allow him to. The fire looked welcoming; a necessity, even.

He scanned his surroundings. If there was someone up there, he'd have known by now. If they'd seen him in the open space leading to this place, he'd be dead, or at the very least, a word of warning would've been forthcoming. No, there was no one up there. Could have been kids playing, and now tucked inside, nice and warm, with a meal set on the table.

"Fuck it. I'm going up."

*Click.*

"Drop the piece and turn around. Easy does it."

Snipe shuddered as if being prodded with an electric rod.

"Okay."

Dropping the empty handgun into the snow, he turned.

"Walker. Mr Walker. Shit, you scared me out of my wits."

"Snipe Siren. You took your time."

Snipe saw a glint behind a mangled bush; the spokes of a wheel.

"It was you on the bike, way back there," Snipe said.

"It was. Come up and bring tinder with you; the fire won't feed itself."

With his hands on his knees, the old boy pushed himself up the incline to the fire. Snipe frowned, but refrained from asking why he didn't pick him up hours before, if he knew it was him. Not that this man owed him any favours. Far from it. He was old man Walker, the most feared landowner in town. He would shoot first and ask questions later, and after he got his answers, he would shoot you again for the hell of it. What puzzled Snipe was that he'd helped him escape, and his brother... Shit. His brother.

"I asked you to bring twigs, not build a lodge!" Walker shouted down from the flames. His voice was old, but powerful enough to make a man stand up and listen.

Snipe did, and placed the pile next to the fire pit.

Shivering, he held his hands to the fire.

"Careful, lad. Warm those chilblains steady-like, or you'll not know you're burning your flesh."

Snipe smiled back, the warmth of the fire not yet registering as his facial muscles took time to unstiffen.

"Thanks, Mr Walker."

"Call me Ron."

"Thanks, Ron. And thanks for... well, you know."

The Walker brothers were inseparable, and the other not being here could only mean one thing. He would not ask. The man he had feared as a child would have to offer the reason for his brother's absence himself.

"Dead," Walker said. "Buried him in the cornfield."

Snipe looked up at his emotionless face.

"Well, I knew you must be wondering."

"Yeah. Sorry about that, truly I am. You didn't need to be there... and Vic, he shouldn't–"

"Didn't do it for you, kiddo. Couldn't give a shit if you lived or died," Ron Walker said.

Snipe didn't answer. He moved closer to the fire and fed it drying twigs, followed by a larger piece that had already been beside the pit of flames.

"I did it for Mr Harden. True gentlemen, and the reason my sorry ass is still alive."

"I don't understand. Vic saved your life?"

"He kept us alive, and hidden from the bastards. He supplied the land and gave us clothes. Swore he'd take it to the grave. And like the man he is... *was*... he kept his word."

"You're..."

"Yes, Snipe Siren. I'm a non-citizen scumbag just like you."

"Fucking hell, Mr Walker. Ron. Shit, I'd never have guessed. Vic never said a word. I thought he hated you as much as I did. I mean, when I was a kid."

Walker's face dropped, as if troubled by his words. Snipe felt a blast of regret, but before he could apologise, Walker turned toward him.

"Something happened back home, Snipe. After I'd thrown the last bit of dirt over my brother, I heard screams. Horrible, painful screams from near Harden's. I saw it at the ranch."

"Saw what?" Snipe asked.

"People turned to ash. Their flesh, Snipe, it..."

Walker gulped and shook his head. Snipe waited, but he offered no other words.

"Drones?" Snipe asked.

"No, not drones or the NWP or anything."

"Who's dead, Ron? Who's still there?"

"Everyone's dead, apart from non-citizens."

He named the unchipped that Victor had kept hidden among the citizens who lived their normal lives, unaware that there were non-citizens amongst them.

"You're not the only one, Snipe. Mr Harden helped many people disappear off the NWP radar. Something, I don't know what, ate them alive. I saw it with my own eyes. That's why I'm here, and if you're wondering why I didn't help you back there…" He pointed in the direction that Snipe had come from. "It's because I hate you, too. I hate that Victor had to die because of you. I hate that my brother had to die, and I hate that I'm going to have to help you survive, when it should be you that's dead."

"That's a lot of hating," Snipe said. "As for the help, save it. I don't need your help. I'm sorry about your brother, and I'm sorry that you feel your allegiance to Vic has to extend to me. I lived with Vic; he was my only parent. He's gone now. We all grieve in different ways, and my way has no place for you."

"You still sound like the snot-nosed kid I used to chase off my land," Walker said.

"And you still sound like the same old fucker everyone used to fear. I'm heading over to that settlement to find a warm place and bed down for the night. Like I said, shove your help. I don't need it, and if you try to follow me, my size tens will show you I'm not the still same snot-nosed kid you chased off *Vic's* land."

The silence around the fire, broken only by the crackling, popping sound of the forced dried timbers, seemed to last longer than it actually had.

"Help? Everyone needs help, Snipe, especially non-citizens. Who knows where the next scan pods could be? They could swoop down at any minute, or worse," Walker said.

"I don't need help."

"No, but I do. I'm not saying you owe me. I'm asking for your help, Snipe."

"*You* want *my* help?"

"You're a leader of men, Snipe; a survivor. I was much like you when Vic took me under his wing. I might be old now, and not as strong, but I'm not ready to join my brother yet."

Snipe didn't answer, just gave a simple nod of his head, and the power had transferred over to him. He owed Walker; that was a given. He wouldn't have made it to Vic's car if it wasn't for the Walker brothers.

"I'll see you into the settlement, stay with you, and make sure you're safe. No promises after that, okay? And just to make it clear, when we enter, we enter *together*. We have each other's back. And you are wrong about one thing; I *do* owe you."

Walker flipped open the pocket of his coat. A medical pack and two dry food rations fell out. Snipe's eyes lit up upon seeing the food. Walker then pulled out hydration pills and a pouch of fresh water.

"In it together. Let's eat; we'll need the strength to make it up and over this hill, and if I'm going to die, I'd rather go to the next realm on a full stomach," Walker said.

The school bell rang out. Parents were already waiting in the thickening snow on a hunch that kick-out time would be earlier due to the miraculous white stuff. Snow hadn't fallen on the Village for over ten years.

The parents and teachers only added to the children's excitement as they looked down at the settling snow, although they felt anything but settled themselves, as more than just snow had arrived today.

Blake Mathews, the father of Jetta and Mibby, stood in his

usual spot under the weeping willow tree, as he always did while waiting for Jetta and Mibby to be set free from the school day. Today, two other parents huddled under the tree to escape the ever-increasing downpour of snow. Blake Mathews gave them a sideways nod before turning to face the school doors. He recognised the two women. He didn't know their names and didn't wish to. They were the parents of Rond and Joshua, just two of the many non-citizens living life among the normal people of Mount Pass.

His hatred and anger towards them had subsided. He was courteous toward them now, but no matter what the Church said, one of their sorts had killed his wife. He remembered her every day, whenever he looked at their daughters.

"It's too dark to play, Joshua." Poppy stood with her back to the waiting parents; arms spread out to stop them from rushing into the schoolyard. "Everyone line up behind me. Single-file."

The older children objected, but the five-to-eleven-year-olds formed a queue, as requested. The parents, not as organised as the kids, bunched up around Poppy, muttering about how the world stops when it snows, and how much darker it was that day.

Poppy addressed the parents. "Please mind the steps when you collect your children; we've already had one accident. Most of them haven't seen snow before, so it's natural that they'll be a little exuberant. Please take care when you leave the school grounds, and your children have letters on their note screens explaining how we will inform you of any changes if the snow continues."

"Let 'em have a day off so they can play," said the mother of Rond.

Blake Mathews sucked through his teeth, as disgusted with

her comment as he was with the other parents who sounded their agreement. He suspected them all to be non-citizens.

"We'll let the weather decide that, shall we? Jetta, Mibby, your father's here."

Collecting children in the dark was challenging enough, but with the added danger of snow, parents had to help each other hold the little ones upright and guide them out of the school's gates. A handful of the older children were already heading for the field, snowballs clenched in gloveless hands. They were having a great time.

Reverend Phillips had set up a makeshift bedroom in the storeroom, which was the only room with a working heater. While waiting for the congregation to turn up, he often stood beside the stacked Bibles and cleaning instruments just to keep warm. It was all but empty now, apart from one open Bible. The page, selected with thought and care, rested beside the makeshift bed, which would be Fin's for as long as he needed it to be, or until one of his flock came forward to offer him a room in their own home.

"Ah, Fin. You startled me, I know it's not much, but at least you'll be dry and warm in here. It won't be for long; I have every confidence that a loving family will house you soon enough."

Fin looked over the shoulder of Reverend Phillips. "It's perfect. I don't know how to thank you." He felt his eyes well up, overwhelmed by the stranger's generosity.

"You're a sign from God, Fin. Look! You've even brought the snow along with you," he said, raising his arm and patting Fin on the shoulder.

Fin laughed for the first time since he left his family the day he went out hunting. What had happened after was now a mixed blur of events that changed in sequence every time he cast his mind back to that fateful day in the woods: the faint sound of gunshots, a killer whose face he had recognised, feeling suffocated, and then waking up in a white room, strapped down and surrounded by computers.

"Are you all right, Fin? I'm sure it will only be–"

"It's fine. Better than most places I've stayed. Thanks, Rev… Mr Phillips…"

"Call me Stephen," said Reverend Phillips.

Blake Mathews had to explain that there was no room in their house to have Fin stay with them. Jetta understood, but Mibby wasn't dropping the subject. She'd come up with a solution for every objection that he had. The *real* objection was that he wouldn't entertain non-citizens, even if they paid him, but that much he kept to himself. He found it hard enough having to pray with them every night; he was only going along with the whole Church thing to give his daughters a better life. Apart from the whole God and religious thing, they had a reasonable lifestyle here at Mount Pass, and there was no way he would allow a dirty non-citizen to spoil the life they'd made here.

"Lights off, girls. See you in the morning."

"'Night, Dad!" they shouted back in unison.

Snipe helped Walker climb the hill. Grabbing branches and getting a foothold, then pulling him from tree to tree, they'd made it to the brow of the hill. On any given day, without being laboured by a snowstorm and an old man who didn't listen to anything but his own voice, he'd have been up there in minutes. Now at the top, Snipe could see lights in the distance being turned off, one by one. Only a few remained, scattered about.

As Snipe looked for the easiest way down, Ron Walker stumbled. His legs swayed under him. "Stop. I need to stop," Walker said.

"Good news and bad news," Snipe said.

"What?"

"Which one do you want to hear first? The good or the bad?"

"Surprise me."

"The good news is there's a clearing, so it will be quicker getting down," Snipe said.

Walker shook his head. "And?"

"The bad news is we have to slide down, and I can't see what's under the snow. Oh, and the settlement is shrinking."

"Stop talking in riddles. What do you mean, 'shrinking'?"

"Must be early birds. Lights going off by the minute. Look, there's another one. I've got the general direction, but we need to move. I'll go first. You wait until I make this sound." Snipe made a hooting sound. "And then you follow down the same track I've made."

"And what if you don't make that sound because you've been torn to shreds by unseen objects just waiting to rip your crotch out?"

"You'll hear a scream. Then slide down a different way."

"Yeah, well, just know I take back the *leader of men* comment I made earlier."

Snipe kept his head raised and his feet close together as he slid on his backside down the hill. Walker didn't wait for the hooting. He just followed behind him. Moments later, they were at the bottom; wet, freezing, and sore, but neither of their crotches were ripped out. Snipe rubbed his hands over his short, crewcut hair to bring some feeling back to his numb, throbbing scalp.

The most prominent light shone yellow through drifting flakes from what looked like a Medieval Church. They headed toward it.

Fin saw the bubbles within the old tin bath pop as his gut

pulsed. Like fingers pushing out, pockets of skin moved, raised, and then withdrew. Reverend Phillips had made it his mission to cleanse both Fin's body and his soul. First there was a bath, and then food and rest. Fin welcomed his generosity as much as Reverend Phillips had welcomed him into his one-bedroom studio flat. The offer was made with the regret that after his fill, he would need to brave the cold and head back to the room laid out within the Church. Fin had never seen a bath, and now here he was, wallowing in his own filth and preparing for dinner with the Head of the Church. His gut bulged again. He sat upright. This wasn't hunger, and it wasn't natural. *No pain, no problem,* he thought, sinking back down into the dirty water.

Reverend Phillips arranged a pile of clothes; the baggiest he could find within the lost property bin. Placing them outside the bathroom door, he told Fin that food was being served, and to come down when he was ready. Standing, Fin pushed at the thumb-sized pockets of flesh as they appeared on his bloated gut. A sprinkling of sweat joined the droplets of water as it ran down from his head. What looked like prodding from within vanished the moment he pointed toward the individually rounded lumps.

Fin's bulk filled the narrow space within the open-plan kitchenette. Reverend Phillips waved his hand across a sensor. A table surface appeared from a boxed food unit, reshaping and lowering until it filled the space within the living and sleeping area.

"I'm not used to visitors. This place is built for one, as you can see. Here, please sit." Phillips pointed at the stools that rose from the floor. "When you sit, they will adjust in size."

Fin lowered himself onto what looked like a thin, flimsy sheet of plastic. As he did, the plastic grew outward in size and lowered to the height of the table.

"Please don't think I'm being presumptuous, but I prepared you a double portion."

"Fine by me, Rev," Fin said.

Snow pelted the window as steam rose from the roast dinners. The warmth of the printed apartment enveloped Fin, as Snipe and Ron Walker trudged through thickening white powder toward the Church.

# Chapter 13

Lexi had never seen Snipe with long hair. Tucking it behind his ears, he shouted and banged on the screen. His efforts went unheard and unnoticed to anyone other than Lexi, who felt his frustration coming from the other side of the thin sheet that divided the enclosure.

She mouthed the word, *"Soundproof."* Then she lowered her hands to calm him.

She felt hunger hit her gut just as two men, different from the ones before, walked in. One carried what looked like a bowl of curry. The other, taller man was empty-handed. The tall man pressed a button to the right of the glass chamber, and a hatch popped open in front of Snipe's face.

"Here. Eat this, son. There's been a delay. You'll be staying a while longer."

Lexi watched the meal being passed through the open slit, unaware of what had been said.

"Where's hers?" Snipe asked.

"She's free to go," the shorter man said, pressing another button.

The full screen separating Lexi from the outside world opened. The tall man fired something at Lexi, and she wobbled. They held her upright, underneath her arms.

The veins on either side of Snipe's neck stuck out and throbbed

119

as if they were about to burst. His contorted, twisted face did not affect the guards. He shouted, screamed, and demanded an explanation. He lunged at the transparent screen; kicking, punching, and banging on it to no avail. His efforts and the sounds he made remained trapped with him.

"It's okay, little lady. You're going home."

Her drugged haze made their words sound deep and hollow. "Snipe needs to…" Her eyes rolled up as her chin fell onto her chest.

"Help get her legs on," the taller guard said, placing her into the cart.

Lexi's alertness returned as the cart left the marquee, the outside air acting as a shot of adrenaline making her gasp like a new-born taking her first breath.

She saw the same tunnel that had brought her to the outside world. The lights on the walls became a constant, blurred line. Guards stood aside, as if they had been cautioned to do so. A solid metal door slid aside only moments before the cart reached it. Lexi's eyes developed the heaviness of sleep. Her limp body flopped to the side. Perplexed and drugged, she slurred her words as she fell in and out of consciousness.

Kat Brenner walked alongside the travel cart. Lexi resembled a ragdoll, sitting limply on the backseat between the two men who'd brought her in via the underground tunnel.

"I'll take her from here, chaps," Kat said.

"You'll have to sign for the cargo. No way it's going missing on our watch."

"Cargo? It?" Kat challenged.

"Short stuff there. I don't want them blaming me if she falls off the back or you do something before Rush Unix sees her."

Kat signed her name as she would for a cart full of rubbish

that was ready for the incinerator.

Lexi's head swayed. Her right eye fluttered, but her left eye stayed closed. Kat sat next to her, leaned forward, and ran a search for the detention centre. After verifying her identity, the cart took over, and she held Lexi upright. The metal sliding doors– three in total – snapped open as the cart approached, and slammed shut at a frightening speed the moment the cart cleared them.

"Snipe," Lexi hummed through closed lips.

"Lexi, it's Kat. Can you hear me?"

"Snipe... left... Snipe," she said, slurring her words.

Four uniformed officers confronted Kat; Rush Unix's hand-picked secret service. Today, they were detention wardens. The prison – if it could be called a prison – was comprised of twelve cells, all in a row, not dissimilar to any corridor found in the mainstream prison. On the two occasions it had been used, the detainees had committed petty theft. Since it didn't call for even a part-time warden, the officers had changed hats on short notice.

The officers didn't have names; something Kat saw as impersonal; the opposite to what the base stood for, and was named after, for that matter. *Freedom* was the name it had been given by its residents, not *Anonymous*.

The officers dressed smarter than her colleagues. Like tongue-less egos, they had call names or numbers that changed every day. She'd never heard the two shorter men speak, either now or in earlier meetings. They had chiselled features and short hair squared off into a block which enhanced their muscular build. They could have even been brothers, as both had the same stubby nose. The other two were skinny and tall, standing a good six feet, and had a smarminess about them. They'd sat in a few of the meetings with her, in the back of the room like a judgmental committee or fake government agents. The likes of Mike and Tyrone called them the *Men in Black*. They loved the mystery that surrounded them; how they never ate with the others and always hid in the shadows. Kat didn't care for any of the mystery, and rejected their self-imposed importance.

"That's far enough. We'll see her into the cell," said one.

"Like hell you will. I'm not entrusting a vulnerable female with a bunch of faceless bureaucrats."

The four men looked at each other. Their eyes moved quicker than their heads, making them look shifty.

"You want to share the cell?"

"Who the hell do you people think you are?" Kat asked.

The one who'd spoken looked toward the others. With no words exchanged, they picked Lexi up out of the cart. One put Lexi over his shoulder; his counterpart moved closer to Kat.

"Leave her alone. Come closer and I'll–"

Kat screamed as he picked her up in a fireman's lift over his right shoulder. She punched his back as he walked over to the cell.

"Let me go!"

"*Cyka*," he said, grabbing her harder and closer to his chest.

The heavy door slammed shut. After lashing out at the closed door, Kat turned and saw Lexi laid out on the solid slab bench. There were two benches, and both had a thin foam cover. There was a sink moulded into the wall and a toilet with no privacy screen. The walls were a pebbled grey and the light was blinding, casting a shadow of Kat as she paced the floor.

"What did he say? Sounded Russian. *Cyka?* That was it. *Cyka.*"

"What am I doing here?" Lexi tried to stand, lashing out with weakened arms. Kat placed her back down onto the foam-topped concrete slab.

Lexi sat up. Her dazed, hate-filled eyes focused on Kat.

"Look, Lexi, I'm in here because I didn't want to leave you with the heavies. Like you, I don't know what's going on, so cut me some slack, will you?"

Lexi spoke about what had happened to her while she was in quarantine. Kat filled in the details of how they both ended up in a cell. She stopped short of explaining the men who imprisoned them. She was in a cell with a troublemaker, after all, and wouldn't break the confidentiality she held in such high regard. It wasn't like she knew anything about them anyway. All she knew was that one of them had muttered something in what sounded like Russian, and Tweedle Dee and Tweedle Dum didn't look like they belonged.

"Why are you keeping Snipe?"

"I'm not." She snapped her head back. "But we'll find out soon enough, and trust me: after what they've done, locking me away like a criminal, I'll make it known."

"You are," Lexi said.

"What?"

"A criminal. We all are. You're no better than the non-citizen who shits in the street and hides in the sewer. Your sewer's just bigger, but it's still full of rats. Bigger rats, if you ask me."

There was a clunking sound, and then footsteps.

"Leave the talking to me. I'll get us out of here," Kat said.

Lexi rolled her eyes. For a moment, the thought of grabbing Kat and taking her hostage to free herself entered her mind. The thought vanished as the thudding boots drew closer.

The same two tall men stood before them. The Russians – if they *were* Russians – were nowhere in sight.

"Brought you both food and drink," he said.

He slid two trays through a hatch at the bottom of the door. Both smelled nothing like the food that was sold in the cafeteria. It smelled better; like real home cooking.

"You have no right keeping me here against my will. Rush Unix will have you hung, drawn, and—"

"You're not being held against your will. You accompanied your friend. Remember?" Smiling he said, "If you want out, I'll open the door."

"And what about Lexi? What are you charging her with? She left the base – albeit unusually – but nothing more."

"You want out or not?"

"Not if it means leaving a defenceless, unrepresented girl on her own, no."

The top hatch slapped shut, and Kat flinched, then shouted, "I'll have your necks for this! Who the hell do you think you are?!"

"Leave it, Kat. They're not worth it," Lexi said.

They both agreed that the meals had to be the best they'd had since arriving at the base. There was mashed potato – not the powdered stuff, either. Plus, proper veg and lashings of gravy.

With slouched shoulders and heavy eyes, they both sat facing each other within the small, oppressive room.

There was a clunking sound, followed by a snap.

They were in total darkness. The shapes of the walls, the sink, the toilet, *everything* had vanished under a blanket of darkness. Blindness hit Kat before Lexi. It dawned on her that she'd never experienced a total blackout.

"Lexi, it's okay. They have to switch on the lights. How else would we find the loo?"

"Keep looking at me, Kat. I can see you fine."

"How? I can't see anything."

"Your eyes will adjust soon. Mine work quicker; I'm used to bright lights becoming black. It's what happens when you dive head-first into a sewer or a wall cavity."

"I've never had to do that, thank God. You're right. I can make you out a little. You're waving, right?"

"Yeah. Right. So, you've never been chased down before and had to hide in a hurry? Every non-citizen, by right, shouldn't be alive. We all survived against the odds."

"I'm a non-citizen by choice. I'm free to travel and do anything that citizens do. That makes being in this cell all the more frustrating."

Kat snarled. Lexi placed her hand to her mouth to stifle her laughter.

"Well, that's got to be the craziest thing I've ever heard. A citizen choosing to hide. You're plain bonkers, girl." Lexi giggled. "Almost as bonkers as me thinking Snipe and I were going to walk out and be rid of this place. How come you ended up here, then, if you don't need to be?"

Kat thought for a moment before answering. What harm could it do, having a chat to pass the time? They might be here all night. She hoped not. She was warming to Lexi, but a night in a cell?

Kat said, "I was working for the secret service."

"Fucking hellfire. Really? Like a spy?" Lexi blurted out.

"No, not a spy or anything grandiose. I was an Admin and a PA for someone of importance. Well, at that time he was. After the event, everything changed. I spent time in... well, a secret government bunker. Slight job change. They had me working in communications. Governments around the world came together, past differences forgiven. It looked like a plan was being formed to rebuild and bring structure and order back to the world. It was like working in the stone age. Well, not quite that bad, but with all sat-coms down and a lack of fuel, things remained disorganised during my time there."

Lexi held back her natural impulse to ask her to get to the point. After all, she was telling a great tale, so she leaned forward. Their knees touched, and Kat recoiled before continuing. "You see, the event was a blow from nature. Everyone had prepared for war – for man-made disasters, and even most of the ones that nature could throw at us. But a worldwide event wasn't foreseen. Anyway, I went around the houses. I found out about something I wasn't supposed to. I dug deeper than my position allowed. The funny thing is, my superiors, and *their* superiors, weren't aware of it either."

Intrigued, Lexi moved closer. "What? What was it?"

"Let's just say that it was designed as a safety net; something that would engage if mass extinction struck. Codename: *Resin Pines*, something like that. Anyway, that's not the point. Only two countries knew about it: ours and the USSR."

"Why does it matter? If it's a plan to rebuild things, they should congratulate you," Lexi said.

"That's what I thought, but the very fact that we're in cahoots with a country which our allies at that time considered the enemy would have isolated us. None of that matters now, of course, but when the people I told about it died one by one, I freaked. I think they were assassinated, and I thought I was next on the list."

Lexi reached out for Kat's hands, gave her fingers a gentle squeeze, and said, "Thanks, Kat. Now that you've told me, I guess I'm on that list, too. That's great." She pulled her hands away and smiled, unaware that Kat couldn't see her jovial expression.

"You've got no worries, but anyhow, that's how I ended up here. I left my family, for their protection, you understand. It all happened so fast. I was wandering the streets and I lied. I told the rebels I was a non-citizen, and they took me into quarantine. When I failed the scan, it was my credentials that swung it. I'm not the only one. Might be chipped, but we're as much non-citizens as anyone. Plus, we come in useful on recon; buying supplies and stuff."

"Others? Who else?" Lexi asked.

"Listen, I've said too much already, tell me more about lover boy, I'd like to find out how you both met."

"So, what was the plan? How was it supposed to rebuild the world?" Lexi asked.

"Artificial intelligence from the old world; very basic. The thing I read was an agreement between us and the AI. We allowed it full access to the seed bank, which holds every known plant seed, and it can reproduce and terraform land; make decisions and act on them for the benefit of the planet, should life end. It was a self-replicating, non-terrestrial replenishment AI automation unit. Or at least, I think that's what they called it. Or it could have been..." Kat leaned forward and clashed heads with Lexi. "Sorry. Anyhow, tell me about Snipe. How did you guys meet?"

# Chapter 14

Snipe opened the door to the storage room. "Looks like the Vicar's a closet queen."

Walker closed the heavy wooden entrance door and ambled over. "What?"

"He sleeps in the church; now that's real conviction for you."

They both peered into the cramped closet room. A rush of warm air escaped before joining the iciness of the open church. There was stacked shelving, no windows, and a make-do bed with an open Bible to the side of the pillow, all dancing to the light of the widest candle Snipe had ever seen.

"So, what's the plan? Have a threesome with the Vicar?" Walker asked.

Snipe managed a smile. "Can't risk finding anywhere else tonight, so we'll stay in here until he comes back. Vicars are known for their compassion and generosity, so hopefully, he'll recommend a place."

"And if he doesn't, we'll make him, right?" Walker said.

"Wrong. They'll be no killing tonight, and you're in a church, for Christ's sake. I didn't even know they still existed. Just leave the talking to me."

They sat with their backs to the heater. Snipe nudged the door shut with his boot. Walker's rifle stood upright between his knees like a third leg. Taking comfort from the warmth of the heater, they stared at the door.

Folding his arms over his gut, Fin tried to hide his developing disfigurement. He'd already eaten, and had nothing to lose in telling Reverend Phillips of his peculiar, but painless, condition. Still at the eating bar, Fin explained what was happening, and then showed the Reverend his complaint. The bulging, finger-like raised pockets of skin settled, as if they were a figment of his imagination.

Fin lowered his chin to his chest before raising it again to look at the Reverend. "You must think I'm crazy," he said.

The wind howled as ice pellets showered the window.

"No. You've been through a lot and needed to rest. You can't go out in this. By the time you reach the church, you'll be frozen solid. I can offer you the floor next to my bed for tonight, then I'll ask around in the morning and try to find you something more suitable. Will you join me in a prayer?"

Fin nodded. What else could he do after being treated so well?

"I'm not sure I know how to," he said.

"Tell you what: I'll read a quote from our good book."

"Quote?"

"A small story. A poem. Then we can discuss its meaning and your interpretation of it before we both retire for the evening."

Fin rolled his eyes. His actions went unnoticed. Reverend Phillips stood. Fin remained seated. It was strange to see a holy man standing in a dressing jacket, holding an open Bible as if he'd sleepwalked into a prayer meeting.

*"And the kings of the Earth, and the great men, and the rich men, and the chief captains, and the mighty men, and every bondman, and every free man hid themselves in the den and in the rocks of the mountains. And they shall go into the caves of the rocks, and into the holes of the earth, for fear of the Lord, and for the glory of his*

*majesty, when he arises to shake mightily the Earth."*

Reverend Phillips continued for what seemed like forever. Fin's eyes felt heavy, but at least his stomach had settled. Maybe he'd imagined it.

"So, Fin, what do you think those words mean?"

"Yeah, I thought it was great. Well, not great, because they all had to hide underground when the Lord shook the earth. All sorts hid from mighty men, and..."

"You interpret the meaning well, Fin. You're tired and need to rest, and I have to be up early, so how about we settle down for the evening?"

Fin smiled in appreciation, both for not having to go back to the cold church and because Reverend Phillips had stopped preaching.

Snipe watched Walker snore, then whistle, then snore again. He feared that the element of surprise had gone and the whole town might arrive. His own eyes felt heavy, warmth penetrating its way through his body, leaving only his feet cold. He bent forward, wrapped them in the end of the blanket, sat back, and tried to keep his eyes from closing.

His mind raced with thoughts of Victor driving to his death. The goons he'd slain. Lexi missing; he could only hope that she'd made it to the base. A base he didn't know how to find. The ants... well, at least they hadn't been spiders. His eyelids fluttered. He tried to zone out; to clear his mind of thoughts. When that didn't work, he thought as far back as he could.

*Lexi. She was fourteen when we met. Happy times. Vic, introducing me to small, fried potatoes. An old man in an army uniform, different greens and brown prints covering him. My Dad is calling him father, taking me to the flying machine. I touched it. It stopped working. They all did. I was five. I touched it, and everything stopped working.*

*The flying machines fell. Everyone laughed. Everyone was happy, and then they argued. We never saw the old man or the machines again.*

"Dad!"

Walker shook him with both hands. "Snipe, wake up and shut up! You'll bring the whole town to us."

Snipe woke with a start. "Sorry. I was somewhere else. I had a nightmare. You snore like a fat man farting into an empty barrel."

"I've been awake the whole time, listening to you having Daddy issues."

Snipe shook his head. There was little point trying to convince the old man that his nasal tune could've alerted the town to their whereabouts, too. He smiled. He'd never remembered a dream so vivid after waking before. His father was in the army before he became a disconnected hippie sort. The old soldier who had been standing by his side was a man of importance, and his grandfather. But what was with the machine, and the flying drones falling as he touched it? Unfamiliar surroundings. Everything white.

"Well, he hasn't come," Walker said.

Snipe stroked his bottom lip with the tips of his fingers. "Strange, don't you think? Leaving a candle burning all night? I'll bet they know we're in here. Got the place surrounded." Walker tightened his grip on the rifle. Snipe smiled and said, "I was joking. I'm sure it's not surrounded, and even if it were, I'd try talking my way out first."

Those last comments struck a nerve, as he recalled taking out the cannibals. *Talk first. Yeah, right.*

"So, what were you dreaming about?" Walker asked.

"It was weird, that's for sure. Until now, I'd blocked out

the time I spent before I came to live with Vic, but tonight, I remembered."

"Dreams aren't remembering, Snipe. They are just dreams."

"Yeah, well, this one was a memory. I'm just not sure what it all means."

"I dreamt that I killed a dragon once. That never happened, and I'm still waiting for one to fly by," Walker said.

Fin woke with a start, sweating and alert. Reverend Phillips laid asleep on the single bed beside him. Fin looked down. Something was inside him, pushing at his gut and trying to escape. He raised his head, but then dropped it back down onto the pillow. The pain he felt wasn't physical; it was the fear of the unknown.

"Reverend, help. Please help."

Without looking, he moved his right hand through the matted hairs on his chest, then down towards his gut.

"Fin, what's the matter? Are you all right? What's happening to you? Your stomach, it… it's growing."

Fin shot up and backed over to the wall. Reverend Phillips stood naked on the bed, one hand over his crotch and the other cupped over his mouth. His eyes told Fin to look. He did, and what he saw was a growing lump the size of a fist. Showing no signs of slowing, it now stood outward ten inches, like an arm trying to escape. Tears rolled down Fin's face as he repeated: "Help. Help."

Reverend Philips watched in horror as the fist-like bulge separated into smaller bubbles that seemed to be trying to escape the confines of Fin's hairy belly. He gagged, but held back the sick that burnt his throat and prevented him from speaking. The sight of the giant known as Fin shaking, crying, and whimpering like a beaten child sent a paralysing fear through him.

Reverend Phillips ran over to the only window above the wash station, opened it, and shouted for help at the top of his voice. If he could raise someone this early – the baker maybe – then they could wake Dr Gibby – the only doctor, and not a churchgoer. He turned back to Fin, who was now on all fours, his gut hanging low, touching the floor. He growled like a bear. The hair that covered his body stood on end, and his penis had retracted in on itself.

"Lord answer my prayers." Reverend Philips clasped both hands together and prayed over him. "I renounce Satan and all his works. I count them as my enemies. I now close the door to all practices and command all such spirits to leave in the mighty name of Jesus Christ."

A small crowd had gathered below the Reverend's window. Some still wore their nightclothes, but all wore heavy winter coats. Their attention was divided between the prayers coming from above and the two strangers mingling among them.

Zip slid his way over to the commotion, stumbled, then slipped and fell between Snipe and old man Walker, his hands pressed into the powdery snow that had settled overnight. Snipe offered his arm to the baker, who, unlike the others, looked wide awake, as if it was mid-morning and not 5:30.

"Here. Take my hand."

"What's happening?"

"We've just arrived," Snipe said.

As Zip rose to his feet, he stared past Snipe and into the eyes of old man Walker. Old man Walker stared back at Zip Walker, his son.

"Er… am I missing something here? Do you two know each other?"

Screams, followed by a much louder grunt, came from the flat.

"He's being attacked!" Poppy shouted.

Someone ran across the snow toward them. "Fin's missing. He's up there." The man pointed at the Reverend's window.

Dazed, old man Walker moved closer to Zip. "Zip Walker. It can't be."

"I need your gun."

Taken aback by the way he handed it over, Snipe stood aside, eyeing the pair.

"I'll come with you," old man Walker said.

It was too late. After trying the door, Zip let out a shot that blew the entrance panel into the lobby area. He ran up the stairs two at a time until he reached the door of Reverend Phillips' flat.

"Open the door!" he shouted. "Stand back."

Zip kicked the door open. Reverend Phillips was trembling, hunched in the corner of the kitchenette. Shards of flesh hung from his hair. His naked body was red with Fins blood.

Zip turned and saw Fin's torn body. Then he screamed through the door that now hung on one hinge, "*Help!*"

Reverend Phillips trembled as he looked up at Zip.

"You're alive," Zip said.

"He exploded. His back exploded. It's not my blood. The devil was inside him."

Zip stepped over soaked sheets. With every step, he felt an intense, crippling pain in his abdomen. Reverend Phillips tried to stand, but fell back down as something tore through Zip the same way as it had torn through Fin. Flesh splattered the partially open door, hitting the wall in the hallway. Zip didn't scream. He remained alive, with a football-sized hole where his midsection should have been. The rifle dropped from his hand. It fired at Reverend Phillips, missing the left side of his face as it entered a base unit. Zip didn't so much fall, but crumbled into a pile.

Reverend Phillips felt any remaining grasp of reality leave him. He tried to scream, but the scream only rang out within his mind. Vomit flew from his mouth, and he blacked out.

Snipe saw old man Walker's face turn ashen. He pushed Snipe aside.

"Stay here. I'm going."

"I'll go up," he said.

Walker, already at the open door, turned to Snipe and said, "Stay here. If I don't come out, then finish what you started."

They both turned to the door.

Reverend Phillips appeared from the shadowy entrance. The gun he held trembled. Wearing the bloodied remains of Fin and Zip, he seemed to look through Zip's father and Snipe, his attention on the growing flock gathered before him. As he raised the gun, Walker stumbled and slipped backwards, landing on his back.

Reverend Phillips waved the gun upward. It looked more like a snake about to attack than a solid object. The crowd ducked. Two slipped and fell over before the gun came to rest under his chin. Using both hands, one either side of the weapon, Snipe swivelled it counter-clockwise. The gun flew sideways, through the door, coming to a stop when it hit the lobby wall. Reverend Phillips raised his hands as if to pray. Snipe grabbed his wrists and pulled, flipping the Reverend over his body and onto the snow in front of the crowd. Now stained with blood and gunk, he wished he hadn't.

Walker stood and shouted, "Zip! He's still in there."

Then he turned to face the grey, shaking body of the Reverend. "Bastard."

Snipe held old man Walker back, more for his sake than the

sake of the naked man lying in the snow. The men outside crossed the blood-splattered snow and were now piling through the door, intent on seeing what had happened in the flat.

Snipe continued holding old man Walker back. "We don't know what's happening yet." He looked around. Children were holding onto the legs of their mothers. "Get a doctor. Who knows this man?"

A woman stepped forward, "He's our Reverend. Reverend Phillips. He's innocent. Please don't hurt him."

The few who'd run in still hadn't come back out. Snipe looked up at the window, then at the door, then down at the quivering Reverend. "Who's up there? Speak, god damn it."

His mouth moved, but his words went unheard amongst the crying, cursing, and whispering of the few who were left standing around them.

Snipe knelt by the Reverend's side. "Speak, or I swear I'll let my friend finish you. Did you shoot someone?"

The words came slow and slurred. "No. I loved them. The devil, the unseen spirit…"

Snipe turned to Walker. "Do what you want."

"I don't need your permission," he said.

The last man into the building never made it to the flat, and was now running in their direction screaming, his arms thrashing. He ran past Snipe and Walker, and past the mothers covering the eyes of their little ones, shouting, "It's invisible! It's coming! Run! Run!"

Delicate snowflakes fell from the sky, rendering the running man invisible. At least six people, maybe more, had entered the building, and only one had returned, shouting a similar story to the one that had been whispered by the Reverend.

Something was moving toward them. The only sign of it was

the snow changing course from the open doorway.

Snipe shouted, "Get these children inside! All of you go inside, now!"

Old man Walker moved toward the door, swiping his hands at the falling flakes. Before Snipe could warn him, he fell to the ground. He, too, was being eaten from the inside-out. He knew that as a patch of snow drifted over to a Mum and her child, it was too late. The last of the Walker brothers was already dead.

With no time for emotion or regret, Snipe scoped his surroundings, using all of his senses. There was a hint of burning flesh, a bitter charred taste in the air, and an invisible force that could only be seen as the snow changed direction. Parents cursed, children screamed, and an excited dog played amongst the bodies' remains.

Someone called from one of the box houses facing the graveyard, "Friend, get in here!"

Snipe fixed his sight on the thing pushing through the snowflakes. It was heading towards Blake Mathews' house.

"Jetta, Mibby, stay in your rooms."

"But Dad...!"

"No matter what, do not come out of your bedrooms. Lock your doors and don't answer to anyone but me. No matter what you hear, do not come out of your rooms."

"Dad, is the devil coming to hurt us?" Mibby asked.

"Is Reverend Phillips dead?" Jetta asked.

"Girls, I don't know what's going on. The strangers we saw outside are misbehaving, and there's no such thing as the devil. Now, do as I ask."

Both girls ran up the stairs. Blake listened for the locks to click on their doors before closing the window flaps. He peered through a sliver left open in the centre. Snipe was the only person still visible.

Snipe watched delicate flakes drift towards to the house. Their focus was the front door, but moments later, they'd disappeared. The snow now fell in its natural downward motion. Blake stared at Snipe, who was, in turn, staring at his house. Blake picked up a fire wand that was used for starting outside fires. It was metal, and the only thing he had at hand. Jabbed into someone's eye, it would blind them. He gripped the stick for comfort, hoping that the man outside would pick on a different family.

Blake's neighbour called up the stairs. "Rond, leave Joshua alone and close the window! It's freezing."

"Mum, why's that man outside? Is he the murderer?" Joshua shouted from upstairs.

Snipe watched air push out from the door it had entered, an invisible cloud that was only detectable when it – whatever *it* was – moved through the soft, gentle flakes.

It entered Blake's next-door neighbour's house. Snipe paced toward it. A woman stood at the window with her face pressed up against the glass. Her eyes were fixed on Snipe.

"Mum!" Rond shouted as he jumped down every other step until he reached the bottom of the stairs. "Something's wrong! Joshua! Quick!"

Before she could react, Joshua was bouncing down the stairs, screaming.

"What have you done?"

Having heard the screams, Snipe ran to the house. The window where the woman stood turned a thick, dark red.

Snipe stood with the same people he'd told to go inside, along with others he hadn't seen before now. Neighbours left their doors open along the small row of printed houses. Everyone rushed over to the property, except Blake Mathews and his two daughters, Jetta and Mibby.

Cries of, *What's doing this? He must be hiding! Wait 'til I catch the bastard!* echoed in hysteric frequencies that rattled through the softness of the falling snow.

Snipe spotted a yellow transporter, its wheels covered with snowdrifts. There would be no way he could start it. It was modern. It required a retinal scan just to open the door, let alone start it, not that it would even move with its wheels submerged.

Someone screamed the name *Poppy*, and Poppy's innards flew out, leaving her spine exposed to the elements. She crumbled in the doorway of Joshua and Rond's house.

Cupping both hands around his mouth, Snipe took in a deep breath, letting it out only when his chest threatened to explode. "The Transporter. Run to the transporter."

Hysteria was spreading as fast as the living were falling down dead.

"Who owns the transporter? You all need to leave now!" Snipe shouted again.

The door next to where Poppy laid broken in the snow swung open. A tall, well-dressed man wearing a three-piece suit stepped out and pushed his way through the others to stand in front of Snipe.

He pointed his finger hard into Snipe's chest. "You've done this. You."

Given any other time and place, Snipe would have snapped his finger clean off, but something – not fear of the man, just *something* – stopped him from doing so. Might've been the shock from seeing old man Walker disembowelled, or the blood of children running down the window, or the woman who'd had her innards ripped out, or the naked man still laying in the snow, or maybe just the motivation to get the fuck out of dodge and save as many people who'd listen to reason.

"What's happening? Stop this," he said, pointing again.

Others circled him, also seeking answers and a cure for the madness. Snipe had neither.

"I've just arrived. I'm passing through. My friend's over there, gutted, just like her. His son – your baker – too. Listen, it's not stopping, and we have to leave now. Whoever can drive that transporter, and *anyone* who can drive *anything*, leave now. Take as many people with you as you can."

He pushed through and stomped over to the transporter, hoping they would follow, aware that Plan B was to leave on foot if they didn't.

Blake called through the open door of his house. His daughters came rushing out. Mibby gasped upon seeing the remains of her teacher. Jetta hadn't noticed; she ran over to her Dad and clung to his leg.

"We're citizens," Blake told Snipe. "My daughters and me. They're attacking only non-citizens. Look, Reverend Phillips—he's alive!"

The silhouette of a naked man walked toward them.

Prodding Blake in the chest, Snipe said, "Holds no weight with me. We're all made the same way, and you're no better than the rest."

A strong, stale smell of alcohol came from behind him. Snipe turned and saw a portly man, unshaven and bleary-eyed. "I'm Dr Gribby."

"Good for you. Can you drive?" Snipe asked.

"I'm a doctor," he repeated.

"So you said. Whatever's killing these people doesn't need a doctor. These people need to leave."

"I understand. I'll leave now. I'll go to my brother's house," the

140

doctor said.

"What are you driving, a motorbike?"

"No, a rather nice car, thank you."

"Then take as many people as you can fit in it," Snipe said.

The people standing around Snipe all took notice. They had moved away from the bloody mess behind the low-level wall. Some people ducked, as if they could see the thing that was causing the carnage. Others gathered their friends and made their way to their cars.

Snipe understood why the NWP and emergency services hadn't arrived. It was strange seeing a mixture of chipped citizens and non-citizens living in harmony. The risk of being found out would mean the end for both sides. The irony is that even if they had called, there would be no one to answer. Victor Harding had made sure of that when he flattened the military base nearest to Mount Pass. What was also strange was that drones hadn't appeared; not a single one. Yet.

The driver fired up the large transporter. It started on the first try. Snipe piled people into the twelve-seater, trying to keep families together, but at the same time, trying not to play politician as time was running short.

Mothers covered the eyes of the young ones as the men looked on with stressed faces through the steamed windows of the transporter. Two others had fallen in the same way. Steam rose from blood-painted snow. Two men with shovels dug around the front wheels. The others laid clothes and anything else at their disposal in front of the rear wheels for traction.

Snipe turned to face the two fallen victims. Their bodies were a blur through the heavy blizzard. Reverend Phillips knelt as if praying over them. A woman in her late sixties stopped next to him. Within seconds, her innards were stripped by what looked like an innocent cloud of snowflakes.

The transporter's wheels spun. Waving his shovel at Snipe, a man asked, "Are you helping, or what?"

Snipe had a sudden sense of what might be happening. "Are you chipped?"

"What?"

"Are you a citizen?"

"We all are, mate. In it together."

"Tell me, or I swear I'll shove that–"

"Yes, I am. So what?"

"And the naked man?"

The man lowered his shovel, bringing it to rest on the ground. "Reverend Phillips? I believe so."

Snipe opened the door to the transporter. "Anyone who's a citizen needs to stay. It's attacking non-citizens."

No one answered. The transporter moved back and forth before rocking itself from the grip of the snow.

"Answer me, damn it."

Blake Mathews raised his hand as a child would to his teacher. "We're citizens."

"Then it's time to redeem yourself. Go back and spread the word. All non-citizens are to follow this transporter. All citizens are to aid them in their efforts, and I guarantee no harm will come to you."

He was bluffing; he could give no guarantees as to their safety. He'd engaged a part of his brain that was only ever active in the most severe situations. This was one of them. Logic played a part, but not as much as instinct, and the gut feeling that'd kept him alive against all the odds.

# Chapter 15

"Like a gentle animal. He can be a tiger when he needs to be, but he wouldn't hurt a fly. He'd ask me to move a spider, not kill it. *Move* it. He's a real softie," Lexi said. "And what about you? Do you have anyone out there?"

Kat thought for a moment before answering. "Er, yes. My partner Alex and my son Chip, they... well, my work here takes all of my time, but when..." She lowered her head, and Lexi placed a hand upon Kat's knee.

"Painful being without the ones we love, isn't it?" Lexi said. "Can I confess something? As in, you won't tell anyone?"

Kat smiled. "Anything said in the cell stays in the cell."

"I have a knack for fitting into tight spaces, and I'm always curious, but there's one thing nagging me." Her eyes raised, as if recalling something. "I think I found base level, but that's not what's nagging me."

"The school on level seven's the furthest the lift goes."

Lexi's face beamed. For the first time, she had the upper hand. "Why would there be train tracks way below the school? I'm talking *way* below, probably five more *levels* below, and how the hell did they get there?"

"What? Are you sure?"

"As sure as you're sitting here right now. Yes. I know what I saw. And that's not all. There was a dim light coming from a large salt rock or a crystal. It sorta looked like a giant bedside lamp."

"Lexi, you're a bright girl, so please understand that what you're saying could get you killed. Don't repeat this to anyone."

The sound of marching boots echoed along the hallway, followed by a clang of metal, which warned of the arrival of the four who had incarcerated them.

"Sorry to have kept you two waiting so long."

"You'll be hearing from Rush Unix about this," said Kat.

Lexi touched her on the shoulder. "Save it."

"We've met with Mr Unix. He needs to see you both. You're both now VIPs," the American-looking man said.

While he spoke, the three others remained silent. The two Russians – if they *were* Russians – seemed different; somehow less threatening, as if they were under orders.

"He wants to see me?" Lexi asked.

"Both of you."

The Russian who'd locked the door stepped forward, and the door slid open.

"Where're you taking us?" Kat asked.

The man with the American accent spoke for him, "You both now have the same clearance levels as we do. The operations room, that's where we're meeting."

Kat recognised the room; it was the one she'd been in with Mike and Tyrone. It hadn't fully sunken in just why Lexi's status matched her own; that of a high-ranking communications officer. Okay, she liked the girl, but Lexi was no VIP.

"So, you're telling me I'm no different than you," Lexi said. "If that's the case, I'd like to see Spud, and I'm not moving another inch until you bring him here."

"You'll see him soon enough. It's important."

"So is seeing Spud. I'm not backing down. Go get him," she said.

"Okay, but you must stay here."

A short while passed before Spud appeared. His face was smudged with dirt. Lexi greeted him with a licked hand to clear it all away. Kat turned her head, then looked back at them with a smile. She no longer saw herself as better than Lexi, nor did she see herself as equal. They were just different, maybe. But this time, there was no ego attached to the thought. Maybe being locked up had changed her for the better?

Spud, after being told for the umpteenth time that he wasn't in trouble, relaxed, but refused to unclench his hand from Lexi's. His eyes widened as he saw the small stage and the seats laid out in rows. Kat knew what to expect.

Lexi and Spud sat front and centre, with Kat where Tyrone had sat before, and the four mysterious men sitting behind them.

Spud's eyes widened as a circular green light spun around on the raised platform. Lexi gripped his hand tighter. Rush Unix appeared, dressed in a vintage army uniform; green and brown camouflage patches with pips on the shoulders. He wore a plain green beret spooned over his head with a silver star placed in the centre, and black steel-toed boots with overlapping laces. Kat was far from impressed. If she wasn't so pissed at being treated like a criminal, she might have laughed at seeing the transformation from hippie to army man.

Lexi placed her arm around Spud and pulled him closer.

"I knew it. I said he wasn't real," Lexi said.

The hologram gave a thin slit of a smile; it seemed to be forced, since his eyes dropped at the same time. "You might be wondering why I've asked you here."

"No, I was wondering why you locked me up like a criminal,"

Kat said.

"And I was wondering why I was drugged and caged and taken away from Snipe – your son," Lexi said.

"Ah, so you've both been talking. Good. You must work together if we're to survive."

"Survive?"

"Snipe Siren the second – your boyfriend's clone – escaped from his confinement chamber last night. He killed the guards, and he's been missing ever since. Our last recording had him on the far side of the base; the rocks are jagged and the sea's rough. He hasn't shown up on any of our cameras."

Lexi felt her head lighten as if it had been pumped with helium, and a knot like a clenched fist formed within the pit of her gut. Spud shuddered at the news he didn't understand.

Kat gave a side glance at Lexi, then looked back at Rush Unix. "What do you mean, clone? Lexi would know the difference. Why would anyone clone him?"

"That's the reason I've asked you to join me. I'll cut to the chase and then play you a short film."

"Sod the movie, I want answers," Kat said.

"Funny, you used to be the professional one," Rush said. "As you're aware, intelligence gathering can be tedious and unreliable, but we've arrived at a conclusion… a *frightening* conclusion. Kat, the report you gave on the thing that slaughtered non-citizens in the bunkers, both hostile and friendlies… clones infiltrated those bases, and we suspect that the one outside tried to gain entry to base Freedom."

"By who? How? Why?" Kat stumbled over her words. "I don't understand."

"You're about to." The hologram paced the small platform.

Kat saw this as a futile attempt to look real, as if Rush Unix the man – not the light show – stood before them.

Rush continued. "First, I want to set the record straight. I am real and very much alive, just not here in person. The hologram's a portrait of my younger self."

Lexi looked at the hologram, her face unreadable, blank and drained of natural colour. "He's Snipe Siren. The *real* Snipe Siren. I *know* he is. We spoke about things that only we would know. I believe none of this."

Rush addressed Lexi. "He's real. Flesh and blood real, with all the features and memories of the Snipe you know, but he isn't Snipe; he's a clone. The machines took Snipe Siren to the farm – a Zeta prison. They've cloned many others, too. Their aim before, destroying the mould, is to create from it a clone fuelled with nanobots; microscopic robots that, when released, act with a degree of intelligence. They kill to order, and the order in this phase is to delete remaining non-citizens."

Kat bit her bottom lip before saying, "Phase. You said *this* phase. What other phases are there?"

"The census was taken by all citizens."

Kat nodded, all too aware of the intrusive census; she'd completed it. Every citizen had.

Rush continued. "A population reducing program; something that should never have happened. It goes against everything we agreed on. I believe it wants to wipe non-citizens from the face of the Earth. Citizens were chosen from the census results. Those who have scored high will build the human race as they see fit, and by all rights, its job will be complete, and it will – or should – shut down and hand over its power to its benefactors."

Lexi turned to Spud. "It's all right. There'll be a movie to watch soon. Just enjoy the lights." She gave Kat a sharp, disjointed look.

Bridging her forehead with her right hand, Kat spoke to the

floor before raising her head to the thing she now despised. "Rush Unix, you seem to know a lot about the elusive Zeta's next moves, and his moves don't seem logical. I mean, why doesn't he kill everyone and leave the few he wants? Why go to the trouble of cloning? And what do you mean, *shut down and hand over power*? A dictator never shuts down his operation and hands over control. And why Russia? Are we expected to believe what you think might happen after being lied to?"

"At the time, we'd concluded that the machines were peaceful. A self-replicating AI switched on in times of need or global catastrophe. It can terraform, organise, and carry out missions to aid human existence. A remarkable creation. After discovering it, we denied its existence, and kept it away from our allies at that time. After they hacked our plans, the project was put on hold until we reached an international agreement. I was to make sure they stuck to their side of things. I stood in the way of it being militarised."

Kat fired back, "Well then, you failed, and you are responsible for countless deaths and worldwide misery."

Adding to Spud's wonder, the hologram coughed, and then said, "Some would argue that after the event, people had little chance of recovery. The machines performed well at dredging, terraforming, and providing emergency aid. They restored order and provided a sense of normality."

"So, just switch the fucker off, then," Lexi said.

"I wish it were that simple. Nobody knows who started the project, who invented it, or how it's controlled. We discovered it after the event; its creators remain a mystery. No one has claimed responsibility for its creation, and for a while, every functioning country assumed it was the USSR or the Americans. We joined forces with Russia, in part because we didn't believe that their intentions were honourable, and we suspected them of creating it. We tried to reverse-engineer the machines, but there was nothing to reverse. They're made of nothing we have ever seen before. The Russians worked on nanotechnology in the lead-up to the event. When we broke into one of the machines, it disintegrated and turned to dust. The other machines reacted and became hostile toward the team who'd tried to understand its makeup. That's when we concluded that it had intelligence. It was an AI-based man-made marvel, hell-bent on saving humanity."

"Well, I'm glad its marvels excite you. So, who's running it and how can we stop it?" Kat asked.

"Yeah, we don't need a history lesson. We need to stop it," Lexi added.

"We told it to power down; it had always followed our instructions up until that point. Remember that its core program is to protect humans, the Earth, and every single living being on it, including planting seeds and regenerating and germinating the land. It can recognise the problem, and then solve it."

"How do you know, if you don't know who created it?" Kat asked.

"An animated projection appeared on our computers and told us its goal, and that it preserved life. After the event wiped out the greater part of humanity, we drew the obvious conclusion: its creators were like all the others: dead. After proving itself, and after we saw the benefits of its actions, we continued to work with it."

"And you all thought you'd go along with this information; information from a hacker or a secret society with a hidden agenda," Kat said.

"We had no choice. It singled out humans as the problem.

When people didn't conform for the welfare of the many, it sanctioned them. First, it gave chances, and then punishments, and now this. It's out of control."

Kat continued, "If it's AI, could it listen to reason?"

"We tried. Only my son got them to obey him. He told me he thought of the words, and they dropped when he asked them to. He was a child, and he wasn't taken seriously until the others couldn't replicate Snipe's actions."

Lexi pulled Spud off his chair as she stood. "I'm going to find Snipe. He'll know what to do," she said.

"The *real* Snipe, Lexi, not the one who's escaped. He *thinks* he's Snipe, but he's only a carbon copy being lead to his doom."

"And just how do you know?" Lexi asked.

"A simple fingerprint test, that's how. They weren't a match. I need my son – the *real* Snipe. It's a long shot, but he could override their entire system."

Maybe it was because he hid behind an altered projection, but lying had become easier for Rush Unix. There was no hope. He couldn't bring himself to mention the second event; the one that would end all life on Earth. Even at this late stage, he couldn't bring himself to explain that the agreement they entered had backfired. That he did not influence the chosen. He had his part to play, as did the others, and he would give them as much hope as possible – that much he owed them – but the inevitable would happen, regardless of any words he chose, so until the next event, he would choose his words with care.

Snipe Siren was more important than they could ever imagine. He'd always hated his father when he used the words: *need to know*. He now understood the importance of those three words, as those three words would give hope to the many, solace to those left behind, and a reason for the chosen to continue. Zeta had relinquished their agreement and taken Snipe. The one choice he had left would save his only son.

"Your plan's floored. I've heard enough," Kat said.

"Me too. You're fucking crazy, that's what you are," Lexi said.

A screen dropped from the ceiling, and an old-style film counted down from three. Spud sat back down as a little boy ran in front of two soldiers. Other soldiers stood in straight lines with their hands behind their backs. The younger of the two officers – Rush Unix – looked no different from the hologram that flickered as it stood beside the screen. The boy had a bandage wrapped around a cut on his hand. Smiling, he bounced from side to side. Dressed in a fur coat with only his face visible, Lexi knew it was Snipe Siren. It was the eyes. The older officer introduced Rush and his son to the gathered soldiers and men in suits.

Spud jumped back in his seat as a drone flashed on the screen. It hovered overhead. The Rush on the screen addressed his audience and explained that the machine posed no threat to life. He looked down and tugged the boy's hand.

"Hold out your hand, son," Rush said.

Snipe did as his father asked and held up his bandaged hand. The drone landed before shutting itself down. Two other drones that had been hovering unnoticed behind the line of soldiers and suited personnel also fell from the sky. Seeing their smiling faces and their hands clapping like deranged seals angered Lexi to the point that she wanted to throw something at the screen, but there was nothing to throw. Spud gripped her hand. It was enough to keep her seated.

"Why use your son, and not an officer, or anyone other than a little boy?" Lexi asked.

"It was a party trick. If only we understood how to master it.

I left the program after receiving orders which were contrary to my beliefs. Snipe became valuable for all the wrong reasons. I did my best to keep him hidden, even after the attack on my commune."

"Maybe try shooting it? Maybe that's our only shot?" Lexi said.

Kat looked at her, perplexed. The men sitting behind her snorted laughter.

Rush addressed her in the same way as Spuds teacher had, "You need to remember, Lexi: you are the enemy not only to Zeta, but to all citizens who follow his – *its* – lead. There aren't enough guns or people in the world to achieve that. They're designed to withstand and work through a worldwide catastrophe."

He explained that the base was on full lockdown; no way in or out until they found the clone. Somewhere, in the depths of his mind, he saw the creation as a miracle; a god-like entity that had matured over the years into an adult. He thought it was no less a son than his own. It had done what it was designed to do and more; so much more. Who'd have imagined that it would weed out the heart of the problem – that of man – and work with, not against, that problem in every possible way? It had walked the walk by showing the progress that people wanted to see. The very fabric of humanity – the ego, the nonconformists, the ones who'd refused to be a part of progress, – had stood in its way, threatening to undo its achievements. Now, it was fighting back at a frightening speed.

He wondered just how things could have worked out if people had worked *with* it, instead of seeing it as the problem. Would the selection process have been a smoother one? Too much time had passed for a secret government not to have claimed responsibility or taken control. These things had acted on the areas they'd asked them to until they'd either become wise to their true intentions or were now working on pure logic by reducing the population and increasing food supplies.

Rush sat limp within his custom chair, mentally punching the wall in frustration as he wondered why people hadn't evolved and matured and flowed with the plan. He'd sought worldwide peace. Nature – the universe – wanted the same for us. Why else would it have created the event that shook the planet? Why else would it present an escape route?

On this planet, they were a selfish, ignorant, self-destructive species. If there were to be a survivor, Rush would make sure it was his son. Hidden from those who thought he could control the machines, it was time to bring him out of hiding and make sure that he found the door to freedom. Whether the thing that glowed below the base was human-made or otherwise, it offered salvation.

That part of the agreement he'd secured for his only son.

# Chapter 16

Snipe sat next to the driver of the largest transporter within a convoy of twelve. Family vehicles and a school bus made up the other eleven. Wheels spun in nearly zero visibility and found traction, but for how long? The road merged with pavements and fields; Mount Pass wasn't visible through the thickening downpour. Scattered trees with low-hanging branches like bony fingers sticking out of a white woollen jumper, bobbed up and down in the gentle breeze as if trying to shake free frozen fibres. They passed ruins of the old world; jagged brickwork and old wrecks poking up through the drift, the snow taking away any sharpness, stripping away any distinguishing features, and any sense of direction. Everything looked the same.

A toddler was having a tantrum, alternating between screaming and holding her breath as she kicked a rhythmic beat into the seat in front of her. Her mother struggled to hold her on her lap with a look somewhere between anger and embarrassment. Bill, the driver of the transporter, tuned to Snipe and said, "Running low on charge. There's not a charging unit for miles. In fact, I'm not sure where we are anymore."

Snipe stood up. "Just keep heading south," he said.

"South. Yeah, right. There's a lot of south. *Where* south?"

His words went unheard as Snipe sidestepped passed seats to reach the mother of the kicking child.

"Hey, what's all this about?"

The little girl screamed louder. Snipe unzipped the side pocket of the flying suit and handed her the compass that Vic had given him. The girl stopped crying, her attention now fixed on the wobbling needle.

"Now, do you promise to look after this very important thing for me?" he asked.

She nodded back with a smile, then looked up at her mother before snuggling back into her lap. The mother mouthed the words, *Thank you.* Snipe looked out the back window. Three cars had broken away from the rest, and were struggling to keep up, –or they'd stopped; he couldn't be sure which.

"Bill, switch on the hazards and pull over. We're losing the others."

Heads turned toward the rear window. The little girl tapped the screen on the gadget he'd given her. They all turned again, this time following Snipe back to his seat.

"Mum, its magic," she said.

Snipe heard this and winked at her. She winked back.

Bill mumbled the words, "*Pull over,* he says. Like *pull over* means anything when everything looks the bloody same."

The transporter stopped. Bill left the engine running with the heaters turned to full. Snipe was too warm, and there was no chance of stripping away the flying suit.

He stood and faced the passengers like a tour guide on a trip to Lapland to meet Santa, only he looked more like a biker that had been dragged through a bush.

"We're stopping to check and see if everyone's okay. We have a few stragglers; I'm going out to check on them. If you need to… well, relieve yourselves, now's the time."

A woman raised her hand. "How're we supposed to do the

business in the snow, with people watching?"

"Be creative. Go in pairs. One of you can hold up a blanket or something," he said.

The line of cars stretched back further than he'd imagined. Stopping at each one, he asked if they were okay, what supplies they had, and checked the charge gauge or the fuel level for those who were driving vintage vehicles.

He felt his hands tighten, and his face went numb, but he continued anyway. The bus was a relief, and a welcome stopping point to the three further back. It was an old-style bus; something he'd never seen until today. The warmth inside hit him as the doors opened. He made his way to the back, then back up to the driver.

"We're not going anywhere. I daren't turn the engine off in case it doesn't start, and if it doesn't start then, we're in the shit. We'll freeze to death."

Snipe wanted to hear that *almost* as much as he'd wanted to hear the screaming kid. "Try to stay positive for the rest of them. They look scared shitless."

"They've got every right to be, unless you've got a plan?"

Snipe hadn't thought past checking on the three further back, but knew he'd have to, and quick. "I'll be back soon. Turn the heating lower and tick her over until she stops. Entertain the passengers, too."

"How?" he asked.

"Sing a song. I don't know. Just entertain them until I get back to you."

Three powerless cars contained frightened passengers. The first had a family of four that shivered beneath blankets, their faces having turned a purplish colour. The car behind them had dug itself into the snow and sat sideways on the road, blocking the path of the third. Both were low on fuel. After reassuring the stranded families whose heaters were still running, he walked back the family of four – a man, his wife, and two boys no older than seven – and led them to the lead transporter.

The doors opened, and Bill said, "No room on this one, mate. It's not happening."

Ignoring him, Snipe took them onto the transporter one-by-one. They recognised just about everyone.

"Let these people defrost. Take turns sitting and standing," he said, before turning to Bill.

"What happened to Church values, Bill?"

"Never been, never will," he said.

Snipe moved closer, leaned over him, and said, "Well, just know that if it all goes to shit, we'll be eating you first. I'd watch what you say amongst these good people, otherwise I'll make it a reality. Understand?"

"Yep."

Snipe didn't have a plan. His joke – albeit a dark one – about eating Bill shook him to the core. Where did he draw the line on survival? Why him? Why'd he taken on the responsibility of the whole damn town? Could there be a divine purpose? Was he the new shepherd now, after the Reverend had lost control of his flock? His mind swarmed with unanswerable questions. All he needed was answers, Lexi, food, and to get out of that damn flying suit.

Time was running out. They'd been lucky so far – no. It was a miracle. They were, after all, sitting ducks in a pool of thickening snow. If Squirrel were here, she would know what to do. She'd find an underground something-or-other.

"I'm stepping outside. I need to think," he said.

Bill opened the side door, and was about to say something

about thinking fast, but swallowed his words before they could escape.

Snipe listened to raised voices and erratic shouting as far down as the fourth vehicle. He looked up, and a flake of snow hit his eye. The old bus, fourth in the line of twelve, shuddered to a stop. He looked for a building, a rock formation, or a shelter of any kind. He couldn't see further than a few feet in front of him. Another engine stalled, then another. People headed toward the transporter. He saw Bill looking through the wing mirror at the approaching horde.

"Everyone, get back inside your vehicles. You'll freeze. Keep in the heat. Shut that door," Snipe shouted to the driver of the car behind the transporter.

Lexi's newfound status flew around to just about everyone inside of camp Freedom. They couldn't understand how she'd climbed the ranks and had the same clearance as senior personnel, nor could they understand why she wouldn't explain herself. She would need to carry around this burden until they found Snipe – the *real* Snipe.

Kat had explained the reason for secrecy, and Lexi had found a new respect for Kat. She understood the pressure of being different. Kat's part was to organise the search mission. Lexi's part was just to be herself, and when the time came, explain the situation to Snipe and convince him to leave her again for the sake of humanity. She was the middle person between the cure and the disease.

Lexi turned to Kat. "I guess that makes me a spoon, then," she said.

"Sorry, Lexi, what?"

"A spoon. If I'm the thing between the cure and the disease, I'd be the medicine spoon."

Kat laughed. "You're so simple. I mean, *sweet*. You're sweetly simple," she said.

In the base, everyone went about their business as if it were a normal day. Chores were dealt with, and meals were served at the same time as usual. They were given the same slop, too – apart from Lexi, who took advantage of her new ranking by asking for pasta. The woman with the wart served her up a large bowl without arguing. She'd taken Spud to his lesson a little late, but nothing new there. The teacher addressed her as Miss Teal, and asked if she wanted to participate in the lesson. Knowing her mouth might go off on a tangent, she declined. Later, when she asked Kat what *participate* meant, she wished she had said yes, but she'd declined his offer since she didn't understand what he was asking.

Lexi sat, book in hand, at the rear of the dining room. She observed and listened to the comings and goings of the people who frequented it. Most of them whispered speculations about why the base was locked. The weather seemed to be the most popular reason. Others said it was a conspiracy, and that gas would be released while they slept. Some people said that Rush Unix might be Zeta. None of them mentioned the guards that were killed by an escaped clone. And why would they? Only a few select people knew about that. They were getting warmer with the connection between Rush Unix and Zeta, though. In a way, they were no different. Both showed themselves as holograms, although Rush claimed to be a real person, and they *did* have an agreement. Deep down, Lexi wondered whether he knew it would turn out this way. Maybe it had been his plan all along?

Kat appeared at her side. She hadn't seen her coming. "Lexi, I'm ready when you are," she said.

"Where are we going?"

"Follow me."

Being in the communications and intelligence gathering room was another first for Lexi, one of many that day. There were three chairs and one desk. Screens covered the walls, including maps and see-through plastic with nondescript scribbles all over it, arrows pointing this way and that. The word *WOW* was underlined several times, and the name *Snipe Siren* had a circle around it. At the centre of the desk stood an antique computer and a machine with pushdown keys bearing letters and numbers, which was not in keeping with anything that Lexi had ever seen before.

Lexi pointed to the clumsy-looking contraption. "What's that thing?"

"It's a decoder. I rely on obsolete machines used in previous wars. Most of what I use has less power than the rubbish bins you see in the canteen. Zeta can crack any computer code, and has access to the grid."

Lexi went to press down on one of the many metal keys poking out of the heavy-looking contraption. "Guess holograms don't have fingers."

Kat raised her palm towards Lexi's finger. "Guess not. Anyway, I'll give you the guided tour later. I thought you'd want to know what I've found so far, before anyone else."

"Anyone?"

"A balloon landed outside a military base. Snipe was in that balloon. At first, it was confusing. Something about a large bird. Could be a call name. I'm not sure. Now, don't freak out on me when I tell you this. Take a seat."

"Kat... what?"

"There was a typed instruction to gain information before..."

160

"Before...? Kat, *tell me*."

"An explosion. It makes little sense. I'm not sure who destroyed it, but the whole base went up in smoke. Lexi, I'm so sorry, but he could've been in there."

Lexi's tear-filled eyes looked out of place as she smiled. "It makes perfect sense. He would have escaped. He'd have killed them and destroyed the base."

"Let's hope so, babes. Let's hope so."

"We need to find him. He might be hurt," Lexi said.

"I will recommend that we send out spy drones. They're short range, and it's a long shot, but it's worth trying, right? I won't give up until we have answers, babes."

Kat went to hug her. Lexi moved away.

"Send a rescue team. I'll go myself."

"The slightest hint that we've located him, and I will. We could send an army out and it wouldn't make any difference without knowing where to send them. Not that we *have* an army. If – *when* he escaped, he would try to find you. So, it would be best to sit tight and hope he shows."

Lexi raised her eyebrows, forced a smile, and walked ahead of Kat. The guided tour could wait. They needed approval to send the spy drones out and ready a team for when they located him. Kat knew the odds were slim that they would ever find Snipe. The truth was that she knew he meant as much to Rush as he did to Lexi, and also, the world needed him to convince Zeta to stop by raising his hand and thinking the words. A joke came to her which could perhaps be an icebreaker if they did ever meet.

*"Hey, care to lend a hand,"* she smiled. *"He has the whole world in his hand."* She hummed the song, but it went unnoticed.

Rush Unix didn't approve the drones, his reason being the range of flight. They wouldn't make it halfway to Snipe's last confirmed location. He also wouldn't approve Lexi's idea of going it alone.

But Lexi had another idea; an idea that went unvoiced.

# Chapter 17

"We will freeze to death," Bill said. "Or be killed by drones. We may as well try our luck back at Mount Pass. Lock the doors, light the fire, and wait it out. Who knows, it might've gone. If we're going to die, let's at least do it with dignity." Passengers aired their agreement. "We're freezing, and we need to go back. Who's going back?"

Snipe stood next to Bill, raised his arms, and said, "Okay."

"Okay? That's your answer? Okay?" Bill asked.

"Well, it looks like you've made your minds up. After all, I don't know any of you. You have a plan, go for it. Go back and take your chances with the thing that ripped open those people," he said.

"So that's it? You're giving up on us?"

"Sounds like you've already given up."

"So, tell us the plan. Tell us where to go," Bill said.

"I know where *not* to go: Mount Pass. Find blankets. Share them. There's no property belonging to any individual in here. Huddle together, and I'll tell the others to do the same."

He'd left a man calling himself Paddy to organise the people on the old bus. He seemed different than the rest; had more about himself. He walked to the rear window and smeared a mix of frozen breath and condensation from the glass to see a sea of snow-covered cars and thickening snow on the ground. Even if the cars could start, they wouldn't roll with the wheels half-buried. He arranged the seating in a rowboat formation. With the windows steamed from the inside, and the number of bodies in the transporter, the increased temperature had steadied the juddering passengers. He walked the aisles, asking each person what firearms they had, if any. The good, churchgoing folks of Mount Pass didn't think it was necessary to have weapons of any sort. The mother, covering her daughter's ears when he asked, confirmed his efforts as futile. He still had Walker's rifle with enough rounds to hunt, but it would be of little use against Zeta's faithful, and not worth firing against the machines.

Snipe chose the old bus over the warmer, modern transporter. A woman sang Christian hymns to a little boy called Timothy; others joined her. The song sounded familiar, something about God having the whole world in his hands. He wasn't sure where he'd heard it before, but at least they were settled.

Snipe asked if anyone needed to leave. It was better if they went out in groups to minimise the inevitable rush of cold air that would sweep in when the door opened. They either didn't need to or hadn't heard him over their joyous singing. Not that he didn't like the singing, but Snipe craved silence; a place of solitude; somewhere to think. He picked out a neck scarf from the communal pile of clothes, wrapped it around his neck and ears, and slipped on a pair of leather gloves. The gloves gripped his hands, allowing only the slightest movement of his fingers.

On his way to check on those in the Transporter, he realised he'd taken on the role of their Reverend. As far as the sheep following the shepherd, he had power over them, and they had trust in what he said, the same way that citizens trusted Zeta. What if the scan pods did not differ from the elephant tied to a plastic chair with a piece of string? He remembered Vic telling him once that mental bondage was stronger than the real thing. Did the scan pods work? He hadn't seen any since leaving town. Either way, they were like turkeys sitting in an open chest freezer.

"Need to get these through the night. Tomorrow we'll head off on foot and find shelter. I'll leave them and continue the search." His words formed a rolling cloud as he spoke. The creaking of snow-laden branches on the few scattered trees that stood pathetically between him and a sheet of darkness looked menacing. He'd always thought of snow being wondrous and exciting. This couldn't be further from that. This was nature's death wish; a clamp holding them in place for the inevitable.

The faint sound of singing came from behind him as he approached the front vehicle. There was no such sound coming from within the transporter. In fact, there was no sound at all. Not a voice or a cry. Were they asleep or dead? No, couldn't be; he'd only left moments ago.

He opened the door, expecting a comment from Bill, who sat open-mouthed, staring out of the windshield. He glanced at Snipe, his white-rimmed eyeballs bulging and his top lip quivering as if to say something. Snipe climbed in, and the door hissed behind him. The passengers had their heads hung low. They weren't sleeping; they were ducking, as if someone was about to swipe their heads.

Bill pointed. "A drone, it's out there," he said.

Snipe looked, but only saw his reflection and droplets of condensation from the snow. He hadn't seen or heard a drone on the short walk from the bus.

"Where? Are you sure?"

Bill didn't answer. Snipe peeled off his gloves and gripped the rifle. "Wait here. I'll take a look." He was putting on a good show, but if there really was a drone, there'd be no discussing it. It would be too late.

He stood outside, wishing he'd kept the gloves. A faint sound came from the side of the transporter. Near a half-buried tree came a humming, so faint that it could have been a small bird or a confused bee. He started toward the sound and moved closer. It didn't sound like a military drone or one of Zeta's gun drones, and the scanners made no sound at all.

A red dot moved up the trunk of the tree. Snipe took aim and fired. Screams came from behind him. The red dot vanished, and the humming turned to a padded thud.

Using the barrel of the rifle as a guide in the knee-high depth of the snow, he waded over to the tree. Illuminated under the moon's yellow glow, a glint of something black stuck out of the snow. He pulled out a tiny rotator drone. A child's toy, but there were no children in sight. The shot had knocked out its circular blade. He smiled as a rush of relief washed over him. Tossing it aside, he trudged back over to the transporter.

Kat climbed on top of the food counter. "Everyone, listen to me. We can only answer questions when we *have* answers. Calm down, and we'll explain later."

She climbed down and paced over to Lexi. Sitting cross-legged with the same book on the same page, Lexi saw her coming.

"What the hell have you told them?"

Lexi shrugged her shoulders and said, "I need to find Snipe. We all do, and sitting around having meetings isn't going to achieve that, and neither is waiting for a fucking hologram to appear and grant us three wishes–"

"You could've started a riot. How's that helping? People are worried sick, and I've got to explain this to Rush Unix."

"I told a maintenance crew, that's all. I don't know how

everyone else found out."

"Why, Lexi?"

"They've sent out the spy wasp-looking things, that's why."

"On whose orders?"

"Mine. I outranked them. They even called me a VIP."

"Well, you're not. You shouldn't have."

Kat walked around a corner that lead to the testing and maintenance room, and Lexi marched quickly behind her. The two repair guys looked down at a small handheld device. Two other bodies moved forward from behind a solid workbench.

"Mike, Tyrone, what are you doing in here?"

"Your Miss Teal's come up trumps," Mike said.

Lexi nudged Kat into Mike and went over to the repair team. A short, overweight man with a full beard spoke. "He shot it, but the camera wasn't damaged. I'll play it back."

Kat bounced on the balls of her feet over to where Lexi stood. She pointed at the overweight hairy man and his sidekick – a young, baby-faced man with smooth, clear skin. She waved her finger at both of them like a mother to her children and said, "You two are in trouble."

Something moved on the screen.

"Told you," said the hairy man.

"Can you play it on the big screen?" Mike asked.

Kat huffed and placed her hands either side of her waist, standing with one leg pointing out to the left. Mike switched on the monitor; a simple square screen mounted on the wall. The video was a recording from the unauthorised dispatch of spy drones. The one in question showed open ground, a few skinny looking trees, and ruins of the old world that would've gone missed by passers-by on the ground level. There were outlines of buildings that had once stood tall, their shape that of residential houses; a road, abandoned vehicles, a tree, and someone approaching it. There was a cracking sound, blinding white, then total darkness.

"Well, that doesn't tell us much," Kat said.

"Wait for it…" Mike said.

Black turned to a trembling white, and then the hairy man froze the picture.

"Snipe!" Lexi shouted. "It's Snipe. He's alive. I knew it!"

The video played again. There was a clear view of Snipe Siren smiling before the camera turned to black.

Mike turned to Kat. "Told you she came up trumps, didn't I?"

"You did, Mike. So, your foolish gamble paid off, Miss Teal," Kat said.

The word *foolish* didn't register, but Kat calling her *Miss Teal* induced an uncontrollable natural smile.

"Will you get a team out now?" she asked.

Tyrone and Mike looked at her. Their tilted heads spoke for them.

"I'll recommend that we do, Lexi, not that you'll take no for an answer."

"Well, you've seen him shoot, so it's best I go with them."

"Don't push it, girl, but yeah. I'll suggest that, too."

# Chapter 18

The people on the bus had noticed nothing, so Snipe thought it better to leave them to their singing. No point in rocking the bus. He made his way back to the transporter. Cheers and applause from relieved passengers welcomed him. Sweat droplets speckled Bill's smooth, round face. His darting eyes had Snipe's inner voice telling him to make up a story that would shut him up, but he couldn't; he took no pleasure from seeing people suffer, even if they were annoying.

Snipe raised his hands. "Thank you."

"They'll know we're here now. They'll be back. The gun drones, they'll find us, and we won't stand a chance. We're sitting–"

"Sledges."

"Er, what?"

"You were going to say ducks. Sitting ducks. I'd say we're more like sitting sledges," said Snipe.

"How can you find anything amusing? It's serious."

Snipe gave him a soft, but pained smile. "Things are only as serious as you make them, Bill. The drone was a toy, out-of-range. It lost signal with its operator."

"And you know for sure?" Bill asked.

"I've experienced drones, both Zetas and military. I've shot them down. I know the difference, Bill."

Bill let out a slow, controlled breath that must have originated deep in his gut for the time it took to leave his dry lips.

Snipe pointed out of the curved windshield. "Looks to be slowing down. Let's get through the night and wait for sunrise. I'll make this my bed for tonight, if that's all right with you," he said, patting the front passenger seat. "I'll take first shift, Bill, and then I'll wake you to do the second, just in case."

"Like a stakeout sort of thing."

"More like keep your eyes open and wake me if anyone needs help or you see another one of those flying things."

"Then what? What if another one comes?"

"Then I'd like to be awake before I die... I'm joking Bill, get some rest."

On the bus, people had found their comfort zone. Any tensions and awkwardness they may have felt about being in such close proximity to one another had drifted away. They'd fallen asleep with their limbs entangled with those of their neighbours.

Singing from the back of the bus had turned to stories from the Bible and conversations about their sleeping children. Gill sat cross-legged, and her husband Cameron sat with his back to her. Timothy was stretched out sideways on his lap, asleep. Cameron was talking to Paddy about Mount Pass and Reverend Phillips. They'd both concluded that he couldn't have shot Fin, not even in self-defence, and that anyone claiming otherwise would receive the wrath of their tongue. Gill used her husband's shoulders to push herself to her feet. She shook Cameron.

"There's someone outside," she said.

"Probably just your reflection or that bloke," he said, meaning Snipe Siren. "Or someone from the other bus."

She nudged him again, this time waking Timothy, "It's the Reverend. Our good Lord has delivered him to us, and he's alive."

Cameron raised his eyes toward Paddy. "She's delirious. Heard us talking while half-asleep. We'll talk later." He turned, with Timothy now standing bewildered between his legs. "Gillian, you've woken Timothy."

Gill shrieked, "He's coming! He's here!"

People looked up from the carpeted passageway. The door to the bus opened. It wasn't the driver; he had his head to his chest, snoring. A tall, pale-skinned man lumbered up two steps before falling headfirst into the driver. His head hit the driver's chin; his body wobbled until it buckled beneath the cabin. The driver, an old man who, until now, had avoided just about everyone in Mount Pass, swung his fists into the air, shouting obscenities at his own reflection. People stood, others leaned forward to get a better look, and a few cowered beneath the backs of seats.

The driver looked over at his passengers. "Help him."

Paddy pushed his way to the front, followed by Cameron, who apologised, as he too, moved people aside to reach the man with his long legs bent at the knees and his arms tucked under his body. A casual, all-in-one boiler suit hung from him like an empty sack.

"Reverend," Paddy said.

Cameron called to the bottleneck of passengers, now standing on their seats, half in fear, and half in joy at seeing their shepherd.

"Make room. Get blankets. Help me carry him," Paddy said.

Cameron took hold of his arms and Paddy took hold of his legs. They dragged him to the back of the bus. Timothy was crying as he clung to Gill. She stood aside as they laid him down with his head against the back wall of the bus and his legs outstretched. They placed a rolled blanket under his knees.

Cameron stretched his arms out to the side. "Give him room," he said.

Reverend Phillips opened his eyes. His pupils grew as he stared at the curved roof. His body trembled, and his skin felt like frozen meat as he mumbled the Lord's Prayer.

"Reverend Phillips, are you with us? Do you know who I am?"

"Paddy, my boy. My little fighter Paddy O'Brien, is it you? I fear that evil has entered my soul… I'm so cold, Paddy… so cold."

Cameron walked the length of the bus, collecting coats and blankets, and helped Paddy wrap the Reverend up until he was three times his size. Despite the commotion, Timothy had fallen asleep with his head sandwiched between his mother's breasts. She laid him down on the seat and joined the others in prayer. Cameron invited everyone to join him. Some held hands and others lowered their heads.

"Almighty and everlasting Lord, I come before you now in great need of your mercy. You are the doctor and physician of my soul. I humbly beseech thee to send forth your healing power into our friend Reverend Phillips…"

Further down the road, Snipe sat back on the padded chair, trying to keep his eyes from closing. He'd been doing long blinks, which was a sure sign that he was losing the battle to stay awake. The rifle slipped from his hand. Grabbing the barrel before it touched the floor mat, he stared down it. *What's the plan, kiddo? How'd you expect to find this base or Lexi? And what about this lot? Who the fuck invited them? Oh, you did. Well, anyway, stay awake now. Need to stay…*

Bill's face, as round and bright as the moon that shone between the clouds, twitched as a spit bubble that had formed between snores popped. He repeated the process, unaware that a rifle was pointing up at him, held at an angle by Snipe's boots. The rhythmic combination of snoring and popping had tipped

Snipe over the thin line he'd held between wakefulness and unconsciousness.

*What if they don't listen this time, Dad?*

*Hold out your hand and think "fall", like you did when you asked them to fly in circles.*

*Dad, they listened!*

Snipe's eyes snapped open. He was gripping his left hand with his right. Holding it up to his face, then to the side to allow the moonlight to brighten it, he squinted at the soft spot in its centre; the scar now barely visible.

Wiping his eyes, he looked over at Bill. The snow outside crunched. The door hissed open. Bill jumped in his seat and wiped drawl from his chin. Snipe looked into Paddy's eyes.

"What's wrong?"

"The Reverend's here. He's on the bus."

Snipe loaded the rifle. "The naked man?"

"What are you doing? He's stable, and I've just come to let everyone know."

"Is he infected? Acting strange?"

"He's on the brink of hypothermia. We've covered him with blankets."

"Paddy… is that your name, Paddy?"

"Well, it's Luke, but yeah. Everyone calls me Paddy."

"He can't stay there. He has to go."

"He's a citizen. That thing only attacked the non-chipped."

"And you're willing to take that chance?" Snipe asked.

Paddy shouted above the barrage of questions, gasps, and whispers, "You heard right. He's alive, and on our bus. You'll all have time to see him when he recovers. Please pray tonight for our good friend," he said.

Bill waited for the break in their conversation, then said, "I'm

173

not praying for him, the murdering bastard. You saw him. Covered in blood with a gun in his hand. Did you not hear the shot from inside his flat, or are you deluded like this lot?"

Snipe nodded in begrudging agreement. He didn't think the Reverend had shot anyone. He'd seen killers, including the crazed ones, and the Reverend didn't fit into any category, but maybe Bill's paranoia could be of some benefit. "Yeah. Like he said, we just don't know."

"Well, unlike you, we all have faith; and faith, my friend, will overcome any obstacle," Paddy said.

Snipe stood, neither inside nor outside, of the transporter. Strangely, Paddy reminded him of a male version of Lexi: headstrong, stubborn, and wriggled with cognitive dissidence.

*What was I thinking? These loony toons are keeping me from Squirrel. She's alive, I feel it... Faith. Guess I've been running on nothing other than just that.*

Snipe climbed back inside. The door closed behind him. Bill looked unnerved. The others appeared excited at the prospect of seeing the head of their church. Some prayed, while others took solace in hushed conversations. Snipe sat with his arms folded as the snow that had been both his worst enemy and his best friend slowed before finally stopping.

"Bastards," Lexi said. "They have no right keeping me in here. They wouldn't know he was alive if it wasn't for me. Short-sighted, hymnodist bastards."

Kat smiled and tilted her head in empathy. "You're right, they wouldn't have. It was you that rolled the dice and achieved the impossible, I'll give you that, but I still think it's better that you stay here. We've not confirmed the whereabouts of the clone, or even why he's here."

"What you smiling at, then?"

"You said *hymnodist*. Did you mean to say hypocrite?"

"I *mean*, you idiots need to listen to *me* and not that light show. I learned from the best and I... I love him."

Kat took no pleasure in seeing the tears roll down Lexi's tanned face. Until now, she thought Lexi was incapable of any emotion other than anger. She was sure that she didn't wear makeup, so the black lines must have been from dirt. Her anguish was painful to watch, and in a way, painful to understand. Kat had never felt real love, and today, she saw the pain it could bring.

"And it's because you love him that you'll find each other. You have two of our best out looking for him. They have a location fix and they are on their way," she said.

Tyrone turned to Mike. "Can this go any slower?"

"Don't think they gave much thought to heavy snow. This was the smallest all-terrain vehicle in storage and the only one with heating. Should I turn back so we can get the fifty-year-old big bitch?"

"I'm not talking about the vehicle. I'm talking about your elegant driving skills."

"Thanks."

"I said elegant as in *ballerina* elegant."

"I know. Thanks," Mike said.

They'd had the order to shoot the clone on sight if it was spotted within a five-mile radius of the base. Anything further, albeit unlikely, could be the real Snipe Siren. His last location was fifty-two miles northeast of the base, so they watched with caution. Mike and Tyrone were both armed. The third seat of the four-seater buggy held an ammunition box below two high-powered machine guns.

"Twenty-four miles to go," Mike said.

"Would you still shoot him on sight, you know, if he popped

out of the blue?"

"No. We're twenty miles away from that order."

"So, how would we know if it's him?"

Mike tapped the dash monitor twice. A static, grainy picture of Snipe Siren appeared, his smile showing bright white against the black background.

"Because he's wearing that."

Tyrone looked closer at the screen. He was wearing a scarf and a black top, the Velcro neck clasp visible under the fold of the scarf.

"He made a hundred-yard shot in the dead of night and knocked out something the size of a kid's toy. What if he thinks we're the enemy?"

"I've heard he's old-school, and you're wearing white. You could use your shirt as a white flag."

Tyrone didn't reply. He'd known Mike long enough to know his current state of mind.

Keeping to the back roads, they'd avoided driving through two residential zones. They'd been forewarned about scan pods that had appeared around residential areas to detect either non-citizens or citizens, no one knew which. Neither were militarised, but they could take no chances with a prize as important as Snipe Siren.

An impassable snow drift from a large hedgerow to a farm entrance blocked their way. The buggy carried supplies, including a shovel. Tyrone got to work on clearing the snow as Mike climbed a fence post to get a better look at what was ahead.

"Don't bother," Mike said. "You'll be shovelling all night and still not clear this lot. It stretches as far as the eye can see."

As the buggy broke through the hedge, Tyrone's head hit the roof.

"Bloody hell, mate. You could've warned me."

"First rule of driving: wear a seat belt," he said.

Re-joining the back road had taken time, not that the miles flowed with consistency. The last five miles had taken as long as the first twenty, and yes, they were counting. Every damn foot was a relief.

The tracker would last for the lifespan of the drone. It was stationary, and they'd banked on it being thrown down into the snow. If the snow started up again, or the opposite happened, and it thawed, the tracker would stop working. Like a more efficient satellite navigation system, it counted down the miles and converted them into minutes, but with one disadvantage: it was a one-way search signal. Like any vehicle allowed to leave the base, the buggy wasn't equipped with a home beacon, it had no signal to count on, and no electronic or written maps were allowed. If they were hijacked, then for all intents and purposes, the base simply didn't exist.

Mike had thought it best not to mention that slight complication to Tyrone; a complication that had now increased with the detour through the field, the snow covering over the buggies distinct tire tracks, and the high hedgerows on either side of the back roads.

Tyrone pointed at the dash screen. "Well, I hope that thing can get us back."

"Er, yeah," he replied.

# Chapter 19

"Where are you going?" Bill asked.

Instead of motivating and lifting his spirits, the mix of prayer, whispering, and jubilation had gotten to Snipe. Even more than Bill, who he now considered to be the only sane person other than himself on the transporter.

"Out," he said.

"Oi, buddy! We're all starving. If you're going to the others, can you ask if they can spare some food?"

Lifting the rifle, Snipe stared at the man who was as round as he was tall. "No. Fuck off."

Snipe climbed down the steps and tried to slam the door, but it hissed closed even slower than usual.

"Fucking people. I saved their godly asses, and then they invite a bloody leper aboard who'll probably wipe the lot of them off the planet. Suppose they don't care. They all think they're heading through the pearly gates. Well, if I made it, there'd be a closed sign and an arrow pointing down saying, 'This way', and 'Please take a list of your sins with you'."

Snipe climbed onto the bus. They weren't singing, and apart from Paddy and another couple tending to the Reverend, they all looked sedated.

Paddy climbed over Reverend Phillips and stood between him and Snipe. "What are you doing here?"

Snipe wasn't going to shoot the Reverend. He never intended to, but the nagging thought remained.

"I'm checking on him," he said.

"We need to get him to the doctor, and he's back in Mount Pass."

Snipe felt his lungs expand as he filled them with air, only to let the breath flow in a stilted manner through parted lips. "Then take him back."

"We've followed you to our doom, and we have nowhere to go, and you've come here to what? To kill our Reverend?"

Gritting his teeth, Snipe heard a popping sound within his head, inaudible to the flock. Reverend Phillips raised his right arm. His hand trembled as he spoke in a hushed, breathless tone. "Luke, my child, let him come to me."

"He wants to see you," Paddy said.

Snipe walked over and knelt by his side. "He said he wants to see *me*. How about you," he pointed at Paddy and Cameron, "go for a walk and take any surplus supplies to the Transporter?"

"Supplies? We're down to five bottles of water and three food bars, and that's got to serve everyone in here."

"Wrong. It's got to feed and water everyone, including the people within the Transporter, so how about you stop whining like a little bitch and do the Christian thing?"

Cameron held Paddy back as he budged forward toward Snipe. Snipe looked up, tried to find the pupils within Paddy's widening eyes, and said, "I will not fight you, Paddy. These people have seen enough death. If you want me to kill you, you have to wait, because right now, I'm going to talk to your man Phillips."

Paddy grabbed two bottles of water and a food bar and left with Cameron. People stared along the gangway, then looked away when Snipe stared back.

"What's your name, my son?"

"It's Snipe, and let's get one thing straight: I'm not your son, and I've got no ambition to reach heaven. You have no hold over me. Tell me why you've put these people at risk."

"The devil was inside Fin, and it moved to other damned souls. It isn't within me, Snipe. I had to leave. The others, they have turned against me. They blame me for what happened."

"So don't these people? Never mind that." He knew the answer already; those left behind were citizens, and the Reverend knitted the two groups together until the invisible killer pulled at those stitches and tore the fabric of their community apart.

"How did you find us here? We're miles away from Mount Pass."

"I followed the tracks in the snow. I had to get away. They've become possessed. The devil has a hold of their minds."

Snipe looked into Reverend Phillips' eyes. He was telling the truth... or at least, he believed it was the truth.

"I got on this bus to end your life, but now I'm asking for your help. These people that you've brainwashed follow you without question, and I know you care for them."

"Yes, I do," Reverend Phillips whispered.

"Then they need to listen to me. Otherwise, you'll all be seeing paradise before God's got your rooms ready."

"There's good in you, Snipe. I feel it, and yes, I believe we will live long in the battle to reach God's kingdom with a warrior like you. According to the prophecies, that came before you, you will fight a good war. I believe you will win the fight."

Snipe could feel the others watching him with an ominous intensity that could paralyse a man where he knelt. He'd deciphered the Reverend's words to mean that he approved of his leadership and would back him up on any decisions he'd make… or at least, that's what he thought he'd said.

The clock was ticking to find Lexi. He'd thought about leaving them and setting off into the night. They'd told him that the next town was only ten miles away. They'd also told him that the citizens would turn him in and that the only safe town was Mount Pass. With the goons' blood already on his hands, he wasn't going to leave them here to die, and die they would without someone guiding them. No, he'd come up with a plan, and maybe give Paddy the challenge of going back to Mount Pass while they laid low. If he returned, then they could all get their sorry asses back to the Church.

Kicking snow, Snipe walked back to the transporter. Something was wrong. Bill had that open-mouthed, wide-eyed look again. The moon hung low, lighting the front of the vehicle and Bill's shiny, round face. He followed Bill's hypnotised gaze. Something shimmered; a distortion within the moon's glow. He'd seen the same thing up close and personal in Vic's garden. It would have done a head count already, and scanned the two packed vehicles when he was busy listening to the Reverend.

*Too many people to move.*

*Nowhere to hide.*

*No weapons.*

*No time.*

He ran across the road, following his footprints back to the tree. There, he steadied the rifle and fired one shot at the moon's distorted reflection. Before he could reload, it was over him; a deep hum above his head. A blue light combed his body. He continued to run. It was only a matter of time before its big brother showed.

"Snipe!" Bill shouted from the open door. "Snipe!"

Snipe turned, cupped both hands around his mouth, and

bellowed the words, "Scatter! Spread out! Away from the vehicles!"

Turning as he ran, he saw people getting off the bus. He must have covered ground, because the passengers looked small in the distance. He couldn't see the drone, but he felt it moving along with every stride he made. Over in the next field, separated by hedgerows, stood a small barn, or maybe a shed. He headed toward it, knowing it wouldn't offer any protection. The drone was predictable, and it would follow him. First a scan drone, followed by a gun drone, or the more recent body snatchers. On the rare occasions when a second didn't appear, it would be an army of Zeta's foot soldiers instead. He banked on it being a drone, based on the time that it would take anyone to reach them through the snow and the fog. Either way, they'd hone in on their prey, and he was that prey: a wanted non-citizen trying to escape. He looked back toward the scattered vehicles.

"Damn it, Bill, take them away from the vehicles."

His words didn't help the residents of Mount Pass as they hung around wondering what to do next.

The material of his flight suit screeched as he navigated a gap in the thorny hedge. He was nearing the battered stone building. Snipe couldn't hear or see the thing above and could only hope it hadn't doubled back to the buses. The door was locked.

"Locked. Who'd lock a shitty building in the middle of nowhere? Why?"

Each breath burnt his lungs as he stood slouched with his back to the heavy steel door. He held his breath to encourage his senses. The moon's reflection shone bright, outlining the grey patches on its surface. Looking around, and listening with an intensity that made his ears throb, the breath he'd held pushed its way out. He could no longer see the vehicles or any airborne death warrant.

He was alone in a snow-filled field with his back to a window-less building no bigger than a cow shed, but right now, it was more secure than any building he'd ever seen.

Mike slowed the buggy to a stop. They were on the old road, one that had been called a *motorway* before the event. Two vehicles had passed them during the time they'd been on it. One had been a military truck, but not one of theirs. The other had been a family car packed to the brim with household goods. There was at least one child on board, as they'd seen a face peering between stacks of either bedding or clothes.

"Why have you stopped?" Tyrone asked.

Mike reached into the glove compartment. "You'll be needing these," he said, handing him a pair of night-vision binoculars. "Better keep the gun on your lap, too. We're within five miles of the signal. This is the only road leading away from it. I doubt he has transport, but you never know. I'll check the road. You check everything else."

Tyrone looked up at the embankments on either side of the wide expanse of snow. "Yeah, *everything*. Right."

Mike pulled off. The heavy tread on the buggy's wheels gripped and released the softness of the snow like two pieces of Velcro tearing apart.

Tyrone said, "Moon's bright."

"He could be anywhere close to the signal, but I can guarantee where he's not," Mike said, pointing to the full moon.

"Yeah. Right," Tyrone said, refocusing on the embankments. Then he shouted, "There!"

A vibrating hum, along with a static electrical charge that spiked each one of their hairs into thin, upright wires, buzzed through the buggy. Mike slammed on the brakes. The buggy jolted, slipped, and jolted again until it stopped. They both stared at a black gun drone flying off ahead of them.

Tyrone stuttered, "W-W-Why are we not dead?"

"That was a fighter, not a scanner, and it's in a hurry. Look! It's heading to the same place we're going."

"I need to report this to Rush. We're not following that," Tyrone said.

Mike nodded in agreement. Tyrone opened his jacket and pulled a handheld two-ray radio from the inner pocket. He spoke the password: "Cap hand." At first, it didn't understand. Instead, it spelt out: *command*.

"CAP HAND," Mike said, so loudly that he made Tyrone hold his right ear and throw a look of disdain in his direction.

A hologram flicked on, then off the screen, followed by another, before a face they both recognised as being Rush Unix appeared with a smile. Mike squinted, then looked at Tyrone, bamboozled by what had happened. Tyrone mirrored his frown before looking down at the handset.

They both spoke at once. Then Mike halted, and Tyrone carried on. "We're five miles from the signal point and a gun drone flew by. We saw it and felt it. It's heading in the same direction we are," he said.

Rush Unix spoke. "Proceed, you have nothing to fear."

Something wasn't right, but he didn't know what.

"Well, fuck me," Tyrone said, as he slipped the gadget back inside his coat.

Mike waved a finger and mouthed the words, *Lose the handheld.*

Tyrone scrunched his nose up and went to speak, but Mike placed a finger on his lips and pulled it from within its hiding place. He lowered the window to the halfway point and bounced the communicator between both hands like it was a hot rock.

On the third bounce, he let go, and it flew out into the snow.

"Fuck me twice," Tyrone said.

"Er, no thanks. I'll pass."

"What's that all about? Have you finally lost it, mate?"

"Something's not right. I'm in self-preservation mode, bud. Didn't you see the other holograms?"

"Could have been a crossed signal, but yeah, strange all the same. You chucked away our only communicator."

"Until we figure out what's going on, we can't risk them snooping. Something's not right. I feel it, and for the record, we hit a rock and it fell out."

"Okay, Mr Paranoia, got it. Hit a rock. Fell out. Watch the embankments and follow a fucking gun drone. I'm up for that."

Bill convinced a few of them to scatter. Some of them stayed on board, but most of them gathered outside, asking questions that he had no answers to. A group of them decided to walk back to Mount Pass, against Bill's advice, and Snipe had run away like the coward he thought he was.

Bill called out, "Okay! Get your sorry asses back inside! I'm only following… never mind, do whatever!"

Snipe steadied his breath to a manageable level, looked across the two fields, and then to the ground, where his footprints sat double-sized in the snow. Every shadow and every rustle from the hedgerow, heightened his anxiety for what he knew was lurking unseen in the sky. He stopped five paces from the building, held his breath, and looked up at the sky. He saw nothing, but heard a distant, all-too-familiar hum heading toward him.

Then, the hum stopped short. Fearing that it would attack the idle convoy, he lowered his head and ran toward it. He covered six of his original foot impressions before slipping over, and the air in his lungs left, leaving him winded. Looking up from the ground, first at the shimmer that could only be a scan drone, and then over to its big brother that hovered six feet above him, he laid flat, facing up. Snow fell into his ears, but he felt spider legs instead.

Raising the rifle, he knew it wouldn't so much as scratch the surface of the unknown material. He'd unloaded thirty rounds into one once, and it hadn't even moved. With no way out, and at the mercy of something incapable of showing any, he closed his eyes.

If he was to die, he wanted his last image to be of Lexi.

# Chapter 20

Someone called out to him, "Move, god damn it! Move!"

His eyes fluttered open. It was still there hovering above, its mocking blackness waiting for the right moment to strike.

"Move!"

A dull, menacing hum turned into a high-pitched squeal. Snipe rolled over before being dragged away as the drone crashed down in the spot he'd occupied only moments ago. Two men pulled him again as the smaller scan drone fell from the sky.

"Pleased to meet you, Snipe Siren. Let's get inside. Hurry," the younger of the two said.

Both men wore old-style combat gear; a patchwork of green and brown, and their faces were painted the same, with two-tone stripes running from their ears to the base of their necks. He could tell that one was younger by the sound of his voice; a hint of immaturity mixed with the energy that only the young can have.

Turning, Snipe looked down at the inactive, yet complete, drone. The smaller scan drone had fallen somewhere near the hedgerow.

"If you want to live, get inside," the older man said.

A box hung from his stretched arms. It took both hands on the rope handle to keep it above the snow. A tube ran from its rear into the small fortress with a funnel sticking out of the front. It looked homemade, with tape strapping the funnel to the box.

"No. If *you* want to live, tell me who you are and how you did that." Snipe pointed at the disabled drone.

"Can't believe it's you. We're on your side," said the young man as he helped the other man carry the box through the steel door.

"Quick, we have little time," the older man said.

Snipe could tell by the sincerity in their voices and their genuine nature that they were trying to help. The small, windowless fortress didn't look big enough for three men and a box the size of a car engine. He owed them his life, so the thought of being trapped became neutralised by their actions. He followed them.

The door closed behind him. The building's solid, square exterior gave way to a cylindrical interior. There were smooth walls with cables running up to the ceiling and a closed wooden hatch sat in the centre of the room, not dissimilar to the one which hid Vic's armament. Snipe's thoughts turned to the spider that had forced him out.

The older of the two opened the wooden flap. "There's someone who wants to see you," he said.

"Yeah, well, there's a lot more outside freezing to death who also want to see me." He looked at the young man by his side, who now appeared to be a teenager, then back to the older one. "Thank you for saving my life. I need to know how you did it."

"You need to know the truth, and the answers are down there," he said, pointing at the opening.

Snipe edged forward; a collapsible staircase led down to another room. A shadow moved across, too fast to register any of its features.

"What's this place?"

"It's a converted electrical sub-station. We've turned it into a base. We're trying to stop Zeta's efforts to take over the world."

Snipe laughed and said, "You're a bit late. He's had control of the world governments and their people for as long as I can remember."

"Snipe, meet Chip, my son. My name's Alex. If we're going to stop Zeta, we only have a small window of time to do so. Please… follow me."

Snipe knew that he still had two rounds in his rifle, and they hadn't taken it from him. If this was a trap, he'd find out within seconds.

"You first."

"Very well."

Before descending, he looked back at the heavy steel door. There were no keyholes and no recognition computer locks. He'd seen Alex turn a wheel clockwise; the sort of wheel found on a bank safe. The hatch was flimsy enough to break through even if it were locked behind him. He took two steps down, held the hatch open with his left hand, and pointed the rifle ahead of him into a low-lit room. Light from another room cast a shadow of someone standing. The shadow moved.

"Any sudden moves and I promise I won't miss," Snipe said, moving the gun away from Chip.

The shadow turned into someone he recognised. "Where do I know you from? Come forward." The man moved closer. "We're on your side. Come down if you want to know Lexi's whereabouts."

Snipe jumped down the few remaining steps. Pain shot up his spine, and a blanket of pins caressed his lower half. Chip jumped back against the wall and Alex stood in front of him, which confirmed their relationship as father and son.

"You're the face in my head. The memory. The white room."

Snipe looked the man up and down. He was unarmed. "Start talking."

"Lower your gun. If I'm right, then Alex and young Chip saved your life. If that's not proof we're legit, then I don't know what is."

"*Legit*. You said *legit*. I was right. You *are* him. The man in the white coat."

"Mathews. Dr Brian Mathews, and yes, I was wearing a white coat when I saw you last."

"Where's Lexi?" Snipe pushed past Mathews and looked around the room. It was a basic L shape, with a computer, wall hooks –probably to hang the frequency gun used on the drones – and no windows, as they were underground. A reflection of Mathews came from the room that branched off from the area where they now stood.

Mathews held out his arm to stop him from entering. "Wait. You'll need an explanation before you see what's in there." He held out both arms, palms upturned, and spoke with urgency. "Lexi's fine and well. She's with your father."

"My father? You know my father? You know Lexi?"

"She may not realise it, but she's being held within a confinement base. The inmates call it Camp Freedom, but they are far from free."

"You know its whereabouts?" Snipe glanced over Mathews.

"Yes, and we want to reunite you with Lexi, but we can't help you unless you listen to what we need to tell you. We haven't got much time, and your friends outside are in imminent danger."

"So, get talking." Stepping back from Mathews, Snipe took a deep breath and lowered his shoulders. "But if I find out that you're telling me any bullshit…"

"Like I said when we first met, no matter how crazy it may

sound, I'll only tell you the truth as I know it to be," Mathews said.

Alex moved from standing in front of his son and stood alongside Mathews instead, blocking the open entrance to the other room.

"As he said, this will come as a shock," Alex said, looking Snipe in the eyes. "Your father and your grandfather worked with Zeta. We have evidence of an agreement between the two. In exchange for Zeta's loyalty and protection, they gave Zeta access to the DNA of every living entity on Earth. They agreed to furnish the group with samples. They gave them everything from our treasured archives, some of which stretched back thousands of years; from our ancient ancestors' DNA and plant samples long since extinct to our more evolved, present-day DNA and, if I'm not mistaken, even living samples."

Shaking his head in disbelief, Snipe said, "They gave in to the terrorists."

"They had little choice." Mathews added, "After the event, they had a palpable solution to the problems which humanity faced. You'd have done the same. They could never have imagined that they would turn against them and perform such an organised assault."

"And Lexi?"

"She's okay, and sources say she's climbed the ranks within the base."

"Base Freedom. A prison, you said."

"A prison of sorts. More like a gathering of non-citizens and those who help them."

"What sources?" Snipe asked. "Can I speak to Lexi?"

Mathews ducked under Alex's arm, which rested on the wall leading to the other room. Alex lifted it, then put it back, as if gating the area. "There's no way of contacting Lexi. Our contact within the camp…" He looked over at Chip, who glanced back, blinking, as if trying not to cry. "Is my… her name's Katrina Brenna. She worked within British Intelligence."

Snipe saw his eyes redden. He could see that his intentions were genuine, and that he was trying to help. Alex flinched, as if he wanted to stop Chip from climbing the steps.

Banging came from the darkened room behind Alex.

"Can you help those freezing people in the convoy?"

"After the event–"

"Did my father cause that, too?"

"No. The event, as far as we're aware, occurred naturally, brought on by external influences. We believe that the Zeta agreement came after the event. The only way to help the people outside, and everyone else, is for you to remember how you disabled the drones. We received a coded message, moments before you arrived. It told of a video that was made when you were a child. You stopped Zeta by raising your hand and touching a machine. Rush Unix said it was because they understood your thoughts, but I'm inclined to think that you are holding a code that can disable them; a safety feature, part of the agreement between Rush Unix and Zeta, perhaps. If you are some sort of antivirus, that would explain why your father handed you over and hid you away from the reaches of the governments and Zeta, and unlocking that potential is of paramount importance."

Snipe smiled and said, "And you believe that."

"I believe what I saw," Alex said. "We need to get you to your father."

Snipe looked down at his palm, rubbed it, and recalled the dream he'd had. Coincidence?

"What's their goal?" Snipe asked. "What does this Zeta organisation hope to gain from these samples, the DNA, the census, and killing the people they should protect?"

"We can only draw conclusions based on what we know to be true," Alex said. "The census was carried out to find out the most suitable people, based on their physical ability, personality traits, and acumen, something your father wanted no part of. He insisted that survival skills and the ability to adapt were more pertinent. All non-citizens were disqualified, and the estimated number of citizens that could be chosen was limited. We can only assume that the plant and animal research had something to do with biological warfare, and that the population reduction was for control. Before you ask, I don't know when the selection will take place, but after the fall, Zeta will control those remaining."

"The fall?"

"After the selection, those who were not selected will be killed. There's no better word for it. They will be turned off, their brains fried. They will be murdered, leaving only those selected."

Snipe smiled. He neither wanted, nor meant to. "This all sounds–"

"Crazy, I know," Alex said.

"No. I would say laughable, impossible, and ridiculous." Feeling the energy and pent-up anger start to drain, he felt fleeting relief, and although he was underground, he'd thawed to the point that he could feel the flow of blood in his face, starting to tingle in his ears. "I want nothing to do with anything that you think might happen, but I do want to see Lexi, and if possible, guide those losers outside to shelter. They've latched onto me. It's my fault, but I now feel responsible for their well-being."

"I don't think you understand."

Snipe raised his gun toward the hatch as it opened. Chip slid down the ladder stairs. His face was red and his breathing was laboured, as if he'd ran the whole way back. A pair of binoculars swung from the back of his neck, threatening to strangle him.

"Chip."

"Dad, they're here."

"Slow your breathing, son. Speak slower."

"Two people driving a buggy with huge wheels. They're not wearing military gear, but they're armed. They just passed old oak. They're approaching the convoy. Dad, they could be there already."

"Okay, okay. Compose yourself," Alex said, before turning back to Snipe.

Snipe started up the stairs, lifted the hatch, and looked down. "As I said, I feel responsible, so I'll check them out."

"You won't get far with that thing." Alex pointed to the rifle. "Prepare to lose your hand. That's what they want. Or they may just kill you and take you back to their base. You won't get to see Lexi that way, but she'll get to see you, I guess."

"Two bullets. Two men out there. You look after your boy. I've got a real issue to sort out."

"Before you go, you'll want to see who's around the corner." Alex pointed past Mathews, who appeared from the shadows. "It'll only take a second. Then do as you wish."

Alex and Mathews stood aside. Snipe moved stealthily into the other room. A man was standing within a glass enclosure. A light shone green above the airtight door seal. At first, he only saw his own distorted reflection. Then he moved closer, and the man's head rose, and he smiled a familiar smile. His green eyes looked straight through him, as if he was working out Snipe's next move.

He hadn't looked in a mirror since leaving Vic's, but this was just as good.

"What's this? A hologram?" he asked.

The man in the enclosure spoke with an insane mixture of words and laughter. "Surprise, fuck head. You're not the only Snipe Siren, and by the looks of you, I don't think you could be the real one, either. They tell me you are, but you're all battered and you look like shit. Did they tell you I was with Lexi? She's okay. They had us imprisoned and they took her. The base is impenetrable. This lot transferred me to yet another glass box, so if you'll be so kind as to let me out?"

"That's enough," Mathews said.

The light inside the enclosure switched off, leaving only a silhouette of the man who claimed to be Snipe Siren.

Snipe went to leave, but instead, he turned back. A dizziness hit him as he frowned at the silhouette. "Answer me three questions. Where did you first meet Lexi?"

"We met near the old birch tree. I headbutted a guy that had been giving her shit."

"What brunch did Victor Harden cook for me?"

A face – *his* face – stared back at Snipe through the glass. "Brunch?" he laughed. "Never had a brunch, and how the hell do I know what he cooked you? I wasn't there. The little potatoes he keeps in the deep freeze would be my guess."

"Where did he keep his guns?"

"What do you mean, where did he keep his guns? Has he moved them from under the floor?"

"No, they're still there… Well, they were before…"

The clone's nostrils flared. He looked up, blinking, as if holding back tears. Snipe knew that look. He also knew what was coming next.

The clone cleared his throat. "Well, how is the old fool?"

Snipe lowered his head. "Victor Harden's dead."

The clone growled, and Snipe flinched when his fist thudded against the glass. "Dead? When? Who killed him?"

Snipe pressed his right eye up to the glass. The clone covered his face.

"Vic died saving my life. I'll work this out. Sit tight and wait for me," he said.

"*Sit tight*? Like I have anywhere to go. If you were me, you'd have killed them and got me out already."

Snipe didn't reply. Pushing past Chip, who stood between him and the steps, he climbed up and let the hatch slam down behind him.

# Chapter 21

Stopping at the hedgerow, freezing fog blurred his vision. Two male voices ahead and the perfumed smell of diesel were the only sign that anything laid beyond the seemingly impenetrable grey curtain. The tiny building behind him had disappeared, enveloped by the fog.

There was a crunch, and then another, and then Alex appeared. "Don't mind me. I'll not interfere until you're dead."

"What?"

"Well, I can't let them take your body. Might stop the machines. Who knows? Me and Chip might be the last ones standing, and we'll need to disable the enemy."

"Yeah, right. Join the queue. Or help me out. I'll listen to what you have to say and check out any evidence. I can't think past getting to Lexi," he said.

"And Chip needs his Mum," Alex said.

Snipe placed a hand upon Alex's shoulder. "Alex, you're a good man. I know the difference, and I believe that you believe the things you're telling me. If there's a morsel of truth in what you've said, and if it means that I'll see Lexi again, then I'll be at your mercy. You're a soldier, right?"

"A carpenter by trade."

"You're holding... let me see, a Glock 17. Loaded?"

"Seventeen rounds, loaded and ready to go," Alex said.

"Have you killed with it?"

"I haven't killed anything or anyone. Fired at trees for target practice," Alex said, handing Snipe the gun. "Here, take it. Go on, have it."

They swapped firearms. Snipe crossed the field to flank the buggy. Alex agreed to be the wondering huntsman, and approached the vehicles swinging his arms and whistling away to himself.

Tyrone swung around. His eyes widened as he saw Alex approaching. "Hey, stop! Identify yourself."

Alex held the rifle above his head. "I don't want any trouble. I was just taking a walk."

"Move closer. Keep your hands where I can see them," Tyrone said, looking around for Mike. "A walk, you say?"

Alex shouted back, "Well, I was trying for a rabbit or two, but the snow's driven them underground. I've not committed any crime, sir. I was just out walking."

Tyrone held out his gun. Alex saw him trying to steady it in his hands. Mike's voice came from behind him. "Ty, drop the gun and slowly turn around."

"Er..." He turned on his heels to face Mike.

Snipe had the barrel of the Glock pressed under Mike's chin. "Do as your friend says and you get to live a little longer."

Tyrone dropped the gun.

"Well, quite the actor," he said as Alex walked over. "You can lower the arms now."

Mike spoke through parted lips. "Are you–"

"Snipe. Pleased to make your acquaintance, and you two must be Easy Pickings One and Daft Lad Two. I mean, they could have sent someone trained for the job. I'm disappointed."

"Snipe, look," Alex said, pointing to the transporter. "Oh my

God! Look what they've done!"

Snipe didn't move his eyes. Instead, he told Tyrone to sit away from the buggy, then pushed Mike toward him. "On your bottoms. Legs crossed and hands on heads."

The silence suddenly made sense when he saw the remains of Bill trailing from the open door. Dark flecks dotted the snow outside, leading nowhere, fading into speckles further from the door.

Snipe slid to the side as Alex bent forward with his hands pressed into his gut. Vomit melted the snow on impact. Otherwise desensitised, the smell made Snipe retch as he moved away.

Mike and Tyrone had melted a patch where they sat. Snipe could see it was more than the cold that was making their bodies spasm. Their faces looked hollow; empty of emotion. They were in shock. He ran to the bus carefully so as not to slip on the now well-trodden route from the transporter, and called out the names he could remember. "Paddy! Cameron! Anybody?"

The only sound was that of Alex, coughing and spitting. The bus materialised, looking ghost-like through a blanket of fog. Silence and dark smears on the window told him that anyone inside was already dead. With laboured breath, he peered through five lines on the window where he'd last seen the Reverend, but the window was too high. Taking a deep breath, he went to the door, but it wouldn't open. The remains of a small child, held together by his mother, kept it closed.

Swallowing down whatever was coming up, he looked down the side of the bus at a patch of fog that was crystalising and swaying as it exited the emergency door.

Snipe bolted toward Alex, who was chewing on a handful of snow to cool the acid burn in his throat. "Move. Run. Get back."

Mike and Tyrone lowered their hands, then put them back up again as Snipe plunged forward. "You too. All of you, get inside." He let off a shot between Mike's legs. "Get up and run. Alex, move them inside," he said.

The hedgerow scratched at Chip's arm. The gun shook in his hand as thorns pricked into his skin. "Stop, or I'll shoot. I'm not kidding. Stop." he let off a shot which hit the snow between his Dad's legs.

"Get inside. We need cover; all of us do," Alex said, before pushing Tyrone. "Not much farther. Keep moving."

Chip held the heavy steel door open. Alex was the first one in. "Shut that damn thing. We have visitors."

"What's wrong? Why are they here?" He let the others in before slamming the door shut. "I didn't mean to shoot. Something stung me and–"

"Get down there and prepare hot drinks."

"But I thought you told me not open the–" Chip took one look at his father's face and retreated down to the basement.

Without instruction, Mike and Tyrone sat down and took the same position as before. Alex grabbed Snipe by the arm and pulled him away from them. "What are you doing? You've just blown our cover. Who's next? Do *you* want to die? Because *we* don't." Raising his hands at Snipe, he spoke through gritted teeth. "Did you see what they did back there?"

Snipe looked past Alex. "Did you kill those people?"

Mike shook his head. Saliva flew from his mouth, hitting Tyrone, who didn't react. His face was ashen, and his eyes were those of a man who'd seen carnage for the first time.

"What do you expect them to say?" Alex said.

"You think they look capable? Whatever killed them was the same thing in Mount Pass."

The hatch opened. It was Mathews. "It's happening."

"Oh shit, no… I have to go down. I'll leave you here with them. I'll come back up. It's happening to… to… your other self."

Alex disappeared and closed the hatch behind him.

"What's happening? Wait! It's dangerous down there. You don't understand," Snipe said, before turning to Mike and Tyrone. "We're on borrowed time." He pointed the gun at Mike. Tyrone was in a world of his own; the protective bubble that closed a man away from anything external after a traumatic event. "You have until that hatch opens to tell me why you're here."

Mike looked up. A tear rolled down his cheek. "We've come to bring you back to the base. To see Lexi. Rush Unix, your father, told us you'd want to come if we explained the situation to you." He gulped as Snipe readied the gun, pointing it at Tyrone. "They told us that you're important, and that you can stop the machines. Don't shoot. We didn't kill those people. Ty, snap out of it and tell him we didn't."

Tyrone's face looked absent from the moment. His head dropped again as the hatch swung open. Alex was the first one up and out, followed by the clone with a hood tied around his neck. They'd strapped his hands, as well. Snipe thought he saw his tight-fitting top bulge at the gut. Mathews' arm appeared only to close the hatch when he was clear of the opening.

"He hasn't much time, and he has agreed to leave and distract whatever caused the massacre. He can't stay any longer. This isn't going to plan."

"There's a plan?" Snipe asked. "And you're putting all your faith into a clone?"

"He stays and we're dead. He goes and we stand at least a chance," Alex said, as he pulled the hood off his head.

There was a dull pop as Mike's head hit the smooth, rounded wall behind him before rolling onto Tyrone, snapping him out of his trance and into a scream. Tyrone's lips danced. His head shook as if it were being pulled by strings. Mike opened his eyes and they both shuffled back as far as the curved wall would allow. Their eyes darted between both Snipe Sirens.

Alex cut the cord that tied the clone's hands. Snipe held out the Colt, prepared to shoot the mirror image of himself. The tie snapped free. The clone spun into Snipe, grabbing the gun and jamming it under his arm. "You better be the real deal." He lifted the gun upward. "As you know, I'm already a dead man. I'll take whatever's inside of me as far away as I can, and if you *are* the real me, then go get the bastard that's doing this, take control, and kiss Lexi from me." He kissed Snipe on the cheek before handing the Colt back to him.

Snipe saw the clone of himself run into a frozen wall of vapour. He should have felt embarrassed and ashamed for being outmanoeuvred, but even with his ego shattered, all he felt was admiration. Would he have done the same, or was the clone somehow less tainted? Less fearful? A better version of himself? It had the same memories and the same love for Lexi, but it lacked the time served. The clone's memories, values, experiences, and the love it felt – even if they were only electrical impulses – were implanted. Without the time served, those memories would never come to fruition. They wouldn't have been there, and nothing would be transferable. He was the real version, if only because he'd lived a full and sinful life. But still, he envied it. The clone's implanted memories stopped at the point of his imprisonment. It knew nothing about the pain he'd felt when Victor Harden sacrificed his life; nor did it know about the cannibals he'd slaughtered.

A misty, near-solid mass swayed through the air, out of place within its surroundings. It was moving toward Snipe with a life he'd seen before. Unlike when it had moved through snowflakes, it now appeared more defined, and almost solid in structure, similar to how a swarm of insects was only visible in numbers. They must've entered the Reverend, and he'd unwittingly killed his faithful flock, and the robot-like virus was now—

"Wahoo! Come on, you invisible bastard! Your friends are inside me! Wahoo!"

The white swarm followed the buggy across the field. Cracking and scraping came from beyond Snipe's visual range. He knew it was the hedgerow crashing under the weight of the buggy that was being driven by his other self.

"Close the door. I know what killed your friends," Alex said.

"So do I. It's following the clone."

"You don't know that for sure. They're invisible to the naked eye." He turned back to Mike and Tyrone. "He's taken your mode of transport. How's that even possible?"

Mike looked up from where he sat. "There's no scanner, just keys, and he left it running," he said, pointing at Tyrone.

"What are you smiling at?" Alex said to Snipe. "Am I missing something here, or what?"

"Just an identity crisis, that's all, Alex. Did you say something about hot drinks? I think our friends could do with one, and I know I could." He looked at Mike and Tyrone, then towards the hatch. "If we're going to save the world, we need that hot drink," he said.

Chip arranged the seating. Mike and Tyrone sat atop an overturned ammo box, Alex and Mathews sat facing them on the fold-out chairs, and Snipe moved papers to one side and sat on the only desk in the room. Chip made drinks and stood in the corner, pretending to clean yet another Colt sidearm as Alex asked for names and gained background information on Mike and Tyrone.

"So, you think we're going to believe that you have no idea how to get back to your base? Keep this up and my lad over there will pistol whip you until you tell the truth." He turned to Snipe, who was slurping his drink and making a mocking sound that echoed in the mug.

"What's so funny?"

"*Pistol whip*. Never heard that one. Might borrow that for the next time I have to interrogate someone."

"Think you can do a better job?" he asked, as he brushed Mathews' hand off his shoulder. "Well?"

"I'll give it a go. Never been much of a talker, but from what I gather, you two are the only ones who seem to know anything about me being able to save the world. What did you call it? The antivirus." Leaning forward, he continued to address Alex and Mathews. "It makes little sense. You say that Zeta's a computer program. The thing that controls the machines, right?"

"Yes, but—"

"So, if that's true, then Rush Unix controls Zeta. Am I getting warmer?"

"Not sure. All we know is that an agreement exists," Alex said, with his arms folded across his chest. "And may I remind you there's a bloodbath outside?"

"Yeah, I know. The dead aren't going to help right now," Snipe said.

"You cold—"

"When you've seen as much death as I have, you'll know where to focus your attention. They can wait; this can't. Fill us in, Alex. Bring us into your realm, and then I might have a better understanding of the tales you're telling."

"Let me explain," Mathews said, noticing Alex's impatience towards Snipe. "Your grandfather and father worked on a military project that was designed to take control after a nuclear war. Your father–"

"Stop calling him that."

"Very well. The man called Rush Unix had other plans that didn't fall in line with those of his senior personnel. He wanted the program de-militarised; a red cross in times of despair, something that would bring balance to a world that has already suffered enough. All assumed an organisation would take responsibility for creating it. When no one did, a joint operation between the old USSR and Britain started. Neither side trusted the other; both had a mutual understanding for one another's work leading up to the discovery of Zeta."

Reaching into his pocket, with a tear of Velcro, Snipe pulled out the map that had been handed to him by Victor. Chip moved aside, allowing him to spread it across the table top.

"What do you make of this?" Snipe asked, beckoning to Mike and Tyrone. Alex led the way. "This was given to me by a reliable source claiming it to be your base." He pointed at Mike. "Does this look like home?"

Mike and Tyrone studied the torn map. Alex peered over their shoulders, while Mathews stood aside with Chip.

"Looks like a pyramid," Mike said, rubbing his finger on the creased paper. "Disguised as a hill. Nature's not good with squares and right-angles."

"Do you recognise it as the base?" Snipe asked Tyrone, who hadn't spoken yet.

"Yeah. Only this diagram shows more levels than what ours goes down to, and that doesn't exist either," he said, pointing to what looked like an oversized crystal. "But the school and pretty much everything else is right. The sea's there, and the wooded area looks right enough. I don't get it. How come you have a diagram of Base Freedom?"

"Until now, I thought it was called Piper's Academy." Snipe underlined the faint pencil scribble on the top centre above the diagram with his finger. "Does that mean anything to you?"

Mike looked at Tyrone. They both shook their heads. Mathews walked over upon hearing the name.

"Let me have a look. Piper's Academy… could be a code. You said these measurements were decoded into reference points?"

Snipe nodded. "Yeah. Vic took the first number, and… well, I'm not sure now, but he got these." He pointed at the ripped corner. Seeing Vic's handwriting made him smile and remember how Vic had chewed on his pen and told him to think like his father.

As if on command, Mathews pulled out his pen and chewed on the end of it while waggling it between two fingers. Snipe watched as he wrote *Piper's Academy* on the back of his hand. He looked harder at the writing in the area that Mike and Tyrone said didn't exist.

"Can you read that?" Mathews asked the group at large.

Snipe looked and found two letters: U and S. Alex couldn't make out anything, and questioned whether they were even words or just wonky arrows.

Chip bounced up to the table holding a round piece of glass. It hit the table with a clunk, emphasising its weight. Sliding it over the centre of the diagram, he made out three words: Latest, Use, and Colonise. Mathews wrote them down; the words ran past his wrist and underneath his shirt sleeve.

Alex tapped away on the only computer; a big box of a thing

which, until now, Snipe had thought was a part of the frequency machine.

Alex turned to Snipe. "*Pyramid Escape*. Piper's Academy turned inside-out and shook up makes the words *Pyramid Escape*."

"I got *My Rapid* for the pyramid," Mathews said.

Snipe walked over. "Found something?"

He watched as Alex pressed a wide button on a handheld radio. "Try Pyramid Escape," he said. "Zeta Earth Mission, too. They're anagrams. Hope it helps. Over."

"What was that?" Snipe asked. "Are they codes?"

"Could be nothing. We'll find out soon. The word *pyramid* keeps popping up, though, and if the base is a pyramid..."

Sitting up on the table, Snipe looked at each person before saying, "Am I the only one here who thinks that pyramids belong in deserts? You know, made by Egyptians thousands of years ago?"

Tyrone nodded in agreement.

Mathews stepped forward and said, "Pyramids extend beyond the desert. The southwest of England has several, and they're across every continent and the vast ocean floors."

"Pyramids?" Snipe asked again, this time unable to contain his widening smile. "Actual pyramids with pointy tops? The sort that the pharaohs made?"

Pointing at the map, Mathews said, "That's one."

"Looks like a hill in a field," Snipe said.

"And to anyone else," Mathews said. "But it's more than a hill. It has a square base and defined edges leading from its base to its peak. Nature has taken hold, blending it into the surrounding countryside, but surely even you can make out the shape of a pyramid. They say there are pyramids on Mars, too."

"A pyramid suggests nothing useful," Snipe said, slurping dregs of coffee. "What about the crystal?"

"Could be a weapon or a treasure store. Maybe a horde of valuables?" Alex asked.

"That's not true," Mike said. "There's no such thing at the base. We don't even have enough food to go around, and our technology goes as far as the drone that we sent out to find you." Mike pointed at Snipe. "And even that was a stroke of luck. It had a short range. Lexi took a gamble in sending it. I'd know if something like that existed."

Snipe climbed down off the table. "So, how come I'm still alive? If Zeta wants to reduce the population, how come they haven't killed me? They could've, back when they had me cornered."

Mathews took in a deep breath before saying, "They took you on the night of the cleansing; the night they flushed out the remaining non-citizens. You went to a prison known as *the farm*. They made a replica of you, along with replicas of many others. The program aimed to introduce the cloned replicas back into society, where scan pods would monitor their movement. Each clone carried a robotic virus, with the aim to cause an epidemic among non-citizens. Those infected non-citizens went back to their family homes, their hideouts, and their secret communities, and what you saw outside happened. When your father heard of your imprisonment, he ordered me to break you out, and told me that he would have you collected at the drop-off point. I told the governor of the prison that I was taking your replica back home, as I'd done with the others–"

"Give me one reason for not putting a bullet between your eyes," Snipe said, lifting the gun. "I'm waiting…"

"I never knew about the virus. I swear. I got out as soon as I could and saved you… Remember that. I saved you."

"There's been enough bloodshed tonight," Alex said, standing between the both of them. "We need him. Snipe, think."

Lowering the weapon, Snipe looked at Mathews with an intensity that stated he was on borrowed time. Subdued, Mathews nodded and lowered his head. "You'd found your way back home by the time the second team arrived and collected the clone, thinking it was you. Caught in the crossfire, I was picked up by Alex. I wanted out, Snipe. You have to understand that I wouldn't have left you, but I had no choice back then." Mathews gulped the cold dregs from his cup. "When the citizens rebelled, and took pity on the non-citizens, the selection process started."

Snipe looked toward the ceiling. "The census."

Alex edged forward. "It has the power to demobilise citizens. They aren't its problem. We are."

"Suppose I get to the base," Snipe said. "And somehow turn off the program. Would that solve the problem?"

"Tell him, Dad!" Chip said. "Tell him about the second event."

"We don't know for sure, son."

"You told me it was coming. You know we're gonna die. All of us: citizens, non-citizens, Rush Unix, Zeta. Gone. Finished. Dead."

"Chip, make some drinks," Alex said, waving him away with the back of his hand.

Snipe laughed. "What? Another event?"

"The force that passed our planet was only a fragment of the object that was projected to cross our path. We don't know for sure. We have few details—"

"But at least that makes sense. Why do something so drastic unless there's no other choice?" Snipe asked.

"It's all in the timing, Snipe. Those two," Alex pointed at Mike and Tyrone. "Need to get you into the base to disable Zeta. Only then will we find other options."

"There aren't any, Dad," Chip said. "You said it yourself; we're as good as dead."

"First thing's first, son… if we *are* going to die, I want us to be together, as a family, and I'm sure Snipe wants to see Lexi with his hand still attached."

"What's the hand thing?" Snipe asked.

"Well, that's what disabled them when you were young. You tell me. You did it."

Tyrone's arm trembled as he raised it, as a child would in a classroom. "So, you're not going to kill us?" He looked at Mike, who didn't look relieved, so much as pissed off.

Mike said, "So, we came to get him." He pointed at Snipe. "Take him back to the base to disable the machines, and that's what you still want us to do, only now, for no purpose, as we're all doomed? Great. Might as well save the drive and sit it out here; at least it's warm. Oh, wait." He looked at Tyrone. "We have no buggy."

"We might stand a chance… if we get to the other world and pass through, as Ivan did," Chip said. "You know about the stories of a man called Ivan going to another world, don't you?"

Alex shook his head, and embarrassment blossomed in his cheeks. "Fairy tales, Chip, that's what they are, nothing more, and even if it *was* true, we're not on the chosen list, son."

Snipe stood beside Chip and said to Alex, "Fuck being chosen, and who decides who's on the list? Zeta? Rush Unix? If there's a chance, we take it. We make our *own* list, not of who can do what or who's higher in the rankings. We send who *deserves* to go."

Chip punched the air. "Yes!"

Snipe knew better than to be suckered into the crazy notion of other worlds, and he didn't believe he played a part in stopping the machines. If anything, he thought he'd be killed to prevent them from being shut down.

The one thing he couldn't shake from his mind was the name *Ivan*. Vic had told him bedtime stories about such a man. He'd gone into great depths to describe him and the new world.

If their foibles lead him to Lexi, then he would play along.

# Chapter 22

Snipe opened the driver's side door to the family saloon. Alex peered in, avoiding the windshield, all too aware that carnage was awash within the transporter that stood ahead of it.

"Five seater with a large boot. It's for sale. No fuel included and only one murdered owner," Snipe said.

Alex's disdain for Snipe's dark humour was clear. Twisting his lips, he sighed through flared nostrils. "Good, it takes diesel. We have plenty of that. Do you think we can get it past the transporter?"

"Let's see," Snipe said.

"Rather not. I'm still tasting my innards from the last time. I'm heading back."

Snipe caught up with Alex. "Should be all right if you've got a shovel. I'll carve a way out."

"Is that a yes, or are you still taking the piss?"

"We can do it, Alex, if you have fuel."

Chip gathered their belongings. Alex handed the drum of diesel over to Snipe while Mathews, Mike, and Tyrone pondered the best way to gain entry.

"Chip, get another barrel and syphon it into two cans; the last thing we need is to run out of juice. It might be a good bargaining tool if we run into any unsavoury characters." He looked at him as only a father could look at his only son. "You'll be all right, son. I'll be back before you know it."

"*Back?* What do you mean, *back?* Are you leaving me? You said we would be a family; see Mum again."

"They're expecting two of their own and Snipe Siren. I'll be going... I'll bring her back, son. Trust me, I will."

Snipe smirked. "Never trust a man who says *Trust me.*"

Alex's shoulder budged him into Mathews. Alex clenched his fist and pulled his arm back, letting it hang suspended in mid-air. "Don't interfere... do you have kids?"

"I'm not a kid. I'm seventeen," Chip said.

Dropping the grin, Snipe stared back at Alex. He neither wanted to match his ferocity, nor strike back. He'd gone too far. Raising his chin to the right, he said, "Go on, then. I wouldn't blame you."

Alex lowered his arm and stretched out his fingers. "I'm not going to hit you, I'm just... it's the people outside, and now this... it's no easy job, being a Dad."

Snipe lowered his eyes. "I'm sorry. You're right. I didn't understand. I've always worked alone. Trust me, I never meant to raise your arse hairs."

Alex smiled. "Never trust a man who says *Trust me.*" He extended his hand, prompting Snipe to raise his. There was no power play and no overly firm handshake, just an understanding between two men. "And I'm sorry for losing my temper," Alex said.

Mathews wiggled his fingers, as if asking for permission to speak. "Now that you two have made friends, Mike and... sorry–"

"Tyrone. Ty."

"...Mike and Tyrone play the biggest part in this, so we should listen to what they have to say."

With renewed confidence, Mike said, "It makes sense, things Kat said. Little hints and questions, which at the time, I thought were nothing. She knew about the crystal and that Ivan fellow. I remember walking in on her, and she made every excuse to distract me. I thought she was just being... *Kat*, but looking back, she was onto something; something she kept close to her chest."

"And what about Mr Lifeless?" Snipe asked.

Mike helped Tyrone up, and he shrugged Mike's hand away. "I'm all right... I think. I mean, it's not every day you see dead bodies, meet the feared Snipe Siren, and find out that we will all die in a second event. Apart from those few details, I'm tickety-boo."

"You had me worried for a while," Snipe said, shaking Tyrone's hand. "You've got a firm shake. I like that. So, how do you think we can gain entry and stop those damn things?"

"They're expecting the buggy," Tyrone said. "They'll stop us before we reach the outer rim, but other than that, I can't see a problem with us bringing back more people. After all, we're talking about Snipe Siren. If you had refused to leave your friends stranded, then we would have been forced to bring them, too. I feel like they'll think we did the right thing. At least we recovered their prize."

"Okay, run us through what we might encounter," Alex said to Mike. "Do you think they'll open the door and wave us through? And if they do, what then?"

"They'll want to take us to a quarantine area and check to make sure that we're not infected or bugged. You're all non-citizens; a quick scan and you're through. What happens next is down to you guys. Hopefully, you stop the machines. Then we can all sit tight and wait for Armageddon. Who knows? The base might withstand the second event, and without Zeta, we get to live a full life. And as far as the other world thing… I'm sorry, but I can't think that far ahead, and I'd take my chances and stay at the base."

"I don't think we've been invited, mate," Mike said.

Sucking air through his teeth, Alex said, "You'd be in for a bumpy ride, son. There are only five seats, so you'd be in the boot."

"He can have my seat," Mathews said. "I'll only be holding you all back. Too many questions will follow, and they think I'm dead, anyway. I have enough supplies, and when it's time, send someone to pick me up. If no one arrives one week from today, then I'll make my plans."

A haze of mustard yellow rays danced between dark grey clouds. It was light enough to see as the fog had thinned and sat low on the field. Alex thought of ways to make sure that Chip didn't see the sights that had emptied his gut. Short of blindfolding him, there'd be little chance of hiding the twisted remains jammed in the doorway of the transporter. Instead, he spoke to him as they walked over to the family saloon. He was in for a shock, regardless of any preparation that Alex could give him. After letting Snipe, Mike, and Tyrone go ahead, they hung back, said goodbye to Mathews, and gathered any pocketable items – a knife, snack bars, water bottles, and a faded picture of Kat.

Snipe walked toward them. For a moment, Alex thought there was a problem with the car, until its engine turned, and a roar sounded in the distance.

"Think you can beat me back to the car, lad?" Snipe asked Chip. "If you can, you'll be the first to beat me in a race. Tell you what: I'll give you a head start."

Alex frowned, unaware of Snipe's intentions to distract Chip.

After he counted down from three, Snipe ran after him. Alex shook his head. "Crazy son-of-a-bitch."

Sandwiched between Snipe and his father, Chip tried to look past them. "Ready to go, boys? Stay left, a foot away from the edge." Snipe said.

As the car rolled past the transporter, Alex glanced down at mounds of snow piled over what he knew was blood and body parts. Turning to Snipe, he mouthed the words, *Thank you.*

"Shouldn't they be back by now?" Lexi asked. "Have they radioed to say they've found him?"

Kat blanked her screen and swivelled in her chair to face her. "God damn it, Lexi, have you never heard of knocking?" Kat asked. "Sorry, come in. Ah, you already are. I lost communication with them on route to the location after Rush spoke to Mike."

"What do you mean *lost communication?* Who's that?" She pointed at the screen. An Asian man stood, dwarfed by what looked like a giant diamond.

Kat switched the screen off. "I don't know who he is."

"Why're you not trying to find them? They should be back by now," Lexi said.

Kat tried to smile, which only angered Lexi further.

"Instead of looking at people underground, you need to look for the people above it," Lexi said.

Kat tilted her head, frowned, and asked, "Why do you think I'm looking for people underground?"

"The man on the screen. He's below the base, and we need to be looking–"

"What makes you think he's below the base?"

"Because I've seen the thing next to him. I told you this in the

216

cell. Damn near got stuck trying to get back out. That's how I got the name Squirrel. I can get to places others find impossible." Spreading her arms on either side of Kat, Lexi gripped her chair. "Can we send out another drone to see if they need our help? Or better still, I could go out. They might have crashed or slid off the road. Kat, they could be in danger."

"Babes, listen, their communicator might be faulty, and they have to take it slow due to the weather. I know that you're worried, but we're only talking about hours, not days. We wouldn't get permission to send a search party. I promise, I'll do everything I can and let you know when they arrive." She looked past Lexi to the open door. "Babes, close the door. I want to show you something."

Lexi shut the door and pulled up a chair. Kat tapped the screen. "Have you seen this man?"

"No. I told you, I saw that big crystal."

Kat flicked her hand across the screen. "What about this one? And this one?" She flicked again, and yet another similar picture appeared, each with a different person, in different surroundings, standing next to what looked like the same glinting tower of glass.

"The crystal's the same, but the people are different," Lexi said, "Kat, I know you're holding back on me. I've already told you enough to have me thrown back in that cage, so why not tell me what you've found out?"

"I'm looking into a scrambled signal, and those people appeared on Mike's handheld communicator at the same time as Rush Unix. Like a conference call."

Lexi scrunched up her button nose, cleared her throat, and asked, "Anyway, can you let me know when they arrive?"

"Lexi, until you told me you'd seen it, I never knew where it was, and I still don't know why it's there. It looks like there's more of the same, and the people standing next to them share our com-link." Scooting the other chair across the floor, she said, "Here, sit down. I need your input on this."

Lexi sat down beside Kat and said, "I know nothing. I only saw it from the vent."

"There must be another way. You mentioned tracks. Train tracks."

"You know what, Kat? It could have been two pipes. It was dark. I saw an opening in the wall with what I thought looked like rail tracks, like for a kid's train. I'm not sure."

"Ever heard the name Ivan?" Kat asked.

"No, never."

"Okay," Kat said, turning to the computer.

After a few taps on the screen, a password-protected file appeared. The blank box flashed, prompting her to enter the correct words. She typed: PYRAMID ESCAPE.

Another appeared. She'd passed the first; one more to go. She typed: ZETA SOUL SELECTION.

The box blinked a mocking wink. After typing: USE LATEST COLONIZE, swapping the words every time it winked back at her, she turned to Lexi, who sat silently, watching Kat's fingers tap harder with each try.

"Lexi, I think the answers are in this file. I'm no hacker, I haven't got a program to get me in, and I can't risk approaching a computer geek." Placing her hands on Lexi's knees, she said, "So, it's up to us gals to sort it out. I need you to think of a word or a number that will allow us access. I've got a list of over five hundred so far."

"Try Snipe Siren," Lexi said.

"Already on the list. Damn, we're so close."

Lexi frowned and asked, "How'd you get the first one?"

"A tip. Pyramid Escape is an anagram for Piper's Academy."

"So, try another anagram, if that's his thing. What's an anagram?"

Kat looked down the list until she found the name *Snipe Siren*. Patting Lexi on the knee, she said, "Let's keep what you saw in here a secret... okay?"

"Not that anyone's bothered, but yes. I was never here."

"Thanks, babes."

Kat locked the door behind her, sat back down, and ran a location search. The signals appeared to be coming from separate locations around the world. With only the local internet, and without global satellite communications, it wasn't as if they could disguise their location. She wrote the coordinates down, accessed the copy net, and then zoomed in from what would have, at the time, been a live feed. Now it was only a copy of the original, frozen in time and taken one week before the event.

*Pyramid. It's a pyramid.* Kat zoomed in on another, and although it was very different in size, its square base and the darker shading to its centre pointed to that of a pyramid. The other locations showed only a blurred patch, normally reserved for military bases. Surrounding the blur, she saw different landscapes, all looking natural and innocent in their appearance.

She pulled out the memory chip and hung it back around her neck, tucking it under her turtleneck top. Patting her chest, she left and locked the door behind her.

She knocked twice before entering the maintenance room – otherwise known as geek central. A short, overweight man ran his fingers through his beard. "Ah, Miss Brenna." His soft-spoken words became clearer as he walked toward her. "Nice to see you again. If you're looking for Lexi, she's not here."

"Why would I be looking for Lexi?"

He found it difficult to keep eye contact as he said, "No reason. Only, the last time we met, you were looking for her. I think… it was a while ago. Do you remember?"

"Yes, I remember. There was another young man." Kat looked around the room. They were alone. "Where is he?"

"I'm by myself today; he's ill. Did you find your friend, the one we saw on the handheld?"

"Yes… well, I'm not sure. They're not back yet, but that's not why I'm here," Kat said, lowering her voice. "I wanted to ask you a few questions. *Private* questions that are to stay between us and not to be repeated."

His eyebrows wiggled. "Um, yes. What sort of questions?" he asked.

"We've met twice now, and I've never asked your name…"

"Mac, but most call me Prof."

"Prof… is that short for something?"

"Professor Cunningham," Mac said, running his fingers through his beard again. "Prof for short."

"Sorry, I thought you were the maintenance man," Kat said. Her prejudgments became visible as blood pumped through her neck reddening her cheeks.

"I'm that, too… with a passion for physics. I'm what you'd call a spooky scientist."

"Spooky… the paranormal?" she asked.

"You could call it that. Some of the guys in my fraternity do, but I like to call it quantum mechanics. In particular, the study of quantum electrodynamics."

"Wow, I never knew."

"Why would you? Unless…" Mac's beard bounced as he cleared his throat. "So, what can I help you with this time, Miss Brenna?"

Kat held back on plugging in the memory chip and asked instead, "What significance would a pyramid and a large crystal have?"

"…Is there a punchline?" Mac's eyes darted around the empty room before focusing on the closed door behind Kat.

"No. I've always been interested in the two, and I know crystals store energy, and it's rumoured that pyramids conduct…"

"I'm sorry, Miss Brenna. I would love to help you with your quiz, but I'm busy right now, and could do with getting back to work."

Kat followed his fixed gaze over to the tiny camera jutting out from the corner of the ceiling. "Ah, okay. I understand. Maybe I can show you around my office sometime. We could have a chat and a drink. It'd be nice to get to know you better."

Mac wiggled his brows once more. Kat gave him the sweetest smile she could stomach and waggled her fingers in a goodbye.

*He knows more than he's letting on. He warned me about the camera… or at least, he looked in its direction. How could I not have known about his qualification? I know everyone's position in here. If I find out he's lying to get into my knickers…*

Kat shuddered at the thought of it as she strode down the hallway leading to the rec room. She craved the outdoors; wanted to breathe in fresh air and touch nature; feel a leaf, kick the mud, taste the salt air blown in from the sea.

She longed for the day when she could see Chip and Alex. The grudge she'd held for Alex not agreeing to live at the base had dwindled; it had worked out well. At first, she'd let him know the whereabouts of Zeta's faithful. This led to leaking more information, for his benefit and hers. An outside source of events. That, and it gave her a reason to keep in touch.

The love she had for Chip was unconditional, and although

she'd have liked to feel love for Alex, the flower had never bloomed.

# Chapter 23

The rec room canteen had thinned out after the breakfast rush. Kat chose the coffee machine rather than the counter. A latte popped out; the froth vanished before her first sip. Warmth ran from her hand to her arm, helping her to focus her mind on the task ahead.

Locking the door, she sat, pulled the chair up to the desk, lowered her head, and slid the chain over the banana clip that held her hair in place. Rubbing the prized memory chip between her thumb and finger, she leaned forward to the computer.

*Knock. Knock. Knock.*

"Hello. Just a second," she said, slipping the chain back over her head.

*Knock. Knock.*

"For God's sake," Kat said, unlocking and jolting the door open. "Yes. Hi."

Mac stood before her. In the short time since they'd been apart, he'd changed into a smart-looking suit. Wide pinstripes ran from his collar down over his breast, where a white hanky stuck out of a small pocket. The stripes became distorted as they rounded his potbelly, and the canvas shoes he wore hurt the otherwise formal attire. "You said pop over, and I thought I owed you an explanation."

"Yes… well, you'd better come in, then," she said, rolling her eyes. "You've changed…"

"Oh, the suit. Well, it's not every day that I get invited… anywhere."

Kat offered him the only other chair. "I hope that I didn't give you the wrong idea. I already have a partner. You're a nice guy, but–"

"That's just as well. I'm not into women… not in that way."

"Oh," she said, feeling the heat rise in her face. "Sorry. I thought… never mind. Welcome to my office. It's small, but adequate."

Mac flicked his eyes around the room.

"No cameras or mics in here," she said.

"That's why I came over; to explain that I couldn't talk."

"I guessed as much," she said, facing him with her back to the computer. "I took your hint to cut the conversation short, but why?"

"Well, you mentioned crystals and pyramids. I wanted to tell you what I know," Mac said, shuffling back into the chair. "I'm sure you've worked it out already, you know, the connection," he said, winking. "But if they're not ours, then who built them?"

Trying to disguise her confusion, Kat coughed, covered her mouth, and clenched her throat. "Sorry, would you like a drink?" she asked. "I have flavoured water, or I could make a hot drink."

"Water's fine."

With her back to him, she bent over and took two bottles of water from the mini-fridge. "So, what do you make of it all?"

Mac blew into his hanky. "They're not ours. Probably not even from this planet," he said.

"The crystals?"

"The drones," he said, taking the bottle from her. "I was hoping that you could help decipher the hieroglyphics. They're all made of pyramids at various angles. I ran the fragments I had through the identification process; even experimented on them myself. No such element appeared on the periodic table, and upon closer inspection, they appear intelligent. The fragments were small, but they reacted to the experiments as if they were connected to the whole. Quantum entanglement on a level never experienced. Quite amazing. I'm convinced that the specimen wasn't man-made. I'd go so far as to say that, with our current understanding of such complexities, it would be impossible to duplicate."

Like parallel train tracks, Kat knew they were in separate carriages. Mac didn't know about the crystal deep under the base, or that the base was a pyramid; unrecognisable at ground level, but identifiable from space.

"Tell me more, but without the geek speak," she said. Realising how insulting that sounded – even to her – she laughed and tapped his knee as she sat down in front of him.

"They gave me samples; bits of lightweight metal. I ran the usual compound tests, and the substance doesn't exist."

"A new military material, maybe?" she asked.

Mac shook his head, dismissing the possibility. "I ran my tests, and the three samples reacted to the fourth."

"Sorry, you just lost me again," she said.

Mac spoke slower, with an intensity that made Kat move closer to the edge of her seat. "I heated the fourth sample, and the temperature on the other three rose to the same as the fourth. I measured the vibration of the fourth when it was put under pressure, and got the same reading on the other three. I ran thirty-two individual tests and got the same results back for all four samples. It works across distance, too. I rigged one sample and another one on the opposite side of the base. Guess what?"

"You got the same results?" she asked.

225

"Yes. You're following me now." He looked around, as if checking for prying eyes. "I don't know for certain, but they might be biological. I extracted fluid. It acted like nothing I'd ever seen. Under the microscope, I found what resembled blood cells. It could be cross-contamination, as the samples weren't sterile, but I found a foreign body within the sample."

"Sounds strange," Kat said. "You said the samples had hieroglyphics?"

Mac twiddled the end of his beard into a point that rested above his chest. "Not so much hieroglyphics as microscopically minute polyhedrons. All have a common vertex, but are displayed uniquely within their space. I've spent weeks trying to find a pattern or a meaning. They're like fingerprints; unique and random."

"Have you run them through a pattern recognition program?"

"That's why I came. I didn't have access to any such programs, and was hoping you did," he said.

"Only what's on the archived net. You have the same as I do."

"You don't have cameras pointing at you, watching every move you make. If there's a pattern, and if these things aren't man-made, then everything we know is a lie…"

"Any good with anagrams?" Kat asked.

Mac's chest bounced as he let out a deep laugh. "Give me a word and I'll give it a go."

"Snipe Siren," she said.

"That's two words, but okay. Snipe could be… and Siren… let me think. I've got one if we use the letters from both. *Sinner's Pie*," he said, wiggling his bushy brows.

Kat turned to the computer, entered it, and got the wink. She tried it the other way around. The box flashed again.

"Try *In Ripeness*," he said.

Kat typed: IN RIPENESS, then RIPENESS IN, and got no results.

"Try *Resin Pines*," he said.

Kat thought she'd make this her last try. There were another five hundred on the list, and she might not get another chance to dig into the mind of the Professor for a while.

RESIN PINES. The box flashed, and the screen changed to a blue background filled with text.

"Yes!" she shouted as she bounced up and down on the swivel chair.

Kat's ears bent as she whipped the chain over her head. The chip flashed twice, showing that it now stored whatever was in the file.

*Knock. Knock.*

"Miss Brenna." The door handle moved. "Miss Brenna! Open the door."

Unlocking the door, it flew inward, and two men she recognised as security entered.

Kat rubbed her arm where the door had hit her. "Damn fool, you hurt me. What is this?"

"Miss Brenna and Mr Cunningham, I am charging you with treason. Either come quietly, or we are authorised to use force."

"Under whose authority?" Mac asked. "And it's Professor Cunningham, to you."

"Treason, you say? Didn't know we had a government," Kat said. "You can put that away and take me to Rush Unix."

"You can follow me," he said, holstering a baton.

Heads turned as they were both paraded down the corridor from Kat's office.

Lexi was taking Spud for a late breakfast when she heard the commotion. Upon realising it was Kat and the maintenance man – as she knew him to be – manhandled past the canteen, she looked at Spud. "Wait here. I'll be right back."

Kat noticed Lexi walking her way. Pushing the security man into the coffee machine, she ran toward her. Kat pulled the memory chip from her neck and handed it to Lexi. "Hide this and don't talk about what you've seen."

Lexi didn't have time to reply. Both security guards had a hold of Kat's arms and were dragging her back to where they'd left Mac handcuffed to a TV bracket.

"What are you doing? Let go of her."

"Lexi, no…" Kat said, shaking her head and looking at Spud.

Stuffing the broken neck chain into the back pocket of her jeans, Lexi walked over to Spud. "So, what do you want for breakfast?"

"Mum, what was–?"

"*Mum?*"

"*Lexi.* What were those men doing to Kat?"

"I don't know, Spud, but she told me to take care of you, and she said the eggs are good today, so what about it? Eggs on toast?"

Spud followed Lexi to the counter. As Lexi approached, she noticed a wart on the woman's face and whiskers sprouting from her chin. The words she'd said a few days ago came flooding back. She saw Lexi as the sole cause of her husband's death. Lexi didn't want Spud to witness any more drama before breakfast. Keeping her eyes down, she ordered him eggs and toast.

"What's on your face?" Spud asked.

Lexi's eyes widened as she faced him. "Don't be rude, Spud." Turning back to the woman, intending to apologise, she saw two security guards talking to the overweight warden who sat in his usual chair, positioned to the left of the tunnel's arched opening.

He pointed in her direction. The guards glanced her way. One pulled out his internal radio while the other rubbed the side of his baton.

"Er... we'll cancel that order, thanks. Sorry for the wart thing."

The woman pulled her head back, creating a third chin, before puffing a sound between her painted lips.

"Spud, I have a chocolate bar in my pocket for you. We need to go hide," she said.

"What's wrong? What are those men pointing at us?"

Lexi held his hand, slid a bar of chocolate from the counter up her sleeve, and said, "It's *why*, Spud. *Why* those men pointing at us?" Spud had to run to keep up as she paced forward. "Fancy playing in the lift?" she asked, glancing over her shoulder at the approaching guards.

"Can we?"

"I'll race you."

Lexi let him run off to the lift as she sprinted after him. The guards picked up their pace, aware that she was fleeing. Lexi knocked chairs over as she dodged tables, reaching the lift as the door pinged open.

"Beat you," Spud said, already boarding the open lift.

Lexi ran in, her forward motion stopping when her palms slapped the flimsy metal at the rear of the motionless lift.

"Come on... come on... come..."

The doors slid closed.

"Phew," she said. "Here, you've earned that." She handed him the bar of chocolate. "Spud, those men want to catch us like they did to Kat. We're going to hide for a while until they've gone, just like we did from the drones." She wiped his watery eyes with her sleeve. "Hey soldier, we're tough cookies, you and me, and nobody's better at hiding than us. I won't let anything happen to you."

"I know, Mum."

This time, Lexi didn't correct him. Smiling, she said, "You'll be all right, son. Together, we can take on the world."

"Level seven? Why are we going to school? I'm not changed into the right clothes."

"We're not, Spud. We're going on an adventure." She bounced up and down, trying to speed the lift's descent. "Remember the story I told you about the dragon and the magic crystal?"

"Yes, I do, but you said dragons weren't real."

"That's right. Giant crystals are, though, and we're going to find one."

The lift bumped to a stop. Lexi readied herself to fight whoever might be the other side of the door. The door slid open. There were no security guards. It wasn't a school day. An absence of screaming kids and the bellowing voices of teachers gave the vast space an eerie feel.

"Hello!" a male voice called.

"Quick, follow me," Lexi whispered.

Lexi breathed in and squeezed her body between the wall and the buzzing backside of the vending machine. "Just need to get this off," Lexi said, pricing the louvred plate from the wall. "You first, Spud, I need to reattach this."

"Who's there?"

The voice was deep and mature. Spud lifted himself into the vent. Lexi followed behind him, head-first. The last time, she'd done it backwards, enabling her to reattach the metal cover. A boxed area allowing room to sit was at the halfway point. Leaving the metal plate on the floor behind the vending machine, she crossed her fingers, hoping that they wouldn't look behind it.

"Quiet as a mouse, Spud. Keep going." She patted his leg. "I'm right behind you."

Lexi tapped his leg twice. Spud knew from his time in the tunnels what this meant. He froze and held his breath. Lexi listened with an intensity that made her ears tingle.

"She couldn't have vanished. Where is she?"

Lexi waited for a reply. The voice she'd heard as the lift closed said, "I've already told you; I saw no one. Look around, but don't take your frustration out on me. *She*, you say. Who is this *she*?"

"Her name is Lexi Teal, and we think a boy who goes by the name of Spud is with her. She's petite, wild brown hair, tanned skin, and the boy is of mixed race, looks like a girl. Has black hair." The security guard rose a flattened hand to the top of his leg. "Stands about so high."

"Ah, well, if I should see such persons I will let you know… maybe."

Lexi now recognised the voice as Mr Ranger, Spud's teacher.

"You'll let us know for sure, otherwise *you* will be the one in jail."

"I'm too old to be threatened by someone who displays such low acumen. I'll inform you if I see them."

Footsteps followed, then the pinging of the lift as the doors closed.

"Well, I wonder how this has fallen off the wall," Mr Ranger said.

The words echoed through the vent. Lexi squeezed her eyes shut tight, knowing he'd not only seen the cover on the ground, but had also spoken directly into the ventilation shaft.

"I'll just have to hang it back on without a clasp. Never know when access will be needed. I hope little Spud remembers what I told him about bullies and how we deal with them…"

Footsteps trailed off into the distance. Lexi tapped Spud's leg. He shuffled forward without speaking. Lexi followed.

# Chapter 24

Ice patches strewn across otherwise crisp snow hindered them to the point where they'd had to scatter ferns and sticks under the wheels of the family saloon to gain traction.

"Let's see how far we get this time," Alex said to his reflection in the passenger window. Chip hadn't stopped asking Snipe questions since the start of the journey. Snipe didn't mind telling him about his adventures, but instead of building them up, he toned them down, and even added happy endings to supplement the otherwise abysmal things he'd done. Leaving out the gory details and adding the phrases *narrow escape* or *finished him off* seemed to do the trick.

They'd made it as far as the dual-carriageway and picked up speed when Mike stepped on the brakes. The car slid.

"Roadblock. Roadblock," he repeated, turning into the skid.

"Shit, we've got rebels up ahead. They've got shooters," Tyrone said.

Alex readied the Colt. "Keep your head down, Chip."

A vehicle was ablaze, blocking their way. Mike noticed the roadblock from a distance. The car stopped after a long skid. Snipe made out three men, but there could be more in the truck parked behind the inferno.

"Let's try to avoid a shootout," Snipe said, flicking the safety catch off. "I'll go have a chat with them."

Tyrone peered up from beneath the glove compartment. "They're non-citizens. It's an ambush."

"Unless you have a crystal ball down there, you don't know. My guess is they're collecting taxes." Snipe reached over the backseat and pulled out a container of fuel. "Alex, when I open the door, you and Chip go 'round back. Mike, get ready to cover me. Tyrone, give me your gun."

Three men, spread out in a line, edged forward, each holding a hunting rifle. Shoving Tyrone's gun between the strap on his flight suit and the arch of his back, Snipe opened the door. Mike did the same, with his gun pointing through a gap between the door and the rubber seal. Alex and Chip whipped around to the back of the car and remained crouched behind the boot.

"Morning!" Snipe shouted as he swaggered toward them. "Do you want a hand putting that out, so we can clear the road?"

They raised their guns, but only gut-high. Snipe knew that they weren't ready to shoot. "Whoa, steady on guys, I'm not going to shoot," he said, raising his hands. The Colt hung loosely from his finger. The container of fuel came to rest on the back of his other hand.

They stopped. So did Snipe, leaving a dozen or so feet between them.

"Toss that over and keep them hands high," the one in the middle said. "On your knees."

The two men on either side of him were younger. Snipe figured they were his sons, since they wore the same smirk as their father.

Snipe tossed the Colt. It fell in the mid-point between them and him, swallowed up by the snow. "That's a good gun, and I've got fuel here if we can cut a deal, but I'm not kneeling. This suit's a little restrictive."

"You're in no place to make deals. Tell the people with you to come over, or I'll make an example out of you."

Snipe took a deep breath. He didn't want to kill them with Chip and his father looking on. He'd told enough stories and didn't fancy reciting this one, knowing there was little chance of a happy ending.

"There's three of you with hunting rifles and five of us, each holding seventeen rounds of death. So how about you stand aside and help us pass, and I promise I won't kill you?"

Mike stood up from behind the open driver's door. Tyrone did the same. Both held their guns outstretched.

Flames licked the sky, flicking through swirling smoke funnels like a pit of serpents set ablaze. Hissing and squealing gave way to a bang. Heads ducked, and the man to Snipe's right moved as a wheel raced past him.

"Snipe, it's the buggy. The buggy's on fire," Mike said.

A haunting screech rang through the air. The smoke changed shape; thickening, moving fast, stopping, backing up, then tearing away from the fire.

"Mike, turn the car around. Head back. Away from the fire." Snipe ran back to the car. Turning to the three men, he said, "You three drive away now. They're coming from the fire."

Mike turned the wheel as Snipe, Alex, Chip, and Tyrone pushed it level until it gripped. Blackened snow flew up from the rear. The roar of the engine summoned them. Chip held the door open for Snipe, who turned the moment a gun fired. A wave of smoke circled the older man's head before entering his ears and nose. Then, when he screamed, his mouth.

Three shots followed. The screaming ceased. His two sons didn't have time to watch their father get disembowelled, nor did they raise their guns at Snipe.

Mike drove in the direction they'd come from. Seeking a back lane, they turned right, and then right again, onto a narrow lane. The towering hedgerows scratched against the body of the car as it bounced into unseen potholes.

"You killed them. You said you wouldn't kill them."

Snipe looked at Alex before addressing Chip. "They were already dead, Chip," he said in a low, subdued voice. "When a painful death is moments away, sometimes stopping it can be the only humane thing to do."

Alex put his arm around Chip. "He did the right thing, son. I'd have done the same."

Chip trembled as he forced a smile for Snipe, but Snipe knew that the boy would never again look at him the same way he did when he'd given his stories a happy ending.

"It was the clone, wasn't it?" Mike asked, navigating the lane. "We can re-join the road in about three miles."

No reply came from the backseat. Alex and Chip were in a father-son embrace, Snipe watched snow fall from the hedgerow as the car brushed by, and Tyrone sat with his hand on his forehead, wishing he was someplace else.

Re-joining the main road not far from the incident, the twists and turns of the snow-filled back allies had cost them an hour in time. The roadblock was out of sight. Charcoal grey, entwined with thick black smoke, dirtied the sky; a reminder they'd wasted a lot of time and had survived another attack from the microscopic intelligent virus.

"Need to refuel," Mike said, looking down at point five on the fuel gauge. "I'll pull over."

"Already?" Snipe asked. "There must be a leak; that was a full tank."

"Don't shoot the driver. I'm only going on what that says,"

Mike said, tapping the gauge. "Straight run from here until we reach the woods, and by then, we'll have more than fuel to deal with."

Snipe glanced out of the rear window as the car chugged to a stop. The smoke was a starch reminder of the kills he'd made.

"I'll fill her up," Alex said.

"I could do with a… wee," Chip said, having almost let slip the word *piss*.

"Yeah, let's all stretch our legs and do a straight run after," Tyrone added.

Chip clambered up the embankment to relieve himself. The fuel was in, legs were stretched, and the others were ready for the final leg of the journey.

"Chip, shake and make, or we'll leave without you!" Alex called.

Chip slid down the embankment a little too fast. Snipe and Alex stopped a momentum that would have seen him fall face- · first in the compact snow. His face jutted, as if he'd seen the end of days.

"What's wrong?" Alex asked.

"A truck's coming, but how, when the road's blocked? There must be more of them. They're coming, Dad."

The roar of an engine and a missed gear confirmed his story.

"Up the embankment," Alex said.

Supported by the thin trunks of sparse trees, they waited. The truck slowed to a stop beside the family saloon.

Alex breathed the words, "I'll handle this," to Snipe, who was approaching.

Snipe waved him back. "Wait to see how many," he said.

Alex joined his finger and thumb with three fingers curled skyward. "Okay."

A middle-aged couple climbed down. They slid on tire tracks.

"This is better," the woman said.

"Yeah, if it's got fuel in it. This one's full," he said, thumbing over his shoulder at the truck.

Snipe let off a warning shot three feet from where the couple stood. The woman collapsed as if he'd hit her, and the man fell to his knees with his hands held high. "Don't shoot! Don't shoot!" he shouted.

"I said, leave it to me," Alex said, hanging onto branches on the way down the embankment.

"Needed to know if they were packing," Snipe said, following him.

The others joined them at the saloon. Chip turned to Snipe. "You're not going to kill them, are you?"

The woman, now kneeling alongside her husband, said, "We're not armed. I have jewellery. Take it all. Spare our lives."

"Were you with the others down there?" Snipe pointed down the road. "Is the truck yours?"

The man answered, "We couldn't get past them. They're all dead. The road's blocked, and we had to get past."

"The keys were in it. Take it. Please don't kill us," the woman pleaded.

"We're not going to kill you," Snipe said, offering his hand to help her up.

The man stood, too. "You're citizens... thank God, you're citizens."

"We're not citizens, and we don't wish to kill you. Who are you running from?" Snipe asked.

"You're not?" The man gulped. "People in the village are dropping. Falling to the ground. They're dead."

"Dead?" Snipe asked. "Where do you live?"

"Mount Pass," he said. "Do I know you? My God, you're the

man passing through. You took the non-citizens out on buses. What's happened to them?"

"Did it do to the others what it did to non-citizens?" Snipe asked.

"No, this was different." Halfway through speaking, the man got choked up, and his eyes welled.

The woman spoke for him. "We were talking to Blake Mathews. Little Jetta and Mibby were drawing in the snow, and he fell to the ground. Jetta was next, then Mibby, and then others just died on the spot, without warning. The devil's rife in the village, and we had to get away," she said.

Alex took Snipe aside. "Let them have the car, and we can take the truck. We're running out of time."

"Where are you heading?" Snipe asked.

The women answered, "Anywhere." She hung onto her husband.

He asked, "Can we follow you? There's safety in numbers."

Mike stepped forward. "Er, no, you can't. There's no way I can convince them–"

Snipe stepped to Mike and asked, "Who put you in charge? You drive and get us there, and I'll worry about the welcome party." He turned back to the couple. "Follow us in the car if you want, but if I give you the hazard flash, then double back or leave any way you can."

They introduced themselves as Jane and Timothy, and after the others had told them their names as well, the group left. Tyrone drove, Mike sat up front, and Alex, Chip, and Snipe sat on a tubular metal bench that stretched the length of the old army truck. Snipe sat in the rear. The canvas had a thick green rope that tied the door tight. He peered out at the saloon that followed, thinking about Lexi and whether he'd ever see her again.

The saloon lost traction and swerved, causing Jane to bang her head on the side window. "Careful," she said.

"*You* try to keep this straight. Look, we're lagging," Timothy said.

"You should have asked where he'd taken the others. We could have joined them."

"I was more worried whether we'd live. Stop your yakking and let me drive, woman," he said.

Jane placed her hand under her chin. Tears fell onto her wrist. Timothy glanced her way and sniffed. Trying not to cry himself, he said, "God wills—"

Jane started a scream that never surfaced. Crossing two roads, the car hit the embankment. The engine continued to rev, and the rear wheels spun until they smoked, as if trying to climb.

"Stop the wagon!" Snipe shouted through the length of the truck.

The truck stopped with an unexpected jolt, sending Chip sliding along the bench.

"It's the car. They've crashed the car," he said, turning to Alex.

Snipe jumped from the back. Hitting ice, he fell. Alex climbed down to help him up. "Snipe, you can't help everyone. We don't know what's waiting. If we get there," Alex said, "we'll check, but then we need to get going."

"Thanks," Snipe said, holding his rear.

Alex said, "You're hurt. We need you fit. Get back in. I'll check on them."

Chip helped him climb back through the thick green curtain. Snipe knew that Alex was right. He, too, had a woman; the mother of his son at the base. Now Snipe had another punch to his ego and sore buttocks.

Mike called into the truck, "Everything all right back there?"

Turning the saloon's engine off, Alex moved Timothy's limp hand and applied the hand-break. Jane's mouth hung open as if she'd dozed into a blissful dream. Timothy's laughing eyes looked through him. His mouth parted, as if in mid-sentence. Alex checked their necks for a pulse. Both were dead.

Grabbing Chip's arm, Alex climbed through the gap in the fabric door, looked at Snipe, and shook his head. No one spoke until further down the road, when Chip asked what had happened. The tactful explanation got Snipe wondering whether he could ever be a father. Would he want to bring a child into this pit of hell they called the new world? Shaking the thoughts from his mind, he remained silent and in pain, with only a view of where he'd been. He'd seen several cars stranded along the way as he peered from behind the canvas and wondered whether they had met the same fate as the couple from Mount Pass.

The truck crawled to a stop. "We will be hitting the first checkpoint soon," Mike said. "There'll be a wooded area to our left and a long drop-off to our right. The checkpoint will look innocent enough; two sentries on duty, maybe only one, but there'll be eyes in the wood and guns at the ready, so I take it that I'll speak to them about the extra passenger?"

"We'll talk about the extra passengers and I'll play it cool, but just know that even with a sore ass, I'm quick on the draw."

Snipe looked at Alex, expecting a reaction. Alex nodded in agreement, turned to Mike, and said, "No funny business."

The chunky truck tires slipped as it climbed the hill to the first checkpoint. Alex held Chip's gun, passing it back over to him with a warning not to use it until he had permission to do so. Snipe loaded his with the missing bullet from the warning

241

shot he'd given earlier, as Alex smiled through tightened lips, readying himself for whatever was about to happen.

# Chapter 25

"You want some?" Spud asked, sitting up for the first time since entering the air duct.

"I'm all right, Spud. You eat it," Lexi said.

She remembered the square where they now sat as being at the halfway point between the vending machine and the crystal. Then it dawned on her that she'd used the space to turn around, and until this point, she'd done this first stretch facing backwards, which hindered the time it took to reach the open square.

"Are we close, Lex?" Spud asked with a mouth full of chocolate.

"Not long to go, Spud. Then you'll be able to stand up properly."

Swallowing the final chunk of chocolate, Spud nodded his agreement, then set off, this time with Lexi leading the way. Spud backed off as Lexi's hair flapped in the cool air that surged through the vent and over their bodies, giving them the feeling of flight. He was looking forward to seeing the giant crystal, even though he knew they were on the run *again,* something he'd been used to his entire life. He knew Lexi would escape; she always did.

"Lex, do you think the crystal will give me superpowers? If it does, I could fight them all, and we could even fly."

Lexi was smiling. "You never know, Spud. Don't be too

disappointed if you don't get the powers you want."

"Mum? Er… Lex? Will we see Snipe again?"

Lexi felt her throat tightening; she hadn't bought a drink, and her tongue was sticking to the roof of her mouth. "He's on his way, Spud. We need to hide until he gets to us. Then everything will be all right. And Spud, its okay, you know. If you want to call me Mum, I'm good with that."

An excited squeal came from behind Lexi, followed by Spud saying, "Mum, when he gets here, he'll win the fight against everyone. He's really big and strong. I think he's already got superpowers."

"Yes, son. He probably does."

Lexi was regretting not bringing a drink, not that shopping had been a priority. The cool air had gotten warmer and was hitting her face, causing her lips to crack.

"Mum?"

"No more talking now, Spud. I'm dried out and I need to keep my mouth closed," she said.

"I've got a bottle of water," he said.

"Bloody hell, Spud. I've wanted a drink forever. How come you've got a drink when we didn't bring one with us to the eating area?"

"Nicked it when you nabbed the chocolate. You always told me to be prepared. You're not mad, are you?"

"No, son. I'm not mad, I'm *glad*. Pass it up," she said, reaching back for the bottle.

After passing the rest of the water back to Spud, she asked him questions and let him talk the boots off her feet. This tactic seemed to work as they'd covered good ground with no complaining flowing upwind.

The air duct narrowed the further they went. Lexi knew this

meant that they were close. She also recalled getting stuck a little further down and having to heave herself through the final few feet before rounding a tight bend and breaking through the plastic cover.

"Are you feeling strong, Spud?" Lexi asked, being careful not to shout and alert anyone who might be waiting for them. She was prepared to wait it out, rather than be taken to prison. She was fine with sitting or standing, just not lying on her stomach, but if she had to, then she would, as she had before, when Spud was younger.

The tunnels grew bigger, and she was impressed by the boy's patience when required. They even made up silent codes that only they understood.

Lexi didn't have to ask him to push. She felt his hands grip her feet and as she wiggled forward, he pushed. She was through.

Relieved to see that the plastic cover hadn't been replaced with solid steel, she peered through the gaps and into the room she remembered.

It was more of a cave than a room, as it had jagged stone walls and what looked like train rails as the room opened out. It was dimly lit, as if by a candle, but neither a candle, nor a lamp, was evident. The ground was smoother than what she'd expect within a cave, and it looked like it had been swept and maintained.

In the middle of the room was the crystal, standing about ten feet tall with a base circumference of five feet, spiralling up to a needle. It was a jagged, rough-cut, glass-like object, softened by a faint mustard glow which was emitted from its tip. The flowing light merged into pink before splashing into a deep purple base, like a backlit waterfall. To Lexi, it looked alive, as if it was willing her closer. Looking at it made her feel alive, refreshed, and vivacious.

"Lexi? Lex, are you still stuck?"

"No, Spud. We're here... and what happened to you calling me Mum?"

"Is it still there?"

Lexi pushed off the cover, and plastic slapped stone. Leaning forward, her hands touched the cold ground. Her legs followed until she was in a handstand position.

Spud couldn't contain his excitement any longer. His eyes widened, and his mouth fell open. Like a ventriloquist's puppet, he turned to her. "WOW!"

"I know. Isn't it amazing? Told you it was like out of the stories I tell you."

"It's beautiful, like you are," he said.

Lexi gripped under Spud's armpits. He'd gotten heavier. Swinging him, she put him down, kissed his cheek, and said, "Well. thank you."

"Can I go see?"

"Don't touch it, but yeah, go explore, and stay where I can see you," she said, taking the memory chip from out of her back pocket. "Spud, I said..."

"I know... where you can see me."

Spud was running around, releasing pent-up energy from being confined for so long. Lexi walked around the solid stone walls, looking for somewhere to hide the memory chip. She gathered that it must be important, and she was sure it had something to do with the crystal.

"Spud, come here. There's a cave with railway lines in it."

Spud ran over to her, gazed at the dark, cold tunnel and said, "I don't want to go into another tunnel."

Lexi didn't blame him. He'd spent most of his life in poky,

overcrowded tunnels. Spud was enjoying himself, running in circles, and God knew he needed the exercise.

"I'm going in, so you stay here, okay?"

"Can I run around it?" he asked, pointing to the rugged-looking object. "Please, Mum?"

"Yeah, go on…"

Lexi didn't have a torch, but entered anyway. The light from her watch provided more comfort than light. After a minute or so, she gathered that the tunnel went on for a distance beyond her reach. With no train visible, or anything other than a damp, almost fetid stench, she turned to head back.

As she neared the opening, she covered her eyes, but that wasn't enough. Light seeped through her fingers, causing her to shut her eyes tight. She let her eyes adjust, but to what? It wasn't much brighter in the room. She opened them again, and the room was how she'd left it.

Except there was no out-of-breath child, no one clinging to her leg or asking what she'd seen. "Spud… Spud, it's not funny! Come over here!"

She ran around the crystal, and even looked in the air vent. "Spud, if you're hiding, you win. I'm getting worried."

There was nowhere to hide and no way out, apart from the tunnel she'd been in and the air vent. She ran over to it and shouted through the vent. The only sound was the echo of her shrieking cries. Clenching her fists, she banged her temples and shouted his name until the air in her lungs depleted.

*He must have gone through the vent. Someone's taken him. No, that's not true. No one could have made it through the vent that fast, or the tunnel. I was in the tunnel.*

Something made her look at the crystal; not a sound or a movement, but a feeling; an instinctive, almost maternal feeling that *it* had done something to him.

# Chapter 26

The truck stopped.

Alex gripped Snipe's arm. "For the love of God, stick to the plan this time," he said. "Good luck, mate, and no hero stuff."

Snipe jumped down and walked toward the driver's side. Mike and Tyrone got out.

"So, where's the welcome party?" Snipe asked.

"That's odd, there should be someone here," Mike said, looking at Tyrone. "Wait for it..."

They waited, but nobody arrived.

"What are we waiting for? Let's keep driving," Snipe said, as Tyrone ducked under the branch of a low-hanging tree.

Tyrone shouted through twisted trunks and thicket, "Mike!"

Mike started to run.

"Hold on. I'm coming with you, and remember, I'm a crack shot," Snipe said, holding his gun toward him.

Alex knew that something wasn't right. He climbed from the back of the truck and joined Snipe as he vanished into the dense woodland.

"Who's not sticking to the plan?" Snipe asked.

"Holy shit... look," Tyrone said, pointing at the ground.

Green ferns made it hard to tell what he'd seen. They followed his trembling finger down to the ground. Two uniformed men were lying face-down in the snow with their guns by their side.

"Well, I think we've found our welcome party," Snipe said.

There was no sign of life or death. The bodies were warm, and their flasks still contained a hot substance.

"Something's wrong," Mike said.

"Would it be the two dead bodies, by chance?" Snipe asked.

"Not that… well, yes, that… and also that no one has come for them." He checked his wrist for the time. "They're either on the way, or they're also dead. The base is minutes away. Without contact, they should be here by now."

Tyrone was visibly shaken, and grieved for the name he kept muttering; he must have known one of the two. As Mike consoled his friend, Snipe and Alex mounted the truck and took their seats.

The truck woke with a violent shake as the engine turned over. They were back on the move, this time downhill. If there were any others in the wooded area, they'd have been alerted to the intermittent squeal of brakes as the truck made its descent down the icy mud road. No one showed. Apart from the background rumbling of the truck's engine, it was silent under the polypropylene fabric.

The hypnotic rumble of the truck changed tempo. Its low, humdrum sound was interrupted by several booms, followed by swishing noises as drones skipped over the flimsy covering that protected them.

Chip fell to the ground and rolled under the tubular bench. Alex ducked with his arms covering his face, expecting them to break through the material. The sounds continued as the truck swerved and skidded. Metal fenders hit trees and the back end swung wide, threatening to topple over. Alex and Snipe flew to the front as the truck hit a force that was not willing to bend or break.

Chip found his footing under the bench, and was the first to speak through a tightened, raspy throat. "Dad, what's happening?"

Alex opened his eyes and looked at Snipe. Helping each other to their feet, they drew arms, pointing the handheld Colts up at the roof.

A God-like voice bellowed from above the truck, *"All living persons selected for teleportation, make your way to the meeting room without delay."*

The message repeated, as if on a loop. By the third time it sounded, Alex and Chip followed Snipe out of the truck. Mike and Tyrone were nowhere in sight. Snipe rushed to the driver's side, fearing that the impact of the truck hitting the low stone wall had sent them through the windshield, but their seats were empty, and the windshield was intact.

"They've bailed," Alex said, looking up at the sky. Snipe followed his gaze. The sky was alight with a reflective distortion that was only broken by the larger gun drone that hovered without making a sound, watching every move they made.

Alex wrapped a protective arm around Chip. They didn't have an escape plan. They could barely comprehend what was happening and where they were. Random tents pitched in the dirt wouldn't offer protection. They looked toward the hill, expecting to see an entrance to a hidden base or people, but there were no people. Both turned to Snipe, who was scanning the area with narrowed eyes. His fingers tapped the handle of the Colt.

"Over here," Mike said. "Alex, Chip... quick," he said, waving them into a patched green and beige tent.

Snipe waved Chip and Alex in. Following behind, he never took his eyes away from the growing cloud of shimmering entities. His finger twitched on the trigger, not drawing the weapon for fear of reprisal. Then he, too, entered.

A square cut into the ground led down, far past the perimeter of the tent. The incline stopped at a solid door. Tyrone held it open as Mike pulled them inside.

A robotic voice bellowed from above the tent, *"You have forty seconds to comply... you have thirty-seven seconds to comply... you have..."*

Snipe slammed the door behind him and caught up to the others, who were already entering another heavy door.

"This way," Mike said.

The second door lead to a tunnel that was not dissimilar to an underground train tunnel, except it didn't have rails. A cart stood idle to one side. Ignoring it, they ran past, and through the underground passage until they reached two bodies, one lying atop the other. Both looked uninjured, with no clear cause of death. Further down, another larger man laid twisted, blocking their way. His leg was trapped under an upturned chair, as if he'd fallen while asleep. He, too, had no life force running through his hollow self. Mike and Tyrone did a double-take. Their faces twisted in mutual bereavement for the guard they'd made fun of for sleeping on the job.

High-pitched hysteria echoed through the tunnel as they ran for the recreation room. A food hall stood to the side of the entrance of the tunnel. There were eating pods, tables and chairs, a wall of vending machines, and reading areas. An open book laid flat on a padded chair next to an upturned cup, and pages dripped as if weeping for the dead.

Pockets of people gathered in clusters around their fallen friends and family. Their incomprehension for what was happening showed in their flailing actions, like they were at a rave on acid and were reaching the pinnacle of a bad high. Until now, they'd gone unnoticed, but this changed when a woman pointed toward them.

Surrounded by people that wanted answers, they found themselves back-to-back, unable to distinguish an individual voice. Their fruitless attempts to calm the growing crowd left them powerless.

Snipe rose his arm and fired three shots. He used a chair to step onto the service counter and shouted, "Lexi! Has anyone seen Lexi?"

Alex joined him and called out, "Katrina! Kat, has anyone seen Kat?"

The crowd scattered. Some re-joined in small groups, and others cried over the litter of lifeless colleagues. Those who were too numb to speak sat with their palms pressed above their eyes, trying to make sense of it all.

Snipe and Alex got down and approached Mike and Tyrone, who were in heightened conversation with two men in uniforms. "Mike, what's happening?" Snipe asked.

Looking at the uniformed men, Alex asked, "Where's Kat?"

Mike turned to Tyrone. "Ty, go see where Kat's got to... and Lexi." Then he led Snipe, Alex, and Chip around to an empty storeroom by the side of the tunnel entrance.

"It's true; the chosen few are assembling in the operations room. Rush Unix is on a video link." He turned to Chip, who was pacing the box room. "Ty's gone to find your Mum. Guys, the clock is ticking."

Snipe grabbed Mike's arm. "What clock?"

"I was told the base has under two hours before... I don't know what."

"The event," Alex said.

Snipe looked at Mike and asked, "Under two hours? How can anyone know that?" Bouncing from foot to foot, he asked, "Where's the operations room?"

The last-ever meeting was nearing its end when they entered the emotion-filled room, packed with edgy people demanding answers. Snipe didn't need a tuning fork to recognise the fight-or-flight vibe; he'd been in similar environments, and all of them had a mental clock ticking which required immediate action and one of the two F's. Only this was different; a classic kiss-your-bum goodbye situation. The clock was physical rather than mental. Fighting wasn't an option, and flight required leaving the planet in under two hours.

In contrast to the despairing gathering of souls, a recording played on a large screen, set back above a stage. Snipe had no memory of his father, but he knew that it was the older version of him talking.

"Make your way to the chute. A carriage awaits you with enough seating for those present. Walk through the light, and be invited into your new home. A land of peace and prosperity. A world you control. Discoveries lie in wait for the chosen few. *You* are those few. Our fallen friends and family have spared their lives for you to carry the human race forward…"

People surged forward past the stage and over to an opening that Mike and Tyrone had never seen before, even in all the times they'd been there. Alex and Chip asked everyone where Kat was. Someone replied, "The lockup. She's in prison."

"Lexi!" Snipe shouted, "Where's Lexi?"

He stood by the opening, determined to disrupt the transition until he had answers. He stared at each person in the eyes as he asked and even threatened those who were unwilling to speak, but it was to no avail. All versions led to the same conclusion: Lexi was seen running away from the guards in the recreational room and heading in the direction of the tunnel they'd entered. The collaboration of truths, their reaction, and their body language all pointed to it being the last time she was seen. Snipe shuddered, more for knowing that she was here than she was missing. The room emptied, and Snipe let those who'd complied through the opening in the wall.

Tyrone walked over to him. "I'll help you look for her. She's our friend, too."

"Where's Alex and Chip?"

"Mike's taken them to the prison section. Someone said she's held there."

Snipe ran the words through his mind: *Lexi, running, guards.* He concluded that she, too, must be in a cell. "Let's go!"

"Where?" Ty asked.

"Prison."

Tyrone tried negotiating with a wall of people that stood in the corridor. Some pushed past to get to the operations room, and Snipe let them pass. Others vented their frustrations to Tyrone, who, at this point, was just trying to appease them with what he knew.

"Keep moving," Snipe said, pulling the gun from the pocket of his flight suit. "Move, or I'll shoot."

Tyrone looked back, thinking that it was he who was being threatened. The gun waved at those in the way. Ty moved through the crowd as Snipe commanded him to quicken his pace.

A man with a look of hatred on his face stood with his arms folded. "Shoot me. We're all dead, anyway." He wouldn't let Tyrone pass. Snipe rose his knee, striking the man in the crotch. As he bent forward, he struck the back of his head with the butt end of the Colt, sending him to the ground.

His swift action hadn't allowed time for Tyrone to process what had happened. Instead, he stepped over the man, who had his hands between his legs and was rocking back and forth in the foetal position. Snipe followed, and the people parted.

"Where now? Quick, we haven't much time," Snipe said, wondering how much time might be left. Maybe there *wasn't* a clock ticking; maybe this whole thing was a trap to gather the remaining non-citizens. Either way, he had to get to Lexi. The world could end if it had to, but when he and Lexi were finally together again.

They soldiered on, pushing past people and families with children standing together, holding each other.

"Down here," Tyrone said.

They ran down yet another corridor and saw Alex, Chip, Mike, and another, much older man leaving with as much urgency as they had used to get there.

"They're not in there. Just two dead guards."

"Lexi's with young Spud," said Mr Ranger. "They were being pursued, and I believe –No, I'm more than sure that they entered a ventilation shaft on level seven. After I told Kat, she asked me to follow her, but I couldn't, so she left without me."

"Where's the air vent lead to?" Snipe asked.

Mr Ranger rubbed his chin and said, "Well, all over I suppose. Its purpose is to supply ventilation. Kat said to head to level twelve, but she must have been confused, because there isn't a level twelve, or any level past level seven. She overcame those guards. Quite remarkable. I'm a school teacher, by the way. Mr Ranger's my name."

Snipe reached into the flight suit, pulled out the map that Vic had given to him, and unfolded it. In his haste to undo it, the map ripped in half. "Shit. Here, hold this," he said, handing a piece over to Alex.

Alex knelt, flattening the piece that had been handed to him. Laying his half on the ground next to it, Snipe joined the two together. "Do you recognise anything on here?" Snipe asked, looking up at Mr Ranger. "Where are we on this thing?"

"Ah, let me see. It looks like a diagram... I don't recognise this, nor... wait. This starts at the school. If the school's... let me see... level one, instead of, as we know it to be, level seven..." He counted down on his fingers. "...Then the object displayed here with a number six next to it is actually level twelve, and if there's a level twelve, then there must also be a level eleven, ten, nine, and eight."

"Never mind that," Alex said. "How do we get there? Where did Kat go?"

Mike and Tyrone paced the floor alongside Chip, who thought that by doing so, it might somehow speed the whole process up.

Ranger followed a light blue line from where he knew the vending machine was, and then around the building and along L6, which he interpreted as level twelve. "That's where Lexi entered, but there would be no way you'd fit through." He then traced two dotted lines from level twelve back up to the operations room. "Looks like you should have gone with the others. They're heading to level twelve."

"Dad!"

Alex turned as Mike and Tyrone hit the wall before collapsing to the ground. Snipe and Alex slid over. Snipe felt for a pulse while Alex clasped his fingers together and counted as he pumped Mike's chest. Chip backed into the wall, turning his head away from Snipe, who performed the same action on Tyrone.

"Come on, god damn it," Snipe said. "Mr Ranger, were these two citizens?"

Mr Ranger nodded. "They're senior staff, so yes, they would be."

"Shit," Alex said, turning to Snipe. "Kat's chipped. She's a citizen, too."


Chip remembered the way back to the operations room. Mr Ranger had told them to run ahead, and that he'd follow, but he was nowhere in sight by the time they entered, and neither was the entrance.

"Are you sure this is it?" Alex asked, pointing to a blank wall.

"It is, Alex," Snipe said, knocking on the wall. It was hollow where they'd last seen the gap. Searching for a secret button or a gap to pry open what they knew was a concealed door, they found neither. Both Alex and Snipe took turns kicking the wall, but there was no give.

"Dad."

They both turned to Chip, who stood by the screen at the back of the stage. The wall where the screen hung moved to the right, revealing a room behind it.

Snipe and Alex drew their weapons and entered. Grey hair hung over a winged back chair; a rasping gargled noise told them it was a person before they moved around for a better look. An old man sat bolt upright. A neck brace with what could have been a voice box protruding from the centre rattled as he tried to speak. Tubes attached to a machine ran fluid back and forth through bloated veins. Snipe looked into his pearly, glazed eyes.

Not wanting Chip to see the living corpse, Alex blocked the view of the winged chair. He looked over Chip's shoulder. "Snipe, the wall; it's opening," he said.

Chip spun around to face the wall as it parted. Alex and Chip ran to it, jumping off the stage and hoping that it would stay open.

"The table," Alex said.

Chip helped drag it over, wedging it into the open space in the wall.

"Snipe, its open!" Chip called to him.

Snipe walked around the chair and knelt in front of the pale, withered figure. "Who are you?"

An inaudible sound. Not quite a voice, more of a tone, came from the man's neck. Snipe placed his ear next to it.

The small box crackled and let off a high-pitched squeal. Snipe flinched his head away and moved back as the shriek turned to words: *"I'm sorry, it's too late, don't trust..."*

"Who?"

The squeal again, this time higher in pitch.

Covering his ears with flattening palms, he asked, "Trust who? Who are you?"

A rhythmic, timed thudding came from outside the room. The upturned table shifted as the wall smashed into it.

"Snipe, I can't hold it any longer. Hurry!"

Snipe raised his voice as the man closed his watery eyes and his mouth slackened to one side.

"Open that up."

Snipe heard rising desperation in Alex's voice.

He moved around the old man. His arm swung, hitting the wing of the chair, turning it as he rushed past. He turned back upon hearing something smash next to the chair. He looked down and saw a photograph of a small boy smiling next to a man wearing a uniform. Like a rubber bullet between the eyes, he knew that the slouched, decaying man in the chair was his father. Hesitating, Snipe leaned forward to pick up the picture.

Screams from behind him sounded hollow. "Snipe! Now, god damn it, *now!*"

Leaving the picture where it was, he hurried over to the wall. The table was in two halves. Alex extended his arm and pulled him through as the wall snapped shut, with only the table leg wedged underneath it.

A mixed look of anger and relief plastered their faces. Snipe blinked, and Alex could tell by his numb, expressionless face and parted lips that he'd had a shock. No words were exchanged as they ran behind Chip, who had nowhere else to run but along curved walls and between tracks, descending like a man trying to catch a runaway rollercoaster.

Stale air filled their lungs the further they went. The light from the slim gap underneath the wall had long since given way to inky darkness. Dust particles, masked by the gloomy tunnel, bleached their nostrils and dried the soft flesh under their tongues as they took each breath.

Alex staggered and stopped. Bent forward, he drew a deep breath and said, "Go. Keep going."

"Get your breath. We'll get there together," Snipe said, listening to the echo of footsteps far ahead of them. "I'd give you a fireman's lift but, I don't think my back will take your middle-aged spread."

Alex laughed, spitting dirt as he did. "Nice to see your sense of humour returned."

Snipe bent to the side, pulling Alex's arm around his neck. They walked for a few minutes until Alex pulled his arm away and started a slow jog forward.

"Dad... Snipe!"

The calling was faint and distorted. They ran toward it,

blackness turning to a haze of purple, growing lighter the further they ran.

Chip stood at the tunnel's entrance, a halo of light surrounding his lean body, changing from pink to purple and merging with a mustard yellow. The cave was devoid of people. The majestic object standing central to the rugged stone walls glowed, as if communicating with them. A mesmerising, haunting chill ran through Snipe's entire body. Alex stood dumbfounded by the spectacle that stood before him. Chip's eyes widened, and his pupils pulsated in hypnotic appreciation for its brilliance.

Snipe felt drawn toward it. He blinked hard in defiance and forced himself to look down at the dust-filled stone floor instead. As he focused on the ground, trying to gain composure, his eyes picked out a boot print.

"Lexi was here… Alex, snap out of it and look down," he said, not daring to lift his head for fear of being sucked back into the sparkling wonder. "Alex?"

Bridging his eyes, Alex looked down at the ground as well. "There's footprints everywhere. Look." Alex pointed at more footprints while keeping his other hand pressed under his eyebrows, only allowing himself to see the ground.

Snipe walked around, stopping only to circle the dirt with his finger when he saw the same boot print. Size three adult boots. It had to be her. They were leading him to the serrated light show.

Snipe and Alex stumbled backwards as a flash, as bright as the sun appearing from an eclipse, struck them. Its intensity blinded them with a sharpness otherwise only felt from a physical impact. White blindness lasted long after the surrounding space had dulled down to only a downcast purple haze.

"Chip!" Alex called out. "Where are you?"

Alex ran to the platform surrounding the crystal. Footprints, some still wet from the tunnel, faced it. Half-prints with only the heel visible, impossible to duplicate in such numbers, vanished, as if the obstruction was placed on top moments before their arrival.

Rubbing his eyes, Snipe watched as Alex walked into the crystal.

He ran to it, stopping short of making contact. He peered at the jagged edges of the razor-sharp glass and rubbed his eyes once more. Fearing that he was hallucinating, he turned away from it.

A warm, welcoming glow cloaked his body; completeness washed over him. He turned to face it. Serrated edges softened to jelly. He reached out with one finger, compelled to touch the thing that made him feel so complete. His finger slid in, and then his hand.

The thought of finding Lexi stopped him, jerking him out of his trance. Fighting an overwhelming urge to jump into the thing that had made him feel loved, cherished, and innocent again, he yanked out his arm.

A hand covered in soft, feminine skin, smaller than his own, stroked and squeezed his, enticing him to be with the girl to whom it belonged.

"Lexi," he whispered, as the jellified substance enveloped his entire body.

# Chapter 27

Having resisted the transition between worlds, Snipe collapsed upon entry. He breathed in a sweet smell; the smell that a child would experience, or perhaps one imagined by an adult reminiscing. A warm, soothing breeze washed a sense of blissful oneness over him. He couldn't feel his body. Did he need one?

*I've died. Yes, that's it. I've died, and this is what it's like being dead... Not so bad. At least it's not final. No running or fighting... Mmm, that smell... and the* warmth.

As his mind wandered, so did his senses. A sweet scent, the warm, blanket-soft breeze, the sound of motor vehicles and people chattering, the taste of soft, delicate lips against his own.

Snipe's eyes sprang open. Lexi pulled away and spat on his arm, then rubbed it and leaned in close. She read her own name etched into his skin.

"Had to be sure," she said.

Snipe felt the embrace of true love. They kissed and spoke without even hearing each other. Two lost souls entwined as one, each completing the picture of a jigsaw puzzle that had been missing two different, yet essential, pieces.

He sat up, knowing that people surrounded him. He recognised a few from the operations room. Alex and Chip pushed through the onlookers to reach them. A woman followed behind Chip, her fingers wrapped up with his. The women hugged Lexi as Alex and Chip smiled. They were talking, but their words were muddled.

Snipe tried to push himself up against a pole with a metal sign attached. A bus, the kind he had only ever seen in black and white movies, growled. Its brakes squeaked as it slowed. Faces clicked past his eyes like a pendulum, swinging in time to the second hand on one of Vic's grandfather clocks.

"Snipe, baby... listen to me. Take your time. It'll take a few minutes to adjust," Lexi said, looking up at Alex, who was already rolling up his sleeves.

He was being carried. Chip had hold of his legs. Alex held him underneath his arms. As he bobbed up and down through the gathering of onlookers, Lexi held his hand and encouraged him, telling him to relax and repeating that she was there for him, that he looked great, and that he would feel normal again soon. He felt foolish, but too weak to protest against being carried.

The spinning slowed. He could see someone standing and holding a door open. The man looked deep in thought as he combed his fingers through his beard.

Snipe stroked the clean sheets, unaware that he was in a bed. Hunger pangs growled, telling him that he'd been asleep for days. Lexi hadn't left his side the whole time, providing proof that he hadn't been dreaming, he wasn't dead, and the people and surroundings were real. He felt reenergized, fresh, and more alert than he'd ever felt before in his life.

Spud ran in and jumped onto the foot of the bed. Bouncing on his knees, he said, "Mum, he's all right. Told you he would be. You are, aren't you?" Spud asked, looking at Snipe's startled expression

A hint of recognition of the boy tickled his mind before vanishing. "Mum?" Snipe asked, turning to Lexi.

"I'll explain after dinner, babes."

Snipe swung the cover off, then on again. The flight suit was missing. He looked at Lexi. She had her hand over Spud's eyes. "That, too, when little man's asleep." Raising her eyebrows, she bit her bottom lip.

Flabbergasted, Snipe saw a full set of clothes hanging up, as if they'd expected his arrival. Not just any old clothes, but new ones. Until today, he'd never wore or owned brand-new clothes. A pair of vintage-style jeans, a white, loose neck top, a set of matching smalls, and trainers. He turned over the trainers. There was a price label in old money, clearly visible, as if they had been purchased yesterday.

Lexi gave him the guided tour. She was given the property on arrival, over a month ago. She'd done her utmost to explain that time worked differently, and that the few hours between her stepping through the teleporter and Snipe following had resulted in over a month passing. It hadn't taken her a month to *get* there, –that had been instant – but for some reason that she didn't quite grasp, a delay or a time shift had taken effect.

"There are other cool things, too, like the water is like a computer." She waited for his reaction. His lips parted with no flow of words. "That's not all. Everything is kinda mismatched; old, but new, if you know what I mean."

Snipe followed her into the dining room. "Lex, babes, I don't know what you mean, sweetie. I'm trying to understand."

"The buildings, cars, and things. Many things. They're from the old world, but brand new."

Snipe fondled a kettle. "1950s, this one. Yeah, looks like everything's old English."

"Not just English. People from just about everywhere back on Earth." She raised her palms, seemingly in shock that she'd finally accepted that she was no longer on Earth. "They're all here. Some streets are East Asian, others are American, and so on. We're in the English part of town."

"It all sounds too perfect, Lex. I mean… all of this." He waved his hand around the lounge as they stepped down into the dining room. "Ouch," he said, holding his finger.

"What's happened?" Lexi wrapped a cloth she got from the work surface over his hand. "It's bleeding."

"Not much. Caught it on that bloody thing," he said, pointing to a piece of metal sticking out from where the sink had been poorly fitted. "Who's in charge? Who calls the shots?"

She handed him a flyer. "We've got to attend a mass meeting on the outskirts of town, on the Chinese side. I think we'll find out then. Snipe, babes, if anything's dodgy, we up and leave. Promise never to leave me. Whatever happens, we're good together."

"After what I've been through, there's no way I'm letting you out of my sight."

"Masterful. I like that. Maybe you can show me that side of you in the bedroom."

Kat called to them from the dining room. Pots and plates clattered on a six-seater table covered with a blush tablecloth and matching placemats, silver cutlery, a salad bowl, and jug of water in the centre. The ornate chairs from a past era had little cushions which matched the dark red tablecloth.

Kat pulled out a chair for Alex, who looked as unnerved as Snipe did, having only arrived a week ago. Chip felt like he had the upper hand, and displayed a slight teenage cockiness for having arrived a week before his father. Kat arrived before them, with Spud and Lexi being the first. Being the new kid at the table Snipe, wanted to know everything that they did.

The bearded guy entered the room midway through a rapid-fire question-and-answer session.

"Hi." He walked over to Snipe and held out his hand. "Professor Mac Cunningham."

"Er, no, Snipe Siren, but you can call me," he combed an imaginary beard, "Professor Siren."

Lexi smacked the back of his hand with the flat end of a knife. Snipe smiled upon seeing Mac's dumbstruck reaction, then he apologised and offered his hand.

"Just breaking the ice, that's all."

"We came through together," Kat said. "Mac took out two armed guards and saved my life."

Snipe noticed Alex drop his head. Mac didn't look the sort to fight, but when it comes to fight-or-flight, sometimes the fight surfaces first, and only when it's over do you look back and think about the consequences. Maybe that's what happened to Mac. Either way, Alex knew that it should have been him rescuing the mother of his son, not an overweight bearded dude. Now Mac was the hero, and he was a professor, too, which meant he was a warrior with brains, which would be a threat to any relationship.

Tucking into the buffet of fresh potato salad, pasta covered with a thick tomato and herb sauce, and hot bread, Snipe told a story of how Alex had rescued him from certain death, and how he'd kept his cool when everyone around them had lost theirs. Alex glanced over at him, giving him a look that was a mixture of *Thanks* and *Please stop before it sounds too unrealistic*. Snipe obliged, turning the conversation back to what Mac knew about this strange new world.

"We know what we've seen and what the locals have said." He looked around the table, seeking permission to carry on. "From what I gather, everything we rely on has little bearing here. Its quantum physics at its most strange. For example," he rubbed his beard, "we all know the internet." He looked at Spud. "Well, *most* of us know the internet. Everything is stored in a digital cloud. Well, here, everything communicates. The water that you drink holds information, just like the digital cloud. I'm not sure quite how it works, but I've started to run experiments in the bathtub."

Lexi snickered at the thought of him experimenting while in the bathtub.

"Not in *that* way; I wore clothes. The water answered the question that I fed into it. I wanted to find out how conductive the water was, and whether it was drinkable. It is, and when I ran electricity through it in a coded manner, it filled in the gaps. It seems to be intelligent. The trees look like any other trees, but they're conscious. To what degree, I'm unsure."

Whether it was information overload or the sight of Lexi mothering a child – the same muddy-faced, desolate child he'd seen the night of his capture – he was unsure. Any words the professor said afterwards flowed past the bubble he'd created, of which, Lexi, Spud, and himself were the only occupants.

Lexi looked at him and winked. "You okay, babes?" She looked at Mac, and then back at Snipe. "Goes on a bit, doesn't he?"

"So, you're telling me that everyone has individual zones here, like back home, but nicer?" Snipe asked, looking at everyone, apart from Mac.

Kat looked up. "No, not like back home. We can go anywhere. I've made it as far as Chinatown. Took me all day. The locals say there's nothing past that town, only open space. I got cold feet and turned back after getting a few looks… you know, the sort you'd get back home."

Alex looked at Mac. "You let her go to a different town in a different world?"

"Hey," Kat said, turning to Alex. "He's not my keeper, and neither are you."

Snipe blamed himself for the tiff and changed the subject again. "So, when's the meeting and who's heading it?" he asked.

The table fell silent. Chewing mouths allowed no immediate reply.

Spud blurted out, "They are, the–" But then Lexi's slender finger fell upon his lips, halting him in mid-sentence.

"There's more, Snipe," Lexi said. "I was waiting for the right time to tell you because I fucking freaked when I found out, and you're only just coming around to the idea of this place, so I wanted to show you all the good stuff we never had."

Snipe raised his eyebrows and lowered his head. "What?"

Lexi explained, "These tall people who belong here." She turned to Kat. "She's better at explaining it, babes."

Lifting her glass of water, Kat swallowed down the remains of her food. "I've never seen one, but they tell me. *They*, being people who've been here longer. They say that the tall people are a different species to us; that they're distant relatives, of sorts. Guess we'll find out tomorrow. I'm just glad to be free again, and away from that hellhole called Earth. Who'd have imagined it? A different planet that can sustain life as we've always known it, minus the shitty bits? When I was privy to sensitive information, I passed it on whenever I had the chance." She looked at Alex. "The rest I couldn't work out until Mac came into my life. All this time, I thought Zeta and the drones were a part of the same destructive program created by us to help organise things, and they somehow gained intelligence and turned on us. It transpires that from the moment they came to Earth, they laid dormant in preparation for the inevitable event."

"Which event? We didn't see the second," Snipe said.

"The first wasn't the first, either. Earth's had many. You know about the dinosaurs, right?" She waited for him to speak, but Snipe just nodded. "They've been there that long. After what we called the *event* happened, they appeared. Top people from around the world studied them. At first, they credited each other for building them, until it became clear that these things had intelligence. Putting it simply, they did what we needed them to. They took commands from the first to make contact."

Snipe frowned and said, "I was one of them."

"I know. I watched the original video of you shutting them down by lowering your hand."

"That's because it has a chip in it, right?"

"Only way to find out is to x-ray it, I guess."

She glanced at Mac, who raised his hand. "Rush Unix told you to think about downing them, and you did. Later, your grandfather and other elites used them to rebuild our infrastructure. They came to an agreement with the machines. Our intentions changed to one of control. That's when they started to regulate and reduce our numbers. Rush Unix didn't want to be a part of their war games and broke from the pack."

"And the pyramids?" Snipe asked.

"Always been there, all over the planet, in one form or another. The crystals came to life after the event."

Snipe rubbed his chin, then looked at Mac, who was doing the same. "But we know from history that pyramids are Egyptian. Well, the ones in the desert, anyway."

"It's true that they reoccupied them and used them for their ceremonial interests. They may have copied them in admiration for the originals. Don't quote me on that. It's just my opinion."

"Was I a part of this agreement with Zeta?" Snipe asked. "That'd explain why they didn't kill me when they had the chance."

Alex coughed before saying, "You were the only one to have ever escaped. If these beings are as logical as we think they are, then you had to be the clone. They wouldn't kill one of their own. Luckily, you weren't spotted together."

"So, they broke the agreement," Snipe said. "If we agreed for them to have human and plant samples, then why the butchering of non-citizens, the disabling of citizens, and how come you made it, Kat?" Snipe turned to her. "I mean, I'm glad you did, but by all rights, you should have been disabled like the rest."

"I was one of the chosen," Kat said. "I'm the only one at this table who was."

"And they don't know we gate-crashed their word?" Snipe asked.

The room fell silent. Mac stuttered out the words, "You being here breaks all logic. An impossibility, as far as they're concerned" He whipped his head around, addressing everyone at the table. "Anyway, that's what I think."

Rubbing his chin, Snipe looked at Mac, who was trying to interrupt Alex. Then he took his hand away from his chin, since the action might be interpreted as him taking the piss.

"What?" he asked.

"May I ask what blood type you are?" Mac asked, looking at Snipe's wrapped finger.

"The rarest. AB negative," Snipe said. "Bit of a random question. Why do you ask?"

Mac went to work on his beard as if he was typing a message. "Mind if I take a sample?"

"Why?"

"I think I may have discovered the antivirus; the thing they fear."

Snipe jolted his head toward Alex and Chip.

"I still don't understand. If they got what they wanted, then why snatch people by force, rip their insides out, and disable the masses?"

"I think I know why they entered living samples," Mac said. "It was for two reasons: First, to rid anything that stood in the way of their plan, like the ones who weren't selected, and those who rebelled. And then second, because they entered a living sample. The masses were killed to end the chance of a human stampede."

Interrupting, Alex said, "The ones who got snatched; Mathews said they killed them after the cloning process."

Kat answered, "Maybe they were, or Zeta might have taken them for further study. If they were chipped after the cloning process, then they might even be here. We only have his word that they were killed. If only I'd looked at the file," Kat said. "Not that we have the memory stick, and even if we did, and it managed to survive the journey, there'd be nothing to plug it into. An advanced planet without PCs. Strange, don't you think?" She looked at Mac. "What did you mean when you said that you think you might have found the thing they fear?"

"I'll know more when I have a sample," Mac said.

Spud raised his finger to ask a question.

"Yes, Spud?" Kat asked.

Spud looked at Snipe. "Can we play outside?"

Smiling, Snipe said, "Yes, we can, and you can show me around." He looked at Lexi. "You coming, Squirrel?"

She smiled back. "Yeah, why not? All this history talk's making us bored, innit, Spud?"

Spud left the table.

Kat shuffled in her seat. "Do you want to know about Rush

Unix?"

"I'm going to take care of the important things first," Snipe said, holding Lexi by the hand and walking outside. Spud had his face pressed up to the glass and was breathing nose clouds from the outside of the window. Lexi offered Spud her hand. He ran to the other side of Snipe and slid his hand into Snipe's palm.

"Let's see the trees. Look, see? Over there." He pointed to a mix of around ten beech and birches, standing beyond an open green space.

"You run on, Spud, we'll catch up," Lexi said.

"Race me, Dad. Please? I'll win," Spud said, pulling his hand away.

Snipe looked at Lexi and mouthed the word, *Dad?*

Lexi shrugged and counted them down from three. Snipe sped off ahead of Spud, before tripping over into a roll. He gave Lexi the thumbs-up and laughed as Spud ran by, reaching the trees first.

Transfixed on a leaf, Snipe rubbed it between his fingers. The tree was the same as any other tree back home, but seemed more alive and vivid in appearance. He looked around, and down at the grass. That, too, looked greener and more vibrant than he remembered grass ever being back home.

Lexi grabbed his waist. "Ha!"

"Is it me, or does everything look the same, but somehow more alive?" he asked, returning to the leaf.

She moved in closer and said, "It's like seeing in HD, babes. Look closer and you'll notice even more."

He did, and saw water passing through the veins of the leaf. "Wow, it's like I've got x-ray vision." He smelled the leaf. An explosion of fragrances blasted his senses. Not one, but many individual, undefinable smells climbed his nasal passages.

"See? Told you it's cool. All you have to do is think about someone, and sniff the air like a dog, and hey, presto! You will know if they've had a shower that morning."

Snipe had to admit; his sensitivity had increased. He felt attuned with this new environment, and at peace. Not at the same level as the others, but he felt less guarded, and more relaxed.

After running around the trees until dizziness set in, Spud eyed a group of children playing with wooden toys. They were taking turns on a catch-cup and playing hopscotch between dirt lines they'd sprinkled onto the short grass.

"Go ask if you can play, Spud," Lexi said, egging him on.

Spud looked up at Snipe. Snipe bent down to his level and said, "Go on, my brave little soldier. Go play. I'll be right here watching."

Spud walked over and hung around, twisting his curls, until a girl passed him the catch-cup. He glanced back, and Snipe gave him the thumbs-up. Pretending he hadn't seen, Spud began to flick the wooden ball with one hand, and gave Snipe the thumbs-up with his other hand from behind his back.

Beyond the field, a set of trees separated the road from the pavement. Snipe eyed a group of people queueing. An old London bus pulled up with an authentic squeak of its breaks. He noticed other vehicles pass by; all of them looked like they were from a car museum.

Laying hand-in-hand in the shade of the Downy Birch, the grass had a pleasant warmth about it, but he couldn't place the sun. The sky was blue and dotted with wispy white clouds, like any summer's day back home, but it was quieter; he could even hear the click of the ball as it fell into the wooden cup. Or was that his newfound superpowers at work?

"Squirrel, look up. Tell me what's missing."

She did. "The sun. I know. I was going to make that my question for tomorrow. The whole sky brightens during the day, then darkens in the evening. Must be up there somewhere."

"No, something else... birds? There are no birds," he said.

Their eyes met, and she said, "I'm the only bird you need. Maybe the squirrels eat them. Damn."

"What is it?"

"We can only ask one question each. I was going to ask where the sun was." She said, kissing him. "But what about the squirrels?"

Snipe returned her kiss. "You're the only Squirrel I need."

# Chapter 28

A sea of people was strewn across the open space. Snipe, Lexi, and Spud stood about a hundred feet from the raised stage. If he was anywhere other than a strange new world, it could have been a rock concert, but the people standing around huddled together in groups, frowning and shaking their heads. There were Asians, blacks, and whites from every corner of the Earth. A wave of mingled languages hung in the air, reminding him how diverse Earth had been.

Snipe tightened his grip around the gadget that had been handed to them on the way through a narrow alley in Chinatown. He thought back to when he lived with Vic, remembering shop and the sacrifice he'd made for Snipe to be standing here today. He smiled, thinking of his wild stories and the words of wisdom that he would slip into any conversation, just when they were truly needed. *Fight logic with chaos,* he'd say. *Do the unexpected; they'll react to it. When they do, you're already one step ahead.* Another one that stuck in his mind was, *they can take your things, even your lifeblood, but they can never take your soul.*

"Well, I hope they get on with it soon. Spud's getting irritable," Lexi said.

Snipe rubbed the boy's hair with his hand. "Afterwards, we'll have a proper look around Chinatown. Maybe we'll find something good to take back home," he said, winking at the lad.

He was impressed by Lexi, the roughneck, mixed-race gal who used to live in dirt-filled tunnels. She was a fighter, a lover, and now a mother. She'd taken the boy under her wing; protected and cared for him. Snipe felt no jealousy or contempt; far from it. She'd put others before herself, which strengthened his love for his little Squirrel.

The assortment of languages gave way to a murmur. A large screen lit up, flanked on either side by two others. An average-looking, clean-shaved man with brown hair wearing a casual white suit, walked out. The crowd didn't cheer. The murmuring grew until he spoke.

"Welcome, humans from the planet Earth. Sounds strange, doesn't it? It did when I arrived. My name is Ivan, and as you can see, I'm very much one of you. I was chosen, in part, due to my profession back home. I'm an interpreter of languages; a linguistic anthropologist. On Earth, I studied Mayan and other Sanskrit languages. However, being as they communicate through me, my talents in this field are, to a large extent, redundant. I like to think that they chose me because I'm handsome... for a human."

Silence fell upon the gathered masses. The speaker's ice-breaking punchline hadn't had the desired effect. Bending down, Lexi lifted Spud onto Snipe's shoulders.

The introduction was coming to an end. Ivan had talked about how they could find out more, and encouraged them to seek information from water, and other things that humans would normally consider incapable of holding information.

"Well, thank you for submitting your questions," Ivan said to the now-silent crowd. "He'll try to answer them all." Following his own footsteps in long strides, like a cheap psychic trying to make contact, Ivan said, "I was asked to explain their ways before he makes contact. Once this happens, it will be his words leaving my body, and not my own. But don't worry. I'm able to translate the information-understandably. Unlike humans, Zetas do not have emotions, and are the original tall greys. You've all heard of, and may have experienced, their offspring; the small greys who have frequented Earth for many years. The Zeta race of the greys is the Daddy, so to speak." He looked at the hard-to-please crowd. Someone shouted something in what sounded like Russian.

"Okay, well, without further ado, please welcome your saviour. I've named him Cal."

There were scattered claps sprinkled from the crowd, but they were few in number, sounding more like the crackling of chips in a fryer that hadn't yet reached its ideal temperature.

A tall figure appeared from behind the screen and stood centre stage behind Ivan. Covered in a taupe cloak, the grey stood a good two feet taller than the man in front. Its slouched posture made it appear old. It had pocked skin over a thin, but muscular, frame. Its black eyes glistened, although they weren't oval-shaped like the much smaller greys that had played a part in human culture and entertainment for so long. Sunken temples gave rise to a disproportionate, hairless skull. Its ears could've been mistaken for human ears, if they had not been attached to such a hideous cranium. Its spread nose merged into its face, leading down to heart-shaped nostrils. A line ran to its downturned mouth. It had no visible lips, and its chin was an extension of its thin neck, covered in patches of grey that gave the appearance of scales, or the wrinkles found in the elderly.

Gasps rippled through the crowd as they experienced transition denial from what had now been confirmed as true. A man of East Asian descent fainted, and was helped back to his feet by the surrounding people. Spud thought it was great, and kept saying

*Wicked* over and over, while bouncing atop Snipe's shoulders. Lexi drew closer under Snipe's arm, as the man standing in front of the grey spoke.

"Welcome to our planet. Our planet, once a star, has been adapted for our use, and now yours. It is five times the size of your home planet, and has been terraformed to offer an inhabitable environment for several species. The area you inhabit is equal to the size of Earth. H20 separates each area."

The speaker held his throat, as if struggling to continue. The grey stood statue-like behind him, without emotion or concern.

"We are your saviours and give this land to you." The man spoke in a raspy voice, as if being strangled. The grey lifted a long, thin arm from beneath its robe and placed its frail hand upon the speaker's head.

Ivan spoke again, this time with the clarity he'd had when he first appeared. "We are Zeta; we are one. We are the original of the masses. Our blood is chlorophyll-based. We do not eat the same as humans, saving on waste material. Zeta gather energy by absorbing minerals through our skin and Zeta use light for photosynthesis. Zeta elders were a thriving civilisation. We had much diversity. We had war and differing belief systems. Radiation from early technological advancements resulted in our species being in crisis. Zeta's failed natural reproductive program, lead us to perfect cloning. By doing so, we controlled the conception process. We saw this as a logical solution. Zeta extracted a range of neurochemical responses in our brain, so that emotionally, our state of being remains consistent and balanced. Throughout thousands of years of cloning, we now have little variation, resulting in our demise. The copies of the original became dimmer and less complete. Zeta understands that the original image will not continue to exist."

The speaker's appearance began to resemble that of the tall grey behind him. Snipe realised that he hadn't blinked. His dormant facial expression looked gaunt; his mouth moved out of sync to what he said.

"Bring him down," Lexi said, reaching for Spud. "It's scaring me," she whispered in his ear.

"Can we go now and look at Chinatown, please?"

"Soon, baby boy, soon," Lexi said, pulling him between her knees.

"I'm not a baby. I'm seven."

"You said you were seven last year, Spud. Let's settle for seven and a half."

Snipe flicked his eyes between the screens. Both angles showed the speaker's legs wobbling. The grey withdrew its hand from Ivan's head and stepped back. The speaker's legs gave way. Snipe watched as he fell to the ground. The crowd reacted, and someone at the front tried to climb the stage, but fell back in line as the speaker stood.

"Sorry. I'm fine. Please calm down. I never said this was an easy job." Ivan laughed, either to make light of what had happened, or perhaps it had genuinely amused him. Snipe suspected that it was both.

"As we're experiencing technical difficulties," Ivan chuckled again, "I'll try to answer your questions, and then we'll give it another go with my friend."

The speaker pulled something from his belt, which had been hidden beneath a loose-fitting linen jacket.

He raised his head after reading something on the device and asked, "*Who's in charge?* Good question, and the answer is you. You're in charge. You're empowered to create your new world as you see fit. Learn from the past, and create a system that works."

He read the next question. *"How did everything get here?"* He chewed it over before answering. "They've studied Earth as much as other planets that had reached their natural end or became uninhabitable. They've built and imported the most suitable home comforts. Humans need artificial surroundings; houses, areas, and stuff. We like our stuff. Other species, such as the dinosaur, need little more than an unspoiled natural environment and a lot of space... a *lot*."

"Mum, they've got dinosaurs. Snipe, can we see the dinosaurs?" Spud asked.

Snipe thought more about Spud calling him by his first name than he did about the notion that dinosaurs existed within this crazy world.

"Dad, can we?"

"We'll go dino-hunting after Chinatown, I promise," he said.

The speaker read another question. *"Is the planet at war?* Another good question. The vastness of the universe guarantees perpetual war. However, this artificial planet has enough defences, should war be forced upon us. War, fighting, and any form of hostility are forbidden. Species are separated, thereby eliminating interspecies war."

Ivan drank from a glass behind the side screen before saying, "I'll make this my last question, as Cal would like to speak. *Where's the sun gone, and how come there are not any squirrels?"*

Pockets of laughter erupted as Lexi elbowed Snipe in his side. The speaker laughed, too, before saying, "Squirrels? I can't recall seeing any on Earth, let alone here. Anyway, that's two questions in one. The sun... how can I explain? You're on it. Zeta draws energy from their star and has built this planet around it. The climate's controlled to suit its inhabitants."

A bombardment of questions flew from the crowd of onlookers, undefinable to the masses and agreed on by those within the vicinity of the person yelling. Hostility rippled through the crowd in waves.

The speaker hushed them, saying, "I can only answer one question at a time."

He turned to the grey before allowing him to speak his words through his body again. "You disrespect your kind by not listening to the spoken word. Your emotions are primitive and uncontrollable. Ours have eroded due to over-cloning. Zeta needs new genetics to ensure the survival of our species. You have so much to learn, but we are unable to teach in our current state of being. We gave humans life. We gave you the planet you call Earth."

A man standing at the front shouted, "God gave us life, not you!"

The speaker, controlled by the grey, listened, and replied, "You are young, and misunderstand the concept of the Creator. It takes little effort to create life. New lifeforms materialise daily. Worlds are adapted to suit new lifeforms. Life's abundant and ever-growing. What you call God is not the Creator of Life, it's what gives lifeforms purpose."

The same man stepped forward, and was pulled back by a family member. Still, he shouted, "So, what's the point if we're all going to die? What's the meaning of life?"

Snipe scrunched his fingers into a fist and punched the air out of appreciation for the man's forthrightness and the quality of his question.

"Death is not final. That is a human concept. Your species are receivers for what you call a *soul*. Life's meaning is universal. Feeding what we call *the greater consciousness system* gives meaning to life. Every experience from every conscious being feeds into this system. When you become formless, your soul enters the ever-expanding consciousness system; the thing you call God."

The speaker wilted as he had before. Then he spoke faster, with more urgency. "We gave life to humans. Offer salvation. We ask for your cooperation. We need access to your soul."

The grey walked off, vanishing behind the screen. The speaker came to, apologising again for technical difficulties. He explained that Zeta needed their cooperation to use their genetics, and their women for procreation, and that no harm would come to them.

As he spoke, Snipe noticed the clouds shimmer. Patches of distortion hovered above the stage. Snipe had seen this subtle disguise before, up close and personal. He watched as a metallic craft lifted from behind the stage, tailed by a black drone. As the Zeta grey flew into the distance, distorted shimmers followed.

Ivan tried to make light of the Zeta's abrupt departure, but Snipe suspected that it was the hidden craft lifting off that had unnerved the onlookers. Ivan went on to explain positives of the new world.

Turning, Snipe reached out his hands to Lexi and Spud. Leading them through a shoulder-packed crowd, he recognised someone. It was only when he'd passed by did it occur to him that it was the man he'd seen being pulled through the clouds, leaving his sports car abandoned.

"Where are we going?" Spud asked.

Someone else smiled at him. He couldn't place her face, but recognised her nose. They'd met at a place and time light-years from here. In a flash, it came to him. The women he recused from certain torment from the barn where her and her daughters were used and sold to those seeking perverse entertainment.

283

"Pulling his arm down, Lexi asked if he was all right. The question went unanswered as he glimpsed someone standing alone, towering above the surrounding people. A scar ran across his forehead.

*The man I sent away from the barn, I told him to live a good life. The man in the woods. Fin.*

"Dad, Mum's talking to you," Spud said. "Where are we going?"

"First, we'll look at Chinatown, then go dinosaur-hunting, but only if you promise to have an early night." He looked at Lexi. "Your Mum and I need to make plans."

Lexi winked and pulled a memory chip from her back pocket. "And find out what's on this," she said.

www.ingramcontent.com/pod-product-compliance
Lightning Source LLC
Chambersburg PA
CBHW022146170626
46807CB00005B/2093